HELTER-SKELTER

Della Galton

Published by Accent Press Ltd – 2007
ISBN 1905170971 / 9781905170975
Copyright © Della Galton 2007

Printed and bound in the UK

For Gran

Acknowledgements

Many thanks, once again, to all at Accent Press. A special thank you must also go to Eileen Dredge whose advice about Parkinson's disease was both inspiring and humbling. Also to Anne Tezer for the technical information about riding lessons.

In no particular order I am also very grateful to Nancy Henshaw, Ian Burton, Janine Pulford, Jan Wright, Su Cooke, Sue Sami, Dunford Novelists and the Wednesday night group.

Chapter One

VANESSA HAMILTON AWOKE TO the sound of a child's laughter. Caught between the limbo of sleep and wakefulness she shoved back the duvet and sat up in the dimness of the curtained room with a smile on her face. And then reality crashed in like a punch to the heart.

She was alone, although she could still hear the murmur of voices downstairs. Saturday morning kiddies' television, she realised. Richard must have left it on. He always watched the news before he went to work. And the child's laughter had reached inside her dreams.

It had been the sweetest of dreams. She and Jennifer had been playing hide and seek in the forest. Her daughter had been running ahead of her, feet crunching over pine needles, the white material of her dress flashing between the trees.

"Wait 'til I say ready, Mummy. No peeking."

"No peeking," Vanessa had agreed, covering her eyes with her fingers, but leaving a gap to check Jennifer didn't wander too far from her sight.

Then she'd woken to find it wasn't real. There were no pine needles cracking underfoot, no flickering of sunlight and shadow on the forest floor, and no Jennifer, and although the reality wasn't as devastating as it had been in the early days it still hurt enough to leave her breathless.

Vanessa knew yesterday's letter from Purbeck District Council had sparked it off. The letter was tucked inside a zipped compartment of her bag, but she didn't need to keep it. She knew it word for word.

'We are writing to inform you we are planning to carry out upgrades to Saint Mary's memorial garden. Disruption will be kept to a minimum, but you might want to remove any personal effects temporarily for safekeeping.'

Vanessa had no personal effects on her daughter's grave, but the letter had opened the raw wound in her heart. She'd planned to show it to Richard last night, but he'd been tired and irritable after a day spent on the phone arguing with a Spanish property developer, so she'd waited. The timing had to be right. She badly needed his support, but he wasn't likely to feel the same way as she did. How could he when Jennifer wasn't his child?

Aching, she reached across to touch the cold space beside her. Richard had been gone a while, but the bed still smelt of him. She breathed in the faint scent of his expensive cologne mixed with the more pungent smells of last night's lovemaking

Then, swiping the last of the sleep from her eyes, she swung long legs over the side of the bed and padded, still naked, to the window. She drew back the heavy velvet curtains. Just for a second she'd expected to see something other than the leafy suburban road that lay beyond the nets. Just for a second she'd expected to see blue skies above a wide sweep of bay and the summer glitter of the sea. Jolted, she drew back into the room, the thick carpet soft beneath her bare feet.

It had been five-and-a-half years since she'd left the cliff-top fairground where she'd grown up and where she'd fallen in love with Garrin Tate, Jennifer's father. Rationally, she knew it should be long enough for her to be able to move on, but sometimes she felt as though the past became more vivid as time went on. Sharper and more brightly coloured, as though she were viewing it through an immensely powerful telescope.

When she and Richard had got married, he'd made her promise she would break all ties with her previous life. At the time it was what she'd wanted, too. She'd been desperate to get away from the grief of losing Jennifer.

Desperate to put the past behind her, but it had crept into her head more and more lately. It was the letter. It had stirred up more than the memory of Jennifer.

Last night as she'd lain beneath Richard, moving with the familiarity of years, she'd looked up into his blue eyes and she'd seen Garrin's dark ones staring back at her. Time had fragmented; memories had sliced through her and she'd felt Garrin's hands moving over her body, a musician playing a hand-made guitar with the grace of the ancients, neither learned, nor practised. She'd moaned softly, caught between two worlds. Then Richard had tensed above her and his face had come back into focus, his eyes smoky with passion, and in that moment she'd hated herself for the deception because he didn't deserve it.

When she'd met him she'd been in pieces and he'd taken her away from Kane's Funfair, 'the best funfair in the world' and he'd given her back her life. He'd been infinitely patient and kind. A rock when it seemed nothing else had been constant. Sometimes she felt she owed him her sanity.

It had been easy to slip into his world – easy to turn her back on the fairground and the people she'd grown up with, because the most they'd been able to offer her was gruff reassurance that life went on. For Vanessa it hadn't – part of her had died when she'd lost her daughter.

Lately, she'd begun to wonder if perhaps all she'd really done back then had been to run away. Annoyed at herself for such disloyal thoughts, she stood under the shower, letting the sharpness of cold water wash away the night.

It was a surprise to be greeted by the smell of toast as she descended the stairs. A nice surprise. Richard met her at the kitchen door.

"Sweetheart, I was about to bring you breakfast in bed. You needn't have got up."

3

"I thought you'd gone to work." She looked up into his smiling blue eyes feeling guilty because she'd been thinking of another man. "So what have I done to deserve breakfast in bed?"

"Don't you remember?" His voice was teasing and he put out a hand to brush back a strand of long dark hair that had worked loose from the towel turbaned on her head. "Fancy a repeat performance?"

The question was rhetorical. He was dressed for work. Although not formally, as on weekdays. His pale blue shirt was open at the neck. He wasn't wearing a tie and his trousers were thin summer casuals. He smelt of aftershave and his fair hair, gold in the morning sun, was freshly washed. She was amazed he hadn't woken her, but then she'd been so deeply immersed in the dream. Maybe now was a good time to tell him about the letter.

"Richard, can I talk to you about something?"

"Of course. Will it take long?"

She noted the quick glance at his watch. Perhaps she should leave it until later, he wouldn't appreciate being held up.

Ignoring her instincts, she plunged in before she could change her mind. "I had this letter. It's probably easier if I show you."

He read it, seated at the breakfast bar in their sunny kitchen. Vanessa held her breath as a slight frown crinkled his handsome face.

"You don't have any personal effects on her grave." It was more statement than question, as he pulled the coffee-pot towards him.

"No."

"Then, why go back, sweetheart? Why put yourself through it?" Long fingers curled around hers. He had beautiful hands – the finest of gold hairs on the backs of them. Manicured nails, perfect. So different from Garrin's

4

hands with his fingernails always dirty from working outside. Why couldn't she get Garrin out of her head?

She took a deep breath. "I want to. I need to make sure she's okay. Is that wrong?" She hated the edge of desperation that was creeping into her voice.

"It's not wrong. It's... self-destructive." He held her gaze. "You know I've only got your best interests at heart, don't you?"

She nodded. It was the one thing she'd always been sure of. "You don't have to come. Although it would be lovely if you did."

His fingers tightened around hers. "I can't let you go on your own. But there's no way I can come with you today. I'm working. I should have already left."

"And that's more important than my daughter, is it?"

"It's not a case of more important, Vanessa. I have things that can't wait. You know I do. The Spanish deal. I'm on the brink of completing it." He dropped her fingers and stood up. She could see the tension in his shoulders as he paced to the kitchen sink and tipped away his untouched mug of coffee. It was pointless pursuing it – she knew it was. Yet there was a part of her that couldn't let it go.

"I could drive down on my own."

"I'd really rather you didn't. At least not today." He still had his back to her so she couldn't see his face. But his voice was rational, level. As though it was her who was being unreasonable. Maybe she was. She had, after all, only just sprung it on him. He couldn't just drop everything. And it wasn't, she thought with a tug of pain, as if Jennifer couldn't wait.

"Can we talk about it later?" she said quietly.

"Of course." He looked at his watch, tutted, and headed for the hall. It was only when the front door slammed behind him that she realised he hadn't kissed her goodbye. He always kissed her goodbye. Unease tangled with sadness

5

and she was tempted to phone him on his mobile. But that would probably make things worse. He'd said they could talk later. She should have listened to her instincts and waited.

She spent the morning catching up on paperwork for his business, printing out invoices and enveloping a small pile of cheques for suppliers he'd signed the night before. He wouldn't be in a hurry to send off the cheques, but she should really get the invoices in the post so they arrived Monday. It was as she was driving to the post office that it struck her she could just carry on into town and surprise him. They could go into Chandlers Ford for lunch. When they were first married they'd done it a lot. They could sit in a pub garden; it was hot enough to eat outside and they could get things back on an even keel. Then, when they did talk tonight, at least he wouldn't be on the defensive. Not that they'd rowed exactly, but she hated the way they'd parted.

Vanessa wondered if perhaps she should phone ahead and warn him she was coming. He might already have made lunch arrangements, not that it really mattered if he had. Waitrose was next door to his office. If he wasn't there she could do the weekly shop and catch up with him later.

Feeling a lot better now she didn't need to wait until the evening, she drew into the supermarket car park, and was just pulling into a space when she saw Richard coming down the steps next door. She turned off the ignition and was about to get out and go across when she realised he wasn't heading for his own car, but to another one parked alongside. Damn, he obviously did have a lunch appointment after all.

Vanessa caught a flash of blonde hair as a woman got out to greet him. It was Tara, one of the shareholders in his property development business. Vanessa hesitated. She'd never felt that comfortable around Tara, who was older than

6

she was and always immaculately turned out. She wished she'd worn something smarter than canvas shorts and a skimpy T-shirt. The June air was sultry and she'd hardly bothered with make-up. Neither had she had time to blow-dry her long dark hair. She'd just let it dry naturally while she caught up on Richard's paperwork, which meant it was a frizzy mess. Perhaps she should leave it, after all.

No, that was ridiculous. She applied lipstick in the car mirror, checked her face wasn't too flushed, and got out just in time to see Richard put his arms around Tara's shoulders and dip his head to kiss her.

For a moment that felt like a couple of centuries, Vanessa stayed where she was transfixed. Even from this distance she could see it wasn't just a friendly peck on the cheek, but something far more intimate: a lingering lover's kiss. A hips-close-together kind of kiss. The kind he gave her. Used to give her, she corrected, certain he would glance up and see her at any moment. He must surely feel her gaze across the short expanse of car park. But then someone moved across her line of vision – a woman with a toddler and a shopping trolley – and Vanessa leant heavily against her car, the heels of her sandals sinking into the overheated tarmac and her arms goose-bumping in the summer sun.

This wasn't happening. It couldn't be. He'd only got out of their bed a few hours ago. Last night they'd made love. They always made love on Friday nights. Richard was a creature of routine. She'd noticed nothing different. Nothing to suggest he was seeing another woman. With another rush of guilt Vanessa remembered the flashback of Garrin's face and wondered if some part of her subconscious had known this was happening.

The next time she looked up, Tara's car had gone. Still leaning against the door of her Mercedes Sports, she got her breathing back under control and wondered what to do.

It felt as though part of her world had just been knocked off kilter. It was still hard to believe what she'd just seen. Maybe there was a simple explanation. Deciding the only way she'd know for sure would be to phone him, Vanessa dug her mobile out from the depths of her bag and dialled his number. He answered almost instantly.

"Hello, sweetheart. I didn't expect to hear from you. Is everything okay?"

"Yes, it's fine." She was amazed at the steadiness of her voice. "I just wondered what you were doing for lunch? It's such a lovely day – it seems a shame to be cooped up in that office."

"I know, pet. But I'm right in the middle of something."

She decided to give him one more chance. Anything but lies. She could cope with what she'd seen if he didn't lie to her about it. Still with her voice on monotone, she went on softly, "Surely you can spare an hour, Richard. You have to eat something, don't you?"

"I grabbed a sandwich earlier."

"And I'm in town," she added, resisting the urge to tell him exactly where in town she was. "I could drop you off a cold drink? Or how about an ice-cream? I'm quite near your office."

He didn't miss a beat. "Sweet of you, but I really can't stop. If I don't get this deal tied up today, it'll be weeks – you know what the Spanish are like. 'Manana, manana'. I'm waiting for a call right now."

How can you be so sure of yourself, you bastard? Vanessa felt pain boiling into anger. It was all she could do not to hurl the phone across the car park. She couldn't believe how easily he lied. Had he always been able to lie like this? Why hadn't she seen it coming?

"I'll make it up to you later," Richard went on smoothly. "Why don't you book a table at Antonio's. With a bit of luck we'll have something to celebrate by then. How does

8

that sound?"

It sounded reasonable, a loving husband reassuring his wife. There was even a faint hint of regret in his voice, as if he really would rather be out in the sun with her than waiting for a business call. Had she not just seen him kissing Tara and driving off with her she'd have been satisfied with that. A little disappointed maybe, but she'd have understood. Like she always understood when he was late home, or had to cancel an evening out because something had come up.

Now she knew just exactly what it was that had come up, every instinct she had wanted to scream abuse at him, but she wasn't going to have this conversation on the phone. Neither did she want him having the whole afternoon to prepare what he was going to say. To talk her round in that calm rational way he had.

She took a deep breath. "All right, I'll see you later," she said quietly and disconnected.

For a few moments she stayed where she was, leaning against the car door, her eyes closed against the heat and against her husband's betrayal.

They would sort it out, all right. She wasn't the type of wife who could turn a blind eye to her husband playing away, as she suspected many of his friends' wives did. But it would be on her terms and in her time. No way would she be waiting meekly at home for him. She needed some space to think. And not at home. She hesitated, realising with a jolt that not one of the few friends she'd made since her marriage would appreciate her turning up on their doorstep with an overnight bag.

Vanessa thought about the letter and got slowly into her car. She'd always believed Richard when he said he didn't want her visiting Jennifer's grave because he didn't want her hurt. A short while earlier it would have seemed underhand to go back without telling him. Now she knew he was capable of cheating and lying to her, it changed everything. There was nothing to stop her going to see Jennifer now.

Still feeling dazed she edged the Mercedes through the Saturday shoppers and out on to the main road once more. Her mind was working overtime. She'd stop off at the house, grab a change of clothes and drive down to Knollsey. She could be there in an hour.

Her hands tightened on the steering wheel and she was glad of the air-conditioned coolness of the car. She was shivering, part rage, part shock, yet there was a corner of her mind that was icily calm.

She would not do anything impulsive. When she'd seen Jennifer she would book into a bed and breakfast for a night or two. It was easier to get things into perspective when you were some distance from them.

Chapter Two

VANESSA'S ANGER BEGAN TO seep out of her as she neared the coast, leaving a deep weariness in its place. The car park scene replayed over and over in her mind and she wanted to believe she'd somehow misinterpreted what had been going on. Was it possible she'd simply witnessed a peck on the cheek between friends? If Richard hadn't lied to her immediately afterwards she might have been able to put it down to her imagination playing tricks.

Her stomach twisted as she remembered the way he had rested his arms around Tara's shoulders, a carelessly possessive gesture and one she thought he reserved just for her. He'd kissed Tara full on the lips. Their fair heads had been close too long for casualness. Their hips had been touching, too. Friends didn't do that. She wasn't imagining it. They were sleeping together and there had been enough familiarity in their body language for it to have been going on for some time.

Feeling sick, Vanessa forced the images out of her head and concentrated on driving. But the closer she got to Knollsey, the more she began to wonder whether this was such a good idea. Richard was right about one thing – going to Jennifer's grave tore her to pieces. During the last six years, she'd only been back a handful of times. In the early days, the pain had been too deep, too unbearable. It had been easier to stay away, bury her feelings in the part of her mind marked 'history'.

More recently she'd begun to worry she might bump into Garrin. And even though it was she who'd walked away and married someone else, it would have hurt her to see him.

11

She slowed the car as she approached the crossroads where she needed to turn off. She was already upset. If she went to the memorial garden now she would feel a lot worse. Perhaps it would be better to wait until morning when she'd had a good night's sleep. Who was she kidding? The chances of getting any sleep with all this in her head were zilch. She glanced at the dashboard clock. It was still early, just after four. Had she been too impulsive? It had always been her biggest fault. Bitter experience had taught her that running away from a situation didn't make it go away. Wouldn't it be more sensible to drive back and have it out with Richard now?

It was time to make a decision. She was at the crossroads. Right to the memorial garden, or left to Knollsey. Or she could turn around and go back to Chandlers Ford. She wondered what Richard would say when he realised he'd been caught out. She suspected he'd try to talk her round. He would have some reason for having his arms around Tara and for lying to her. Quietly and rationally he would explain it wasn't how it looked, until he'd got her to disbelieve what she'd seen with her own eyes. He was a brilliant negotiator, or was it manipulator? He could make people think black was white and white was black. She'd seen him do it in board meetings often enough. In the end he would wear her down and then he'd want to take her to bed, and the way she felt now she never wanted him to touch her again.

For the first time since she'd been married she longed for the solace of a close female friend. One who wouldn't judge, who wouldn't offer advice, but who'd just listen. Someone like Izzy, she thought, with a sting of regret.

Izzy had brought her up, despite being the wrong side of forty when Vanessa's parents had decided they didn't want the responsibility of a baby. Izzy didn't have children of her own, but she'd been surrogate mother to many of the fairground kids. Kind and wise, she was the archetypal mediator. With a petite femininity that belied how strong she was, both mentally and physically, Vanessa could never remember her losing her temper or getting drunk or being anything other than gentle and dignified.

Yet when she'd left the fairground, she'd turned her back on Izzy. Richard had persuaded her a clean break was best. That it was the only way she would heal and be able to move on. The regrets she'd more or less managed to bury skittered to the top of her mind. Leaving Garrin was one thing, but she should never have abandoned Izzy. What she had done was unforgivable.

Her arms goose-bumped in the air-conditioned car. Five and a half years was a long time, she must have caused Izzy untold pain. She wouldn't be able to put that right, but she could at least say she was sorry. She should have done that long ago.

With a pang of sadness, because she knew she was turning her back on Jennifer once again, she took the left-hand turn to Knollsey and headed through the town towards the coast.

Of course, Nanna Kane might order her heavies to throw her off the site before she got as far as Izzy's living wagon. Nanna Kane had not been impressed with Vanessa's defection and she had a temper like a pit bull. Vanessa wondered if there was any mileage in taking the path over the cliffs and climbing over the fence at the back of the fairground. The cliffs were steep, but she and Garrin had managed them easily when they were children.

No, that was stupid. She was not going to sneak about. She would see Izzy, say what she'd come to say, and leave. No one would stop her doing that.

Knowing she wouldn't be able to park very close to the fairground, and finding several roads she wanted to go down were now one-way, Vanessa zig-zagged along the back streets until she found a parking space, deciding to go the rest of the way on foot

The streets and buildings were familiar, even though many of the shop-fronts had changed. She felt herself unravelling as she breathed in the familiar mix of salt air, fish and chips and traffic fumes. It was like coming home. Her lips tightened at the irony because Kane's Funfair hadn't been home for a long time.

It was humid despite the sea breeze, and her thin T-shirt stuck to her as she weaved between families: men with brown beer-bellies overhanging their shorts, tired-eyed women with sunburnt shoulders, and kids carrying buckets and spades, coming back from a day on the beach to get spruced up for the evening meal.

As she neared the seafront, the expectation of seeing them all again brought an ache of longing to her heart. She hadn't realised how much she'd missed this little seaside town. By the time she got to the front she was high on adrenaline, her breath catching in anticipation of her first glimpse of the fair. She stopped so sharply that a man walking behind cannoned into her.

Someone had altered the skyline. It should have been bumped with fairground rides, the big wheel, the roller-coaster and the domed red and yellow roof of the helter-skelter. Instead, on the hillside where the fair should have been, she could see a gleaming white block, its windows golden eyes in the setting sun.

"Excuse me," snapped the man who'd bumped into her.

He had a scraggy German Shepherd dog on a lead and she stared at him blankly. Shaking his head he stepped round her and she looked back at the building. What the hell was that doing there? Had she stumbled into one of those nightmares when you come home one evening and all the street signs are the same, but your house is full of strangers who claim they've been living there for years?

14

Vanessa blinked. It would be all right. In a minute she'd realise she'd taken a wrong turn and feel giddy with relief. She'd backtrack and come out in a different place and there on the hill would be the golden wrought-iron archway and neon sign proclaiming that you'd reached Kane's Funfair, 'the best funfair in the world'. She leaned on the railings that overlooked the sea and took several deep breaths of salt air. The tide was in, lapping at the stone wall, boats bobbed in the harbour and seagulls swooped above the greyish sea. Beside her a painted sign offered Dorset Belle cruises and trips to Brownsea Island and a ferry service to Poole.

Eventually she turned again to look at the alien view across the bay. There was no mistake, she was in the right place, but they were gone: the fairground; Nanna Kane; Izzy; Garrin; all gone.

Developers had been pestering Nanna Kane to sell for years, but she'd been adamant she never would. She must have finally caved in, seduced by an irresistible offer, but why? Something terrible must have happened.

Vanessa hurried on along the sandy pavement, passing ice-cream kiosks and burger bars, the smells of the past sparking off a hundred neural pathways in her brain, triggering memories as bright and fleeting as the patterns in a child's kaleidoscope.

A few minutes later – a life-time later – she reached the security gates that barred the entrance to the flats and now she could see they were surrounded by gardens that led down to moorings and a sign that said *Private Access*. The flats each had their own balconies, strung with hanging baskets of flowers: A world away from the living wagons and the chugging of diesel engines and the painted stalls, all brighter in her mind now they were gone.

There was a brass plaque above an entry phone, which said Fairground Court, numbers one to thirty-five. She stared at the black writing and leant forward on the iron gates and felt sick.

"Can I help you, madam?"

Vanessa swung round and found herself looking at a man who was dressed in a peaked cap, black trousers and a white shirt with the sleeves rolled up. He didn't look very happy. She wasn't surprised; he must be baking in that lot.

"What?"

"You've been standing here for five minutes. Were you wanting something?"

She stared at him and wondered where to start. He didn't look the slightest bit sympathetic, probably thought she was casing the place or something.

"I was looking for my family, they used to live here."

"What number?" He was carrying a clipboard, which he now held in front of him, studying her over it as if he didn't believe a word she said.

"They used to live here before the flats were built," she murmured, realising belatedly that telling him that probably wasn't a good idea. If he thought she was something to do with the fairground he'd probably have her escorted off the premises. Not that she was actually on the premises yet. He'd opened the gate, but he was blocking the entrance with his body.

"No one lived here before these flats were built. This was undeveloped land." He glared at her and she knew she could no more tell him they'd lived in living wagons beneath the stars than she could have changed the concrete monstrosity that had taken their place back into fields.

But she had to do something; she couldn't just walk away without knowing what had happened. "Do you know who the developer was?"

"No." His voice was curt, but something in her face must have appealed to his better nature because he said, "If you hold on a minute I can probably find out for you. There's

16

some paperwork in my office."

She followed him, hope overriding reluctance, into a cell-like building that would have benefited from air-conditioning. He rummaged in a filing cabinet. It seemed to take ages, but finally he found what he was looking for.

"Blake Anderson bought the site, but they sold it on to another firm who did the development." He smoothed out a piece of headed paper. "It's here somewhere; I'll find it for you in a minute. Who did you actually want to contact?"

"I need to know if there's a forwarding address for a Mrs Kane. She used to own the site."

"And you are?"

"I'm a relative." Well, it was almost true. She would have married Garrin if she'd stayed and he was Nanna Kane's grandson.

"The site was purchased from a Mr G Tate." The concierge looked at her suspiciously.

"Garrin's my brother. We haven't spoken for a while."

"A long while. He sold up five years ago."

"Did he leave a forwarding address?"

"If he did the developer would have it. Ah well, I suppose there's no harm in it." He wrote something on a Post-it note and pushed it across the desk. "There you go, that's the company that built this block. They own the freehold and quite a few of the flats, I believe. They'll tell you what you need to know."

It seemed that now he'd started being helpful, he couldn't do enough. Or perhaps he was bored.

"Thanks." She glanced at what he'd written. For a moment she didn't think she'd read it right. "Hamilton's…?"

"Yep, that's the one."

Vanessa felt the blood rushing to her head and for a moment she thought she was going to faint. Hamilton's was Richard's firm. So he'd known about this. He must have come home to her, night after night, while his diggers ripped up the ground, tore up the fabric of her childhood, chunk by chunk. He must have taken her to bed, made love to her, while his company wiped out everything she'd known and grown up with. And possibly, just possibly, she could have coped with that. She could have understood his motives. He'd wanted the past forgotten. He'd wanted to be everything to her. He'd said it enough times when they were first married. She could have understood this, if she meant everything to him. But after what she'd seen today she wasn't sure she did.

She gripped the edge of the desk, aware of the man's curious gaze.

"Are you all right, madam?"

"I'm fine," she said numbly, struggling to get her feelings back under control. "Thanks, you've been very helpful."

"You don't look all right, if you don't mind me saying so. Airless place, isn't it?" He was coming round the desk, but she was up and out of the door before he reached her, shouting back over her shoulder that she was fine, just needed some fresh air.

Numbed at the extent of Richard's betrayal, she walked slowly back down to the coast road, past a candy-floss booth, painted pink and white. Carlotta's candy-floss, the best candy-floss in the world.

Hope rose inside her. A little piece of the fair transported. Cissy Brown – Carlotta – had rented a pitch every year from Nanna Kane, and as Vanessa got closer she could see the old lady serving, greying hair pushed into an orange band, the same smile, the same wrinkled friendliness.

Vanessa joined the queue and when she reached the counter, Cissy looked up with eyes that were blank, "Yes please?" Then she frowned and recognition spread across her face. "Vanessa, my darling, well, well, I never thought I'd see your pretty face again. Trip down memory lane, is it?"

"I didn't know," Vanessa said, gesturing back the way she'd come. "I didn't know it was gone. What happened?"

Cissy took in her expression and wiped her hands on her overall. "I'll just serve these kiddies and I'll be with you. Time I had a tea break anyhow."

Ten minutes later she shut up the stall and led Vanessa into the Egg and Spoon café across the road.

"Two teas, please, Hannah, my darling. Now sit yourself down, Nessa. Must have been a right shock if you didn't know." Her blue eyes darkened with seriousness. "You don't know any of it, do you?"

"I know that Garrin sold the site. Why?"

"Oh, lovie, I'm so sorry. Nanna Kane passed away. Very sudden, it was. Heart attack. Huge shock to everyone."

Vanessa nodded, biting back tears. Even though she'd suspected something like this – no way would Garrin have sold the fairground otherwise – it hadn't prepared her for hearing the words. He must have been devastated, she thought aching for him. He and Nanna had fought like cat and dog, but, beneath it all, he'd adored her. She was the only relative he'd had left.

Cissy gave her a moment to gather herself, her eyes compassionate.

"I'm so sorry, Nessa. I thought they'd have been in touch with you. I'd have got in touch myself otherwise. Oh, love."

"When did it happen?"

Cissy paused. "It was December – just after you went – so what would that be – ninety-nine – two thousand?"

"Ninety-nine," Vanessa said quietly. She'd left in the November. Why hadn't anyone been in touch? Garrin might not have wanted to contact her, but Izzy would have phoned or written. Perhaps she had, perhaps that's how Richard had found out; he had a habit of opening her mail. In the early days she hadn't minded, she'd wanted to cut herself off, and he'd been happy to protect her. Or was it control? She shook her head.

"What happened to Garrin?"

"He moved on. Don't think he could bear to carry on with the place, to be honest. Trade wasn't what it was. I think he wanted a fresh start." Her eyes softened. "Same as you, lovie."

"Do you know where he went? And what about Izzy?" Vanessa could hardly bear to hear the answer, afraid of more bad news as Cissy frowned.

"I'm not sure where Izzy went, but Garrin would know. I've got his address somewhere. I'll get it for you. Will you go and see him?"

"Yes," Vanessa said slowly. "I will."

"Best get back to me stall, then, lovie. I'll get that address for you. And good luck with Garrin."

Vanessa stood on the sandy pavement clutching the piece of paper Cissy had given her. Not that she needed to keep it because the address was as familiar as her own. Garrin hadn't gone far. He was living at Izzy's Uncle Bert's. As children they'd gone there most winters when the fair was shut. Nanna Kane, who'd hated the cold, had usually gone abroad, but more often than not Garrin had opted to go to Bert's with her and Izzy.

Bert had an old farmhouse in the Purbecks, surrounded by acres of sandy land where he'd bred horses. It had been his dream to breed a champion: A horse that would star at the Horse Of The Year Show. He'd never done it, as far as she knew. And he'd been old back then. He must be ancient now.

Standing there in the balmy sea air amidst the humdrum

bustle of holidaymakers, she thought about Garrin. He'd always loved horses. Izzy had encouraged him, teaching him to ride as soon as he could walk – even though they'd both known it would never be more than a hobby. His future had been set in stone.

With both parents dead he'd been destined to take over the fair from Nanna Kane. He'd be part of a long line of showmen, going back generations. Once they'd been travellers, too, but Nanna's parents had bought the scrubby cliff-top site and decided to settle there permanently. This had always annoyed Garrin intensely.

"God knows why they gave up travelling," he'd mutter. "Now we don't fit in anywhere. We're not flatties and we're not proper showmen either. We're in limbo land."

Vanessa hadn't understood why it bothered him so much. At least he still had his gran, whereas she had only Izzy. Belonging was about who cared about you, not about where you lived.

For a long while she stayed where she was, leaning on the sea wall, and listening to the endless hissing of the sea, which had always been as comforting as a heartbeat.

Even though she'd never been back, she'd imagined the fair carrying on without her. Each March she'd visualised them all setting up the stalls and the rides, Nanna Kane barking orders while the gaff boys tested equipment. She'd imagined the place filling up: the noise of the generators; the excited shrieks of the punters; the fragmented music, and the smell of fried onions and burgers threading through the salt air.

Then at the end of the season she'd imagined them taking down all that could be dismantled, putting the giant machines into winter hibernation and scattering to temporary jobs around the country.

But all of this had only happened in her head. The fair hadn't been there for the last five years. It had been an

21

illusion. Like her happy marriage, she thought bleakly, remembering Tara. She was in limbo land herself now.

Her present life wasn't the safe comfortable place she'd thought it to be. And neither was her past. Richard had changed both beyond recognition.

Chapter Three

ACCORDING TO TRADITION, GOOD legs meant quality – both in women and in horses. Garrin had always thought there were other parts of their anatomies that were equally good yardsticks. The bay horse trotting away from him had strong well-muscled hindquarters. The sort that had a nice solid feel if you slapped them. Not too much bounce, but not so firm you'd hurt your hand. If he had to score them on slapability they'd come out somewhere around factor nine, ten, being high.

The girl riding the horse didn't have a bad butt either, and, tightly encased in fawn jodhpurs as it was right now, he was in a good position to judge. She wasn't so skinny that there was no movement when she hit the saddle on the downward stride of the rising trot, but there wasn't enough of a wobble to be distracting. Women with wobbly bums were very distracting and could sometimes put him right off his stroke when he was teaching.

"Change the rein," he shouted now, because it meant she'd have to come past him again and he could have another close-up look. Yes, it really was very nice, he decided as Nero went by, his hooves thudding on the hard packed peat of the school. Pity her riding skills didn't match up. "You're too stiff," he yelled. "Loosen up a bit for Christ's sake. It's a horse, not a seesaw."

She was pretty, but she wasn't very fit. Her face was flushed and a strand of blonde hair that had escaped from her skullcap was sticking to her forehead. They were only ten minutes into the lesson. God knows what she'd be like when they really got going.

"And – walk," he ordered. "No, not like that. You're too

heavy-handed. You should be stopping him with your seat, not your hands. There's a mouth on the end of those reins."

She didn't say anything. She looked as though she was going to burst into tears.

He sighed. "Rein in."

She brought the horse to an untidy halt and he strolled across. "Your stirrups are too long, that's not helping." He adjusted them. "There. That's more like it." He stood back, a slight frown on his face. "Overall, you haven't got a bad seat. You're too far back though; we're aiming for a nice light, forward seat. Like this. Better. Now try again. And for Christ's sake, look where you're going. How's he supposed to know what you want him to do when you've got your chin stuck in your chest?"

"I know. I'm sorry." She sounded tremulous, a little-girl voice, which doubtless got her a long way with most of the men she came across, but cut no ice with him.

"Get going. Keep your head up. And use your legs. Haven't you listened to a word I've said?"

After another twenty minutes he was satisfied. "Better. Much better. Okay, trot him down the poles. Keep him straight. Your hands should be following his mouth, nice and light."

She complied. She was happier now, more relaxed and the horse was more balanced.

"Fine. That's great. Have a breather and if you're up for it we'll finish off over a little jump."

She nodded and walked round on a long rein while he set up a cross-pole.

"Okay. Now, round on the left rein and then bring him down over the poles, keep him straight and he should pop over that, no probs."

"Not bad," he said, "but don't lean quite so far forward. You're ahead of the horse. If he runs out, you'll be over his shoulder. Okay, one more time for me."

He shielded his eyes against the afternoon sunlight as she circled away from him and then came back down the centre. He could see it was going to go wrong before she'd got halfway. Nero was bored with the trotting poles and she was relying too much on her hands again. At the last minute, the bay horse got his head free, put in a sidestep she wasn't expecting, and ducked out of the jump.

She came off in a graceless sprawl, hit the wing of the jump and let go of the reins. Free of his rider, Nero put in a little buck and cantered across the school. Garrin caught his reins as he went past and pulled him up short. "That's enough of that, you little sod." He led the horse across to where his pupil was sitting on the ground, her face in her hands.

"Are you hurt?"

"No, I'm all right." She was crying, though. She rubbed at a mascara smudge below one cheekbone, tears breaking up her voice.

"Then get back on him."

"I can't."

"I said, get back on him."

She shook her head and he knotted the horse's reins on his neck, so they wouldn't trail on the ground, and let go of him. Then he hunkered down beside her on the hard-packed peat. "If you don't get back on him now, it'll be twice as hard next time."

"There's not going to be a bloody next time. I've had enough." She took off her riding gloves and tried to unfasten the chinstrap on her skullcap, but her hands were shaking too much. From defiance, or fear, he couldn't tell.

Garrin pulled her hands away from the strap, and then, still holding on to them, he pulled her roughly to her feet. She wasn't as tall as him, few women were. She'd have to look up to meet his eyes and she didn't want to look at him, but he had no intention of letting her walk away.

"You're covered in peat," he observed, letting go of her hands so she could do something about it.

She brushed at her thighs and bits of peat fluttered back to the ground. Behind her, Nero stood flicking his ears against the flies, patches of sweat darkening his neck.

Garrin bent and picked up her riding crop, which was lying by the side of the jump. He handed it back to her and leant against the wing. The air around them was heavy and breathless. Hardly a breeze ruffled the bushes that lined the far side of the school.

"Now stop wasting my time. Put on your gloves and get back on that horse."

There was a small silence. For a moment he thought she was going to refuse. She picked at a strand of loose leather that had unwound itself from the handle of the crop and then she walked away from him towards the horse. There was still peat clinging to her jodhpurs, he saw, a dark smudge across one buttock. She reached Nero and un-knotted the reins. There was hesitation in the slender line of her shoulders.

Garrin went across to her before she could change her mind and held Nero's head while she re-mounted. "All right. Once more over the poles. Take it slowly."

She okayed this with her eyes, which were a bitter-sweet blue, the colour of the afternoon sky. He let go of the reins and she turned the horse away from him, the hesitation gone now. She was obviously more afraid of him than she was of falling off again, he thought wryly, watching as determination straightened her back and she closed her legs against Nero's sides.

"Better," he called, giving Nero's rump a slap as he went by. Yes, a definite factor nine.

He watched her circle and come back down the poles and over the jump, a little stiffly, but otherwise not bad.

"I was much too stiff, wasn't I?" She cut back across the

26

school and drew up beside him in a near-perfect halt.

"I think you've had enough for today," he said, patting Nero's neck. "So has he."

She looked back at him impassively. "But I still have ten minutes left."

"You were arguing the toss about getting back on him five minutes ago. It's best if we end on a good note, don't you think?"

"Shall I take him in then?"

"Yeah... And get yourself some arnica on your way home, it's good for bruises."

She nodded and was about to turn when Garrin caught hold of the horse's reins.

"Well done," he said.

"So who have you been tormenting today then, my love?"

"No one." Garrin grinned and bent to kiss Izzy's cheek. She smelt of something with vanilla undertones and there was a pink streak in her white hair. She would never be conventional, even here, sitting in a floral-patterned armchair with the backdrop of the sea through the wide glass window behind her. He sniffed appreciatively. "You've been baking."

"Cinnamon biscuits. They're on the side. You should eat more. You're looking peaky."

He laughed. "Your eyesight's going. I'm out in the fresh air all day, for God's sake. How much healthier does it get?"

"I didn't mean your physique." She pinched his arm playfully. "You spend far too much time cracking the whip, my love. I meant your eyes."

"My eyes?"

"Yes, your eyes. They look tired."

"Well, they're not tired." He sat opposite her. "No more than usual anyway. It's tough at the top."

27

"You shouldn't be doing all that lot on your own."

"I don't. I've got staff coming out of my ears."

"I'm not talking about things staff do. I'm talking about…"

"I know what you're talking about." He stood up abruptly. "And you needn't worry about me on that score either. I don't sleep alone very often."

"Heaven forbid." Her voice was dry. "There's more to life than sex, darling, go and put the kettle on, will you, and get the biscuits while you're at it. They're on the side."

He shrugged, marvelling at her ability to get sex and biscuits in the same sentence, and went out to the kitchen, which was huge and filled with every imaginable labour-saving device and the kind of cooker a TV chef would have been proud to own. All smoked glass and dials. A modern, spacious kitchen was one of the two things she'd stipulated when he'd bought her this place. An odd request, he'd often thought, for a woman who'd spent most of her life in a living wagon cooking on a Calor-gas stove. The other requirement had been a sea view and Garrin understood this perfectly. After all, it was what he'd wanted too, the luxury of being able to smell the fresh ozone tang of the sea, without the ever-present undertones of diesel fumes. He piled the biscuits on a plate and took them back into the lounge.

"I mean it, Garrin, you should get yourself settled down – have a family. Time waits for no man, you know."

"Bollocks," he said good-naturedly. "I don't think I'm on the shelf just yet."

"I'm not suggesting you are." She nibbled a biscuit and frowned. "Too much cinnamon. So, come on, I want to know about Amanda Battersby-Smythe. It was today, wasn't it? How did it go? Was she as good as her father thought?"

"About factor eight," he said, grinning because he knew

that wasn't what she was asking. But she'd have got round to it soon enough. Next to his horses, his love life was top of her list of favourite conversations.

"Really. And this judgement was based on observation, I take it?"

"Yeah, I didn't get close enough for anything else. Horse dumped her. I doubt she'll be coming back."

"She will. They always do, don't they?"

Her blue eyes were sparkling and he nodded, even though it was a statement of fact, not a question. It was a standing joke between himself and Izzy that the harder the time he gave his pupils, the more they seemed to like it. Very few didn't come back.

It was something that had often surprised him. Pity he hadn't learnt it when he was younger. He could have saved himself a lot of heartache and trouble. Not with his pupils, but with women in general.

"I expect you bullied her into getting back on, though, didn't you?"

"It was for her own good. Daddy wouldn't have been pleased if his little petal gave up a sparkling career in show-jumping because she'd got a bruise or two. Tantrums are for five-year-olds, not grown women." He bit into a biscuit. "They taste fine to me."

"Ah, but you never were one for subtlety. So how's our protégé coming along?" Her voice had lost its teasing tone now and Garrin relaxed. He could talk about his horses for ever, longer if he had the opportunity.

"Derry's fine. He won again yesterday."

"Why didn't you tell me?"

"You were too busy interrogating me."

"Did you have Tracey up on him?"

"Yes, I had too much to do – more's the pity – and they're only small shows. I don't want to over-face him and Tracey's in her element. As long as she doesn't interfere too much, he'll be fine. He's a natural."

"Heaven help her if she puts a foot wrong." Izzy shook her head. "Does she know what she's letting herself in for?"

"She's not the sensitive type. She wouldn't still be working for me if she was."

"I'm sure you're right. You must let me know when you start working with him yourself. I want to be there when you jump him. I want to be around to witness the whole of his meteoric rise."

"Don't tempt fate, Izzy."

She smiled. "No, you're right, but he is something special. He was always going to be, wasn't he, with a dam like Sorrento?"

Garrin nodded. Izzy might be seventy and prematurely weakened by Parkinson's, but she was still as passionate as ever about horses. Sorrento had been Izzy's pride and joy, the result of years of intuitive breeding by her uncle. Horses had always been the link that had bound them. For as long as he could remember she'd told him he'd be a champion one day. She'd given him riding lessons and dreams as soon as he'd been old enough to walk, even though the chances of him ever owning a horse that wasn't plastic and attached to a carousel had seemed as far out of reach as the stars in those days.

"Of course I'll let you know. You can come and stay with me if you like. Make sure you don't miss anything."

"No, I'm quite happy here, thank you. I'll just pop in each day. You can come and pick me up."

"Like I've got nothing better to do," Garrin grumbled. "You're the one who said I look tired."

"It'll do you good to get out more, even if it is just a couple of miles up the road. You spend far too much time cooped up in that yard."

"Cooped up is the last thing I am," Garrin said, thinking of the patchwork of sandy fields that surrounded his house.

30

He wasn't as close to the sea as Izzy, but it was near enough to smell, and you could see it in the distance when it wasn't too misty, a glittering blue ribbon beyond the cliffs. "Anyway, enough of me. How did it go at the hospital? What did the consultant say?"

"Nothing new. The side effects of the drugs are better than the disease itself."

"Is that his opinion or yours?"

"His, but I don't mind, love, I've told you before. If I have to have something wrong with me, then I'd far rather it was Parkinson's than something nasty and painful."

He nodded, knowing she would never tell him the whole truth about how she was feeling. It wasn't her style. If he could have done anything for her, given her anything, it would be the chance to die peacefully and with grace, before the illness stole her dignity. At the moment it wasn't too bad. On a good day you hardly noticed the tremors. On a bad day she moved constantly and had difficulty with sentences, both his and her own, losing the thread halfway through, and although she always smiled away her discomfiture, he knew it troubled her.

All her life she'd been razor-sharp. He hadn't realised that Parkinson's would slowly interfere with her mind, as it interfered with her body. Garrin hated its relentless invasion. Izzy was the closest he had left to a relative, the one constancy in his life and he loved her more than he'd ever have admitted.

"Are you out tonight then?" she asked him. "Or was this a special trip?"

"Of course it was a special trip, but yeah I'm meeting a bloke in the White Heather about a horse for the school. There's no rush. I said around nine."

"Would you like something proper to eat? There's some cooked chicken in the fridge. It won't take a minute to heat up."

"No ta. I'll grab a pie in the pub."

She smiled at him and for a moment he was tempted to ask her if she missed her old life. If he'd done the right thing bringing her here, away from all that she knew. But then in the end there hadn't been much left that was familiar for either of them, and at least she was comfortable here.

"What's on your mind, Garrin?"

"Nothing." He stood up. "Maybe I will get going, in case this bloke turns up early. I'll ring you about Derry. Next week I should think, if I don't pop by before."

"I'll look forward to it."

"Me too." He went across and took both her hands in his, and then he bent to kiss her face. Her cheekbone felt hard beneath his lips. Izzy had been a beauty in her day, with the pale English rose fragility that belied the toughness within. She was more fragile than ever now, her face lined from years of hard work and the unforgiving sun, but she was still lovely. He smiled at her. Looking forward to doing some serious work with Derry was the understatement of the century. He hadn't been so excited about anything for years. "Don't get up, I'll see myself out."

"Okay, darling."

She looked tired too. He suspected that her concerns about him looking peaky were a diversion tactic to stop him quizzing her. As he let himself out of the bungalow he thought that had she not been so fragile he'd have left competing on Derry himself for a bit longer, but he was worried she might not feel up to coming to the stables every day if he did. Maybe he could persuade her to stay with him. It would be a lot easier all round and it was high time Izzy let him pay back some of the enormous debt he felt he owed her.

As he drove towards the White Heather, his thoughts turned to Amanda Battersby-Smythe. He had given her a hard time and he wasn't really sure why. He wasn't usually so brutal, at least not on a first lesson. Perhaps he'd been worrying about what the consultant would say to Izzy today. Or had he been worrying about asking too much of Derry too soon and ruining him? Garrin frowned. No – none of that would usually have affected his judgement.

He drew into the car park of the White Heather, but it was only as he was getting out of his car that it struck him why he'd been such a bastard to Amanda. She didn't look like her in the slightest, but something in her eyes, a mixture of vulnerability and defiance, had reminded him of Vanessa.

Chapter Four

TOO EXHAUSTED TO DO anything else that evening, Vanessa booked into a bed and breakfast, accepted a tiny room with seagull prints on the walls and sat on the bed and wept. Finding out about Nanna Kane was bad enough. She'd always been so tough, an ageless, vibrant lady, who'd ruled her little empire with energy and humour. She hadn't even been that old, her name reflecting her status rather than the fact that she actually was a grandmother – Garrin's grandmother. Everyone had called her Nanna Kane, just as everyone had called Izzy, Aunt Izzy.

It was hard to believe she was gone. But what hurt most was that Richard hadn't told her. He hadn't given her the chance to return one last time and tell them how sorry she was. What had they thought when she hadn't turned up for the funeral? That she didn't care. Or had Richard made some excuse on her behalf? No wonder they hadn't been in touch.

She'd switched off her mobile when she'd met Cissy. Now she put it back on and listened to a message from Richard. He didn't sound particularly worried, just concerned they'd be late for the table at Antonio's, which she naturally hadn't booked.

Vanessa deleted it and snapped off the phone. Let him wait. She was too angry to speak to him. She'd trusted him completely. She'd made it easy for him, she realised, wondering how many more lies he'd told her.

When they'd met she'd been barely twenty-one: streetwise from her upbringing, but also terribly vulnerable because she hadn't got over Jennifer.

She remembered the first time she'd seen him, strolling

across the fairground, his smart suit and briefcase out of place in the dirty heat-filled day, his fair hair glinting gold in the summer sun.

"Here comes trouble," Nanna Kane had muttered, turning from her living wagon window, silver bangles jangling on her brown arms.

"Shall I make myself scarce?" Vanessa had asked from her position on Nanna's couch.

"It'll be him that makes himself scarce, but we'll have some fun with him first – eh?" There'd been a glint of mischief in Nanna's dark eyes and Vanessa had smiled despite herself. Fun had been a word missing from her vocabulary for a long time.

The man stepped up into Nanna's wagon and glanced around him and Vanessa wondered what he made of the ornate brocade drapes and the beautiful old rosewood display cabinets, which housed Nanna's prized crystal collection. Nanna never had made it into the 20th century.

It was hard to tell what he thought because his shrewd, clean-cut face was expressionless, like every salesman Vanessa had ever met. He wasn't as old as she'd first thought, maybe thirty and he was immaculately dressed. In fact everything about him screamed money, from his well-cut suit to his leather briefcase, which he rested on the floor. Aware of her gaze, he gave her a quick smile.

"This is Richard Hamilton," Nanna said, also smiling. "Come to make me an offer I can't refuse. Isn't that right, laddie?"

"I certainly hope so." His accent was Hugh Grant, but he sounded confident enough. He'd be a nervous wreck by the time Nanna had finished with him. Vanessa felt a pang of sympathy. Nanna didn't often let them in, she usually gave them their marching orders before they got this far.

"So what exactly are you offering, Mr Hamilton?"

"It's probably easier if I show you, Mrs Kane." He

unfastened the briefcase and began to lay out paperwork.

Nanna Kane had kept him in the hot living wagon for nearly two hours, pretending to consider his offer, quizzing him about the designs he had in mind for his flats, maybe it would even be possible for her to live in one – so she wouldn't be too far away from her roots. He'd gone through everything patiently, saying he was sure that would be fine, she could have the penthouse, the site was valuable – they could do a deal. Then at the end of it, Nanna Kane screeched with laughter, told him she'd no more sell her land to him than chuck herself off the cliffs, and sent him on his way with a gypsy curse.

Feeling his hurt, and acutely sensitive to other people's pain because she'd gone through so much of it herself over the last few months, Vanessa caught up with Richard at the gates of the fairground.

"That wasn't a real curse," she said softly, looking at his troubled face. "It's just that she gets fed up – so many people ask."

He nodded and to her surprise he smiled at her. "It's okay, I kind of figured she wasn't going to sell, but you never can tell. Thanks – though – for letting me know about the curse."

Sure he was laughing at her, she swallowed down the tears that were never far away and turned abruptly, wishing she hadn't bothered. And he must have caught her look because he touched her arm.

"Hey, I meant it – are you all right?" The concern in his blue eyes had brought more tears. "No, you're not, are you. Look, I might not be much of a salesman, but I'm a good listener. Why don't I buy you a coffee?"

That's how it had all begun. He had been a good listener too and it had been easier to pour out her heart to this older stranger, who wasn't a part of her world and who wouldn't judge her, than it was to deal with Garrin's silence. With the

36

benefit of hindsight she knew Garrin had been as grief-stricken as she was over the loss of their child. But at the time she hadn't been able to deal with her own pain, let alone his.

Vanessa blinked away the memories. She'd severed all ties with Garrin when she'd married Richard five years ago. She'd had to – for Richard's sake and for her own sanity, but now Garrin was back in her thoughts. Deep down, Vanessa knew there was a place in her heart he'd never left. By resurrecting him, she'd resurrected the guilt too – and it was no easier to deal with this time round than it had been five and a half years ago. Time had sharpened, not dulled the guilt.

The next day she got up early, sore from nightmares. She couldn't face breakfast, but while she was settling up for the B&B, her mobile rang and Richard's name flashed up on the display. She turned it off. He'd have to wait. She had no intention of speaking to him until she'd done what she came for. And this morning was Jennifer's time.

It was a twenty-five minute drive to St Mary's and Vanessa dreaded arriving during every one of them. She was trembling as she made her way along the path through the cemetery, not looking left or right, until she reached the remembrance garden, where she paused, the bars of the gate slippery beneath her touch. The memories were already crowding in like little black ghosts, reaching out for her because this place held no peace. It never would despite the anaesthetic of the years.

She opened the gate and stepped into the flower-filled garden. She was alone, thank God; she couldn't have coped with anyone else's grief. Time slipstreamed around her as she took the final few steps until she stood before the grave. It was well tended. A new pot of freesias spilled pink and yellow petals across the ground, scenting the air.

So Garrin still came then. She wondered if his pain had

faded, or if it gnawed away inside him, still haunted him on the sunniest of days when he was trying to think of something else entirely.

The whiteness of the marble headstone had faded a little, but the words were as clear as ever.

In memory of Jennifer Tate, our beautiful baby girl.
Born 10 August 1999 – Died 10 August 1999

And Vanessa was back there in the delivery room, looking up at the doctor's sombre face. Garrin stood at the foot of her bed, his eyes black with pain. And all she'd been able to do was lie there, shattered from the long labour and stare back at them. Lie there in the breathless air, not understanding why the room, which had been hectic and filled with people the moment before, was now so empty, so silent.

"Where's my baby? I want my baby. Give me my baby." Her voice rose with each word until she was screaming at them. "What have you done with her? Give me back my baby."

The midwife had come to shush her, shaking her head – that gentle touch on her arm more frightening than any words. Garrin hadn't been able to look at her. His hunched shoulders turning away, cutting her out, blaming her – because who else's fault could it be, but hers?

If only she hadn't been so stupid. If only she'd listened to Izzy. If only she could rewind the past forty-eight hours. Vanessa would have given all that she had for a second chance.

And now her throat closed, as she saw once more her daughter's perfect face – eyes closed as if sleeping, her tiny nose upturned, a smattering of dark hair. Exquisite in every perfect detail.

But she did not breathe.

Pearly translucent fingernails, tipping delicately curled fingers. So still and good and beautiful.

But she did not breathe.

Vanessa felt her legs collapsing until she was kneeling on the cinder path, her hands covering her face, sobs wrenching her body. How could Garrin still come? How could he bend and place flowers? How could he take the old dead blooms away? How could he even bear to breathe the air in this place where their daughter lay, their daughter who had never tasted this air at all? Not once. Ever.

Chapter Five

VANESSA WASN'T SORRY TO leave Knollsey. It held nothing but bitter memories and although she'd felt compelled to visit Jennifer's grave – in her heart, her daughter wasn't lying in that cold place anyway. In her heart Jennifer grew year by year. Occasionally she caught glimpses of her, a toss of her dark curls, a flash of her olive skin and sloe eyes. She was always laughing when Vanessa saw her, sometimes in the shadows of street corners, sometimes in the distance when she ran along forest paths, alive and vibrant and free.

Vanessa had told no one about these 'false memories' of her daughter, but they'd always comforted her – made it possible to carry on living some semblance of a normal life. Had she just been kidding herself all this time, she wondered, as she drove away from Knollsey? By imagining Jennifer growing up in some parallel world to this one – was she perhaps just burying the fear that it was her fault she'd died? That the reckless way she'd behaved when she was pregnant had contributed to Jennifer's death?

It was a long time since she'd let such ideas into her head. Feeling numb, she tried to blank them out and her thoughts returned to Garrin. One thing she was sure of was that he wasn't going to be pleased to see her, but she couldn't think of any other way of finding Izzy and she must find Izzy. She must apologise, at least to Izzy, for abandoning her. It didn't matter so much what Garrin thought of her – she could cope with that. Good God, she probably deserved it.

She drove slowly back towards Corfe, along hilly roads with cows in the fields either side of her. Seeing Corfe

Castle suddenly in the distance was a shock. It was always a shock, even though she was expecting it. Those great grey stones against the cloudless sky, so stark and out of place, towering over the stone villages below them. She had some vague recollection of roundheads and royalists, although the dates and the details were a bit hazy. She'd been good at English and maths at the local school, which Izzy had insisted she attend regularly, but history had never been her strong point.

When she and Richard had married, she was aware of the gap in education between them and she'd taken a course in business management. She'd wanted to be involved in the whole of his life. Besides, it made more sense for her to work for his company than get a token job. But she'd never caught up on history. History had always been a taboo subject in their house.

It was almost lunchtime and, realising she hadn't eaten since the previous morning she stopped at a pub, full of hunting pictures and black-and-white portraits of men in old-fashioned clothes. She ordered a sandwich and sat in the garden away from the families of Sunday lunchers, and thought about what she was going to say to Garrin. Perhaps he had bought Uncle Bert's place and married some pretty girl and she'd walk into a scene of domesticity, with toddlers running about the place where they'd spent so much of their childhood. It was an unsettling thought.

She left the pub and drove onwards through villages of Purbeck stone and up tiny winding roads with the sea never far from view. Fields dotted with yellow ragwort gave way to fields of maize, lush beneath the sun. She reached the village of Coomb Carey just after one. Apprehensive, now she was so close, she stopped at the village stores and bought a bottle of fizzy water.

"You on holiday?" The shopkeeper smiled at her.

"No, I'm on my way to Fair Winds."

41

"Ah – Garrin Tate's place. Are you a student then?"

Vanessa looked at her curiously. "What sort of student?"

"A.I.s, I think they're called – something to do with horse riding." The woman raised her eyebrows. "He teaches. He's very good at it apparently."

Puzzled, Vanessa got back into her car. She hadn't liked to ask what A.I. stood for. She drove on, childhood memories pouring back at her from the countryside that, unlike Knollsey, hadn't changed. A mixture of fear and exhilaration made her fingers slippery on the steering wheel and stuck wisps of hair to her neck.

Just before she reached the entrance to the long driveway that led up to the house, she saw the white-painted sign, *Fair Winds*. Beneath it, the silhouette of a horse and rider jumped over a fence. Pride threaded through her trepidation. So he'd actually done it. Realised his childhood dream of owning his own yard; she wondered if he was riding professionally too.

She still couldn't fathom what had tipped his decision to sell the fair that had been in his family for generations, but she knew she would find out soon enough. That's if he didn't slam the door in her face.

Her heart sped up as she drove up the long gravel driveway. He'd transformed the place. She remembered mud and barbed wire. Now there was white-painted fencing. It reminded her of a ranch. Several horses grazed in the fields and ahead of her she could see the house, which didn't look much different. The Purbeck stone blended with its surroundings as easily as if it had grown there.

She parked and crunched her way across gravel to the front door. After about five minutes, during which her heart got faster and her hands clammier, she realised no one was in. There were two ways to the stables – through the house; or through the wooden gate to her left, which had the words, *Private Property Do Not Enter* painted on it in white.

Taking a deep breath, she headed across and found it was unlocked. A stony path led between barbed-wire fencing. The long grass on either side was littered with a selection of tyres and rusting metal objects. He'd obviously only tarted up the bits that showed – typical. She was about halfway along the path before she heard the geese.

A flock of them were heading purposefully towards her – necks outstretched – wings flapping and by the row they were making, they weren't a welcoming party. The one in front was the biggest. As it got closer, it began to hiss and she realised it wasn't just passing, but was coming straight for her. Vanessa wasn't scared of animals – she'd grown up with them – she'd have a dog or cat now if Richard wasn't allergic to them. But this goose looked like he meant business.

Vanessa backed away, but he kept on coming. Then, when she was pressed uncomfortably against the barbed-wire fence, she realised there were more geese behind her. There must have been at least a dozen and they were hissing and honking and making a hell of a row.

She was considering her options, brazen it out or run for the gate, when one of the birds behind her took an experimental peck at the knee of her jeans.

"Sod off," she shouted, trying to avoid his beak and flapping her hands. The group stepped back *en masse*, except for the lead goose, which was hissing, a malevolent look in its beady eyes. She decided running would be good but found she couldn't move. Her T-shirt was caught on the barbed-wire. Turning her back on Mr Macho goose wasn't an option. She wrenched the fabric, heard it rip and then raced back along the path. The geese followed, this was obviously the best sport they'd had in years.

She was almost at the gate when she tripped on something on the path and went sprawling. Putting out her hands to save herself was a bad move. Pain shot through her wrist and she landed heavily on her side, scraping her face. A series of coloured lights danced before her eyes and in that moment of stillness, as time slowed to nothing, she decided it had probably been her life flashing before her. She was going to die in some crummy yard in the middle of nowhere, eaten alive by a flock of crazed geese.

"Can't you bloody read?"

The voice was familiar, but she couldn't see anyone. She couldn't see anything at all. It took a while to realise she was lying face down with her eyes shut. When she opened them it was only slightly better. The gravel directly in front of her was a very odd colour – grey with flecks of red.

"I said, can't you read?" A pair of riding boots came into focus. Vanessa groaned and stayed where she was. The flecks of red seemed to be spreading. She cupped the hand which didn't hurt over her nose and realised blood was pouring from it.

She felt hands on her shoulders. "Come on, let's get you up." And she was rolled gently on to her back.

She had the briefest of advantages, as her hand – not to mention a fair bit of blood – was covering most of her face. She looked up into Garrin's eyes and saw a mixture of exasperation and concern.

"I expect it looks worse than it is. Come on, let me see." He gently pulled away her fingers and disbelief swept across his face. "Vanessa! What the fuck are you doing here?"

Chapter Six

VANESSA WAS TEMPTED TO say, 'not a lot', but the words wouldn't come out and she made a kind of gurgling sound instead. Garrin crouched beside her. The geese, much to her relief, seemed to have vanished – probably scared of him, poor things. She stole a glance at his face and knew he was biting back his anger because he didn't know how hurt she was. If he'd found her in one piece, no doubt he'd have thrown her out himself.

"Come on, sit up." He put an arm around her shoulders. She'd dreamed about him doing that lately, but not like this with blood pouring down her face and something that looked like bird shit smeared along her arm. "Lean forward and pinch your nose," he instructed. "Did you hurt anything else?"

"My wrist," she said, feeling dizzy. Must be all the blood she'd lost. Her T-shirt was splattered with it and so was the path. She stayed with her head between her knees, waiting for the dizziness to pass and glad she had an excuse not to look at him. She'd come back to say sorry to Izzy, but she owed Garrin much more than sorry.

"Has it stopped bleeding yet? Yeah, I think it has. We'd better get you cleaned up. Won't do my reputation much good if anyone sees you. Then you can tell me what you were doing in my yard."

Vanessa clambered groggily to her feet and brushed away his hand, which was a mistake because fire shot through her wrist again. It was swelling visibly and it was grazed. She held it across her chest and Garrin glanced at it too.

"Christ, that's all I need, a five-hour wait in A&E." His

sympathetic bedside manner was evaporating fast. He'd always been so patient with injured people at the fairground and there wasn't much he didn't know about natural remedies. When she'd been pregnant he'd made her all sorts of concoctions until he found one that worked for her morning sickness. Things had obviously changed.

She followed him back through the gate and maybe it was delayed shock or maybe just the sheer ludicrousness of the situation, but by the time they reached his front door, she was giggling. That sort of uncontrollable laughter you can't stop.

Garrin gave her a disgusted look and propelled her ahead of him. "Go and get cleaned up. Don't get blood on anything. I've only just had this place decorated."

Not even his disgust could stop the laughter. She went upstairs and ran the shower. Then she peeled off her jeans and wrecked T-shirt and stood under the spray watching her blood turn the water pink. Somewhere between getting in the shower and getting out of it again the laughter turned to tears and she was shivering when she finally wrapped a faded yellow towel around her.

A sharp knock on the door heralded Garrin's return. "I don't suppose your clothes are much good. Put these on and get downstairs pronto. I want to know what's going on."

She waited until she was sure he'd gone, then opened the door and found an oversized T-shirt, which was obviously his, and a pair of pink shorts, which obviously weren't. They were too small, Vanessa thought irritably, as she put them on, wondering what his girlfriend – or possibly wife – would think when she found a strange woman wearing her clothes. It was a sobering thought and she was straight-faced when she finally went downstairs.

She found Garrin in the galley kitchen. He'd had an archway knocked through to Bert's back room and light spilled through, making the kitchen look bigger than it had

46

before. Weren't places supposed to shrink when you came back to them? The black flagstone floor was still the same, so were the whitewashed walls, which were several feet thick. It must have been hell knocking that archway through. Vanessa tried to work out how long it was since she'd been here.

Garrin was bending by a fridge-freezer. He had the freezer door open and was shovelling ice into a bucket. He glanced up as she came in and then stood, knocking the door shut with his knee. Suddenly things were back in perspective because he looked too big for the kitchen. "Go through," he said, gesturing impatiently to the archway.

He wasn't at all happy, Vanessa thought, going ahead of him into the room, which was familiar, yet unfamiliar. It smelt of leather and sunshine. Bits of bridles were scattered over the dining table and a saddle was propped against a chair. The décor was different and there were pictures of horses on the walls – pictures of him riding, she realised. The room was bright with light from the French windows that opened on to the patio. She glanced out, memories flooding back because the view hadn't changed at all, it was just as breathtaking. Days spent out here with Izzy and Uncle Bert, days of innocence and orange squash and laughter.

Garrin came in behind her, the ice bucket in his hands. "This is for your wrist. Can you move your fingers?" He watched as she wriggled them. "How much does it hurt?"

"On a scale of one to ten, about seven." They'd always scored everything when they were younger: happiness; fear; pain; other people's dress-sense. She caught his look and knew he was remembering too.

He ran his fingers along either side of her wrist, pressing gently. "How about that?"

"About eight."

"I doubt it's broken then, I'll be able to tell more when

47

the swelling's gone down."

She nodded. He was usually right about such things. His mother had been a healer before she'd been mown down by a drunk driver one summer's night. Nanna Kane had been a healer too, and realising that Garrin had also inherited the gift, she'd encouraged him to develop it. None of them liked conventional hospitals; they were consulted only in the direst emergency.

He went back into the kitchen and returned with two mugs, which he put on a coffee table that had an old map of Dorset showing through the glass. He sat on a pale leather armchair, the arms darkened with creases and Vanessa sat opposite him on the settee, the ice bucket on her lap.

His thick hair was the same jet black, but shorter. He obviously had it cut more often, these days. There were more lines on his lean tanned face and there was something different about his eyes. They were still as black as darkness, but harder than she remembered.

"Well..?" he said conversationally. "I haven't got all day. You've wasted enough of my bloody time already."

"I wasn't expecting to get attacked by a bunch of vicious geese."

"You shouldn't have ignored my sign. It's big enough." He gulped coffee and narrowed his eyes over the top of his mug. "So why come back now, Vanessa? You're a bit late for the funeral."

She flinched. God, he hadn't changed. Straight for the jugular.

"I didn't know about Nanna Kane until yesterday."

"Don't give me that crap. You must have known. You're married to the arsehole. I take it you haven't brought him with you?"

His language hadn't improved. Having spent years away from the ribald banter of the fair, it sounded strange to hear Garrin's rough dark voice again. Richard rarely swore in front of her. She'd grown used to his clipped middle-class accent, his soft politeness. She closed her eyes. Even if it had been a veneer for his lies.

Garrin drummed his fingers on the arm of the chair and the air buzzed with his impatience.

"Richard doesn't know I'm here. I'm so sorry, Garrin. I truly didn't know. I'd have come straight away if I had. I loved her. You know I did."

Silence settled around them and Vanessa could feel his eyes on her. She could feel his anger too, although it was a few moments before she realised it was aimed at her. Not understanding, she went on hesitantly, "I saw Cissy yesterday. She told me about Nanna's heart attack."

"That's right. It happened a month after you'd gone. The doctors put it down to stress. Nanna didn't have a cat-in-hell's chance." His voice was casual, but she could see the bitterness in his eyes and suddenly she realised he blamed her.

"I'm so sorry."

"Yeah, so was I. So was everyone. But it was a long time ago. Life goes on. As you can see."

"Richard didn't tell me. He didn't tell me about any of it, Nanna Kane, the fairground – you – I drove down there yesterday. I thought you were all still there. It was a shock."

"You still haven't told me why you're here."

"I've left him." Had she left him? She certainly felt like it, but was she really never going back?

"Got tired of your life of luxury, did you? Well, well, and I thought it was Happy-Ever-After. What's up? Has he fallen on hard times?"

She shook her head. She'd been expecting him to be bitter, but it still hurt. Everything hurt. In the last forty-eight hours her life had crumbled and now her past life was disintegrating too. She wasn't sure how much more she could take.

"Is Izzy all right?" she asked quietly. "I'd like to get in touch with her. Do you know where she is?"

"Yeah, I do, but I'm not telling you. I don't want her upset."

"I'm not planning to upset her."

"She's got Parkinson's. She leads a very quiet life, these days. She might not want a ghost from the past turning up on her doorstep."

Vanessa stared at him. "Is it bad?"

"She's coping. You know Izzy. I'll give you her phone number. But not today. I'll tell her you're here first."

"Okay," she said, knowing she was in no position to argue with him. Anyway, he was probably right. There was no reason to think Izzy would be any more pleased to see her than Garrin was. Ice clunked against her wrist and she glanced at it. Some things you could mend, some you couldn't. How had she ever imagined she could go back there and find them all unchanged?

"Where are you staying?"

"Nowhere yet, I came straight here." She was still reeling from the news that Izzy had Parkinson's. How many more shocks could there be? Five years – a lifetime.

"There's not much choice in the village at this time of year. Besides, you can't drive and I haven't got time to taxi you around. You can stay here if you like. There's plenty of room."

"I don't think so."

"Let's get something straight. I'm not asking you because I want you here. You can go in the morning, the further the better as far as I'm concerned. I'm only offering because Izzy won't thank me for throwing you out. Suit yourself, Vanessa. I've got to do the evening feeds." He got up, took his empty mug into the kitchen and disappeared.

Vanessa found she was shaking, from his callousness, and from his indifference – could you be both at the same

50

time? The Garrin she remembered, along with everything else, seemed to have gone for ever.

Chapter Seven

VANESSA WOKE THE NEXT morning to a pale blue sky with the heat of summer already in it, despite the fact it wasn't yet eight. Disorientated she rolled over, flinched as her wrist protested violently and remembered yesterday: the geese and Garrin's hostility and her acceptance of a room for the night because he'd been right, she couldn't drive. She'd actually gone out to her car and tested the steering wheel with her good hand.

Garrin had stood in the doorway watching and after a minute he'd shouted, "Don't be so bloody ridiculous. What if you crash and kill yourself – or worse, someone else?" And she'd looked at his face and accepted defeat.

She sat up in bed. To her surprise her jeans and a fresh T-shirt were neatly folded on the chair beside her. Ironed too, she saw, getting up carefully. She'd wrenched several muscles and she felt stiff and sore. The swelling on her wrist had subsided, but it still throbbed painfully.

The house felt empty as she went downstairs. She guessed Garrin was outside with the horses. She went into the kitchen and stopped in her tracks. A petite blonde girl was standing at the sink, washing mugs. She turned as Vanessa came in.

"Hi, I'm Tracey. Garrin said you were stopping over. How are you feeling?"

Vanessa stared into blue smiling eyes and didn't say anything. The girl had peaches and cream skin and couldn't have been more than twenty. She felt dowdy and old in comparison, sharply aware of the gravel rash on her face and the darkening bruise beneath one eye.

"Blimey, you did take a tumble, didn't you? You look

like one of those battered wives posters. Want a cuppa?"

"Yes please." Vanessa attempted a smile. It hurt.

"Sit yourself down in the other room, I'll bring it in."

Vanessa did as she was bid. She hadn't expected Garrin to live alone, but this girl was so young and beautiful. No wonder he'd been annoyed when she'd turned up yesterday.

"Thanks for the loan of your shorts – and the room," Vanessa said awkwardly when Tracey brought in two mugs of tea. "I'll be out of your way later."

"Well, don't go on my account. It'll be nice to have some female company. And you can give me all the gossip from Garrin's past. You've known him a long time, haven't you? Has he always been such a bastard?"

The word tripped off her tongue with such lightness that Vanessa stared at her in surprise.

"Well, he is, isn't he? All the A.I.s are terrified of him. But they still come back, silly cows. I think most of them fancy him."

"Doesn't it bother you?"

"No, why should it?" Tracey screwed up her face. "I only work for him – hey you didn't think we were together, did you?" She laughed as if the idea was completely ridiculous and Vanessa blushed.

"Sorry – yes I did – sort of jump to that conclusion."

"God, no. He's not my type. Too moody by half. Mind you, I bet he's good in bed. He certainly gets plenty of practise."

"Does he?"

"Yeah, he's always got some girlfriend in tow, randy sod." She laughed again, her amusement infectious and Vanessa found herself joining in. It felt good to laugh. It was probably relief, she thought, although why she should be relieved that Garrin didn't have a live-in partner, she wasn't sure. She'd given up the right to care what he did when she'd married Richard.

"If you're done discussing my love-life, then you can piss off out of it and do some work." Garrin's voice cut across the air and they both jumped. He was standing in the archway, one hand resting against the wall. "I thought you were making a cuppa."

"It's on the side." Tracey got up, winked at Vanessa, and ducked under his arm. "See you later. We can catch up properly."

Garrin came right into the room. "You look a mess."

"Thanks very much."

"Tracey talks a load of bollocks. I haven't got that many girlfriends."

"What you do is your affair. I'm not interested."

"That's not what it looked like just now." He came across and sat beside her. Too close for comfort. She was aware of his hard muscled thigh close to hers and she moved pointedly away from him.

"I want to look at your wrist," he said, moving his leg back and picking up her hand. "Don't be so touchy." His fingers pressed the same spots as yesterday and she flinched. "Still eight out of ten?"

"Yes."

"I'm pretty sure it's just a sprain. I can spare Tracey to run you to hospital later – if you want a second opinion."

"No, it's all right." She took her hand back from him. "I'll get out of your way."

"How? You still can't drive. And as I said yesterday you won't find a room in the village. It's carnival week. The tourist highlight of the year. Anyway, I've invited Izzy over for supper. She wants to see you."

Vanessa kept out of his way for the rest of the day, which wasn't difficult, as he didn't come into the house much. She saw Tracey a couple more times, but she didn't want to risk

54

getting into another conversation about Garrin, aware it wouldn't take much provocation for him to explode.

She checked her mobile. Richard hadn't phoned again or answered the text she'd sent him last night, saying she'd been to the memorial garden and was staying in Knollsey overnight.

Perhaps he'd worked out what had happened – if he had, he'd know where she was and might even be on his way down here. On second thoughts, that wasn't very likely, he wouldn't want a confrontation with Garrin. He hated confrontations.

She walked down to the village and discovered Garrin was right about everywhere being full. There wasn't exactly a lot of choice anyway – one pub and a pretty house which had a B&B sign displayed, but no rooms left. Anyway, she wanted to see Izzy, and if Garrin wasn't going to give her the address, then this evening was probably her only chance.

He came in about seven and disappeared into the shower. When he came downstairs he was jangling his car keys.

"Make yourself useful and lay the table while I pick her up."

"What are we eating?"

"There's cold meat and salad in the fridge. I'll sort it when we get back. We'll eat on the patio. Izzy likes the view."

Vanessa found cutlery and napkins in his kitchen. Irrational twinges of jealousy swirled in her stomach as she opened cupboards and wondered how many women he'd brought here.

She hoped Izzy wouldn't be as hostile as Garrin. She didn't think she would; Izzy wasn't the type to hold a grudge, although God knows she deserved it, but she still felt slightly sick when she heard the front door bang and voices in the hallway.

She got up nervously as Izzy came into the lounge and was relieved to see she didn't look any different. Her white hair was pulled into a chignon, fastened with a pink slide and her hair had a pink streak in it too. Her eyes were the same clear blue that Vanessa remembered and she was smiling as she came across the room, her hands outstretched.

"Vanessa, my love, it's good to see you."

There were no recriminations in her eyes and somehow that was harder to bear than Garrin's bitterness. Vanessa took her hands and Izzy drew her close. "Oh, come here, lovie. Give me a hug."

They hugged and Vanessa could feel the old lady was as emotional as she was.

"It's good to see you, too," she murmured. "I'm sorry it's been so long."

"We've got a lot of catching up to do." Izzy drew her out onto the patio. "I'll have a glass of white wine please, Garrin, love. Same for you, Nessa?"

They sat in the glow of the late sun and Izzy touched Vanessa's face, "That looks sore. Have you put anything on it?"

"It's not too bad."

"Damn geese, they're a liability, I keep telling him he'll get himself sued one of these days. Has he been giving you a hard time?"

"No more than I deserve. I'm so sorry about Nanna."

Izzy's face clouded. "It was a very bad time for us all. When she went it was as though we were on a rudderless ship. Garrin tried to take over, but he was too inexperienced for all that responsibility and his heart wasn't in it. To be honest, I think the fair had had its time. Or at least our sort of fair. People want super rides, these days, million pound rides – Nanna never had that sort of cash – and she

56

wouldn't go in with anyone else. In some ways she was very old-fashioned. The fair was dying, Nessa. It was probably a good thing he sold."

"What happened to Uncle Bert?"

"He got himself a little villa on the Costa Del Sol. He was ready to retire and he was more than happy to sell up to Garrin. They always got on, didn't they?"

There was a small silence and Vanessa wondered if Garrin would have made the same decision if she'd been by his side. How could he have been expected to cope, torn apart by grief from the loss of his grandmother, still devastated about Jennifer's death, and the pain of her betrayal? No wonder he hated her now.

Suddenly unable to meet Izzy's eyes, she stared away across the sloping garden, towards the distant ribbon of the sea.

Reading her mind, Izzy said softly, "Don't blame yourself, Nessa. We all do what we have to. We all make decisions that are right for us at the time."

"I should have kept in touch."

"It was too painful. I do understand, you know. He does too, beneath all that bloody-mindedness." She leaned across and covered Vanessa's hands with her own, and Nanna Kane's silver bangles slipped down her wrists, a musical ting of sound, more evocative than any words could be. Vanessa swallowed and was glad Garrin chose that moment to come back with their drinks.

Izzy said her goodbyes early, confessing she was tired, and Vanessa contemplated going to bed before Garrin got back. He'd been uptight all evening, although he'd done his best to hide it, chatting easily with Izzy about his horses, mostly about one particular horse, Derry, who they seemed to think was going to be a star. Although they'd included her, and Izzy had made a point of explaining the more technical bits, a lot of the conversation had gone over Vanessa's head. She had a working knowledge of horses, gleaned from days at Uncle Bert's, but Garrin was streets ahead.

He'd taken his teaching qualifications, sailed through them, according to Izzy, and now taught and competed and took in working pupils who were studying for their Assistant Instructor exams – so that was what A.I. stood for. Izzy was proud of him; it shone out of her eyes. Vanessa had seen no sign of the Parkinson's, although Izzy had sipped her wine through a straw, saying lightly it saved her spilling so much.

Vanessa had watched Garrin as they talked. Once she'd been able to read every nuance of his face and she'd found herself slipping back into the habit. She knew he was still angry with her and she'd sensed that once or twice he'd wanted to express it, but in deference to Izzy he'd restrained himself. Vanessa had the uneasy feeling he was going to make up for lost time when he got home.

She abandoned the idea of going to bed because if he was determined to have a go at her, he'd just come upstairs, and she felt better able to deal with him, down here, fully dressed.

She was washing up one-handed when he came back in. He glanced at her and poured himself a brandy.

"Want one?" His voice was mild.

"I've had enough, thanks. I'm ready for bed."

"I want to talk to you first. Leave that."

Half nervous, half irritated, she followed him into the lounge. She might as well get it over with.

He drank his brandy and went back for the decanter.

"Haven't you got to get up early?"

"I'm catching up." He re-filled his glass, drained that too, and she looked at him in trepidation. A drunk and furious Garrin was going to be even harder to deal with.

"What do you want to talk to me about?" she said,

before he had the chance to drink any more.

He came across the room and Vanessa wished suddenly that she'd sat in an armchair instead of on the settee.

"Izzy might have forgiven you, but I haven't."

She didn't look at him and he sat beside her.

"Don't ignore me."

"I'm not. I just don't know what to say." She risked a look at his eyes, which were dark and angry.

"Sorry would be a good start."

"I thought I'd already said that."

"You said you were sorry about missing the funeral. You didn't say anything about being sorry for walking out without a word. Not that I'm bothered about that. I got over that a long time ago. What I can't get over – is that you've never been to our daughter's grave. Not once, have you? Too far to drive, was it? Or were you too busy? Perhaps you'd like to explain it to me. No – let me guess. You've replaced Jennifer with a bunch of blond-haired mini Richards. Like you replaced me. Is that it? Wiped the memories clean out of your head with your wonderful new life."

"You bastard."

He caught hold of her good hand, crushing her fingers and wrenched her round to face him. "At least I'm a bastard with a good memory, Vanessa. Tell me how you could forget about our child, just tell me."

She was shaking; she didn't know whether it was anger or pain. "I haven't forgotten Jennifer. I think about her every single day of my life. I wake up seeing her face. I always will. How the hell do you think I could forget?" She was crying now, the tears stinging her grazed face, not caring, because it was nothing to the pain he was bringing to the surface with his anger.

Garrin's eyes glittered and she knew he was close to tears too. Rage probably – there had always been a fine line between his emotions, passion spilling from anger and pain from laughter. They were the same like that, easily roused, their emotions ruling them.

"For what it's worth," she went on quietly. "I've never stopped thinking about either of you. You're joined in my mind. I can't get you apart. I never will. That's why I had to go. I couldn't bear to stay – couldn't bear to carry on looking at you and seeing Jennifer in your face. I thought if I went it would be easier. But I was wrong. It never got easier."

It was true, she realised, aching. Seeing Richard with Tara had been a catalyst, but she'd have come back sooner or later. She was joined to Garrin. He was part of her childhood, part of the fabric of her life. She would never have been able to erase him completely from her mind. Now she was here again, with him a breath or so away, she couldn't believe she'd ever tried.

His fingers had loosened, although he was still looking at her, years of pain in his eyes. She wiped her face with the back of her hand and winced.

"I should have done something about that bruise. Does it hurt?"

"Nowhere near as much as the rest."

He nodded and time stilled around them and she was reminded of a thousand other moments like this, when they'd sat together, so close it seemed nothing would ever break them. But they hadn't been united by pain then, just love. When she looked back at him, she knew he was remembering too.

"I went to see Jennifer yesterday," she said at last. "I don't know how you can bear it. I – I can't…"

He looked at her and in a movement somewhere between a shrug and an acknowledgement of her grief he put his arms around her.

Vanessa leaned against him, his closeness smashing

away the barriers of time and for a long while he just held her. She could hear his heart beating through his T-shirt; feel the warmth of his skin, and his breath in her hair. He kissed the top of her head, reassurance and comfort, for him maybe – as well as her.

There wasn't an exact moment when she knew they'd moved beyond comfort, just a growing awareness that she wanted to lie in his arms, feel his body pressing down on her. She wanted him so much it scared her.

She felt him shift, picking up her thoughts, and then he turned her face to his and kissed her gently.

"Come on," he said, his voice gruff. "Let's go up."

Still holding hands, they went upstairs. At his bedroom door he put his arms around her and she drew away from him. "I can't."

"Why not?"

"I just can't."

"Yeah, you can." He kissed her again, his lips bringing pain and wonderment and a dozen other emotions, which had been buried but not dulled by time, and she thought fleetingly about Tara. But as she let Garrin lead her into his bedroom she knew Tara was irrelevant. She'd have done this anyway.

His bedroom was shadowed and still warm from the heat of the day and it smelled of him. She sat on the bed and watched him undress. He was more muscular than she remembered – his thighs hard. She was reminded of mahogany, chiselled and perfect. His chest was muscled too, finely covered with black hair, slightly curly. He caught her watching him and glanced up, a half smile on his face. Then he came back to the bed and kissed her, his hands moving beneath her T-shirt, leisurely, freeing her breasts, as sure and as confident as if she'd never stopped being his. Vanessa moaned softly, shifting to help him, knowing this was utter madness and also that she couldn't

61

stop.

When they were both naked he lay on his side and looked at her. "Still as lovely," he murmured. He ran his fingers along her shoulder and down the curve of her back, her hip, her stomach, a voyage of rediscovery.

She touched him too, running her fingertips over his skin, tracing the tattoo of a dragonfly on his thigh. Finding him again was like finding a part of herself, the heat and scent and hardness of him reawakening half-forgotten memories. Unable to wait any longer, she moved on top of him, but Garrin was in no hurry. He teased her with his eyes and his fingers and his mouth, and finally he shifted their positions so he was above her, propped on his elbows, looking down at her face. Then he slid inside her and stayed, utterly still, watching her.

"Have you missed me?"

"What do you think?" She ground her hips against him and he stopped her with his body.

"So impatient."

"I don't want to talk – Garrin – don't – have I ever told you – what an utter – bastard – you are?" She could hardly speak for wanting him, and he was loving every second of it, his eyes black with passion.

"Then answer my question. Have you missed me?"

"Yes." The word was half shout, half gasp. She could feel her muscles clenching and unclenching around him and still he didn't move.

He laughed and kissed the bruise on her face.

"Then we won't talk." He drove into her with such intensity that within seconds she could feel the orgasm building. There was nothing in the world except Garrin, the lines of his face hardened in passion, a fine sheen of sweat on his skin, his love-making a knife-edge of desire and anger.

When she was capable of coherent thought, Vanessa

wondered again how she'd ever thought she could leave him.

"That'll do for starters," he said, sliding out of her, his voice softer now, his eyes gentle. He traced the line of her cheekbone with his fingertips so tenderly she wanted to weep for all the time they'd wasted.

Instead, she caught his hand and pulled him close, scared to let him see what she still felt for him.

Misinterpreting the gesture, he ran his tongue over the lobe of her ear. "You might be ready for round two," he muttered, "but I need a minute or two to get my breath back."

Chapter Eight

HE WAS GONE BEFORE Vanessa woke and for a while she stayed in his bed, ashamed because she'd never dreamt she could betray Richard so easily. The fact he'd betrayed her first was no excuse. None whatsoever. But she couldn't pretend she didn't also feel a sense of slowly rising joy as she remembered the previous night. It was as though a part of her that had been missing for such a long time was back in place.

She went to find Garrin and discovered him in what Tracey had said was the outdoor school. He was lunging a horse, a whip in one hand, a long line in the other, his body making up one point of the triangle. He stopped when he saw her, put down the whip and coiled the lunging rein into loops as he went towards the horse. Then he opened the connecting gate that led through to the field next door, undid the horse's headgear and set it free with a slap on the rump. The horse ambled away from him, lowered its head and sniffed the grass.

Before Vanessa could speak, Garrin turned to her, unsmiling, and said, "I want you to go."

"Why?" Vanessa asked, her trainers sinking into the peat. In the field the horse's legs buckled, front end going down first as it collapsed with a grunt and rolled on the dusty summer ground. Her legs felt close to buckling too.

"Because we can't go back. I can't risk letting you into my life again."

"I thought you already had."

"That was my bed, not my life," he said calmly. "Go back to Richard. The bloke's probably frantic."

"I can't." She looked at his face, trying to find

something of the man he'd been last night, but he'd shut down. His eyes were cold, his mouth hard.

"Well, do what you like, but you're not staying here."

She could feel the sun burning the tops of her shoulders, but it didn't touch the ice that was spreading within her.

"I'll go and pack my stuff, then." That wouldn't take long: most of it was still in her car.

He nodded and added as an afterthought. "Is your wrist okay to drive?"

"That's my problem, isn't it?" she snapped, walking away before he could see how much he'd hurt her. But perhaps that was what last night had been about. Perhaps he'd just wanted her to have a taste of what she'd handed out to him. He'd certainly succeeded there. She straightened her shoulders and remembering something, turned.

"You said you'd give me Izzy's address."

"It's on a pad in the kitchen. Help yourself."

He didn't come back to the house and half an hour later she was driving away, cramps churning her stomach so that once she had to pull over into a gateway because she thought she might be sick. Garrin might be moody and fiery and unpredictable – but he'd never been cruel. Was this her doing? Had she made him like this by leaving?

She went to Izzy's, which turned out to be a pretty ivy-covered bungalow on the cliffs, not far from Lulworth village. When Izzy opened the door, she smiled, and Vanessa had a feeling the old lady had been expecting her.

Izzy made coffee, refusing help, and they sat in a pretty back room, which was dominated by a huge window that overlooked the sea.

"He'll calm down. Give him a few days. You know how he is."

"I don't think so. I think he'd be happier if he never saw me again."

"He might think that now, but it's not how he feels deep down. You've re-opened old wounds, my love. And he's too proud to admit you going was partly his fault."

"It wasn't."

"You're too hard on yourself. I know how he was when you lost Jennifer. He went inside himself. Men do that and I know it wasn't what you needed. You were both grieving in different ways and it drove you apart. I think your splitting up was inevitable." Izzy hesitated. "Tell me if you think it's none of my business, but what are you going to do about Richard?"

"I'm going to divorce him."

"Are you sure that's what you want?"

Vanessa nodded. "He's having an affair with an older woman. How ironic is that? They're supposed to go off with younger ones, aren't they?"

"You sound like you care," Izzy remarked thoughtfully.

"I only found out a couple of days ago. It was a surprise, that's all. I'd have come back anyway..." She tailed off, aware of Izzy's knowing eyes. "Okay, maybe it isn't as simple as that. I did think I loved Richard. He's not all bad, Izzy. He had a terrible upbringing. He lost his dad when he was ten and his mother's a hard-nosed cow. He wasn't even allowed to cry at the funeral. How sad is that?"

"Your upbringing wasn't a walk in the park, but it didn't turn you into a callous selfish individual who doesn't care who they hurt."

Vanessa lowered her eyes. "I had a great upbringing. I had you, Izzy. And I have hurt people. I hurt Garrin badly. And you."

"Not intentionally, you didn't." Izzy frowned. "Nessa love, I'm not trying to talk you into going back to Richard – far from it – you know how I feel about that man – but are you sure this is what you want? These last few days must have been a terrible shock."

"Yes, they have, but it's not just that. As soon as I saw Garrin I realised I'd been kidding myself. I should never have married Richard. I've been living a half-life."

"Nostalgia is a powerful thing."

"It's not just nostalgia. When I was lying in that yard and I heard his voice." She hesitated, closing her eyes against the memory of last night. "Oh, I don't know what it is, but I knew I'd been wrong to leave. You take it with you, don't you, you can't run away."

"Did Richard tell you he was having an affair?"

"No. I saw them. Richard doesn't know I know."

"He's probably got an inkling now. Where does he think you are?"

Vanessa shrugged and Izzy went on quietly, "Don't make the same mistake you made with Garrin. Sort things out properly with Richard. If you're serious about divorcing him, then at the very least you should get yourself a decent settlement."

"I don't want his money."

"You can't live on fresh air, lovie. You need somewhere to settle down, lick your wounds for a while, until you work out what you're going to do. Get what you're entitled to." She leaned forward and touched Vanessa's hand. "Trust me on this. I know what I'm talking about. I've had three divorces and I always made sure they left me with property, even if it was only a living wagon." Her eyes sparkled with laughter and Vanessa smiled, warmed.

"This is a lovely house."

"Yes, but I didn't get this from a husband, none of the buggers had that much money. Bert gave me the deposit. And Garrin put up the rest. Nanna Kane left everything to him and I think he felt guilty. Do you remember Harry and Jean who had the dodgems? He pays the rent on their flat, too. Everyone else was young enough to get another job, but they were well past it. They'd have been on the streets if he hadn't looked after them."

"He's all heart."

"Don't be like that. It doesn't suit you."

"Sorry." You're right. I am a bit shell-shocked I think." More nuclear-bomb-shocked, but she couldn't tell Izzy this. What had happened between her and Garrin was too private and hurtful to share.

"Well, that's because you're in limbo. You need to get things sorted out with Richard and you'll feel much better. I promise. You'll keep in touch this time, though, won't you?"

"Of course I will." Vanessa hesitated. "When did you find out about the Parkinson's?"

"It was about five years ago. I saw this young neurologist, rather dishy actually. He asked me for a sample of my handwriting. One of the symptoms is that your writing gets smaller as it goes across the page. I wrote – I think this doctor is very dishy. He didn't turn a hair, I probably embarrassed him." She smiled. "But he diagnosed Parkinson's. There are a lot worse things to have."

"Oh, Izzy – and there's me moaning on about my problems. I'm sorry."

"Don't be. As I frequently tell Garrin, if I have to have an incurable disease, I'd rather have one that doesn't hurt. It's not painful. Just a little inconvenient."

"What sort of inconvenient?"

"I think the worst thing about it is the dyskinesia – it's the thing most people associate with Parkinson's, the involuntary movements." She stood up and demonstrated how her feet weren't quite in control and Vanessa felt both humbled and proud that she was facing her illness with such unselfconscious courage. Typical Izzy.

Izzy sat down again. "Afternoons are normally my worst time, but I tend to have a nap then, so I don't notice it so much. Anyway, that's enough of me, what are you going to do now?"

"Talk to Richard. You're right. Izzy, tell me something. Did you write to me when Nanna Kane died? Or phone?"

"Yes, love, I thought you'd want to know, but I wasn't surprised when you didn't reply."

The old lady's eyes were gentle and Vanessa wondered if she hadn't been surprised because she'd suspected she hadn't got the letter or because she'd thought she hadn't wanted any more involvement. It was too painful to ask.

"Nessa, if you do get stuck, you can come and stay with me. I've a very comfortable spare room."

"Garrin would love that."

"He bought me the house; he doesn't dictate who comes into it."

Chapter Nine

THE THREE NIGHTS VANESSA had been away felt like for ever. She was half surprised to see 24 Birch Avenue looked exactly the same. The hedge, grown straggly with summer, still needed cutting. The hanging baskets in the front garden looked in need of water. Richard didn't notice plants unless they were dead.

His car was in the drive, so there would be no putting off the confrontation. She let herself in and stood for a moment in their lounge, breathing in air that smelled of stale cigarette smoke and emptiness. She found Richard upstairs in his office, hunched over his desk, a whisky glass and full ashtray at his side. There were papers strewn everywhere and a Mozart CD played softly.

She stood in the doorway without speaking and for a moment he just stared, as if he couldn't quite believe his eyes, and then he was stumbling across the room. "My God, what's happened to you? I've been out of my mind with worry."

Not out of it enough to come after me, she thought, but said nothing, just waited for him to get to her.

He stopped before he touched her, as if he sensed her stillness. "Where have you been?" His eyes were so haunted she felt guilt flickering through her, and then remembering what he had done and why she was here, she gathered herself.

"You know where I've been – I texted you twice, you didn't answer."

"You know I don't read texts." His blue eyes flickered and she knew he had read them, but, for some reason of his own, decided not to respond. Perhaps he wanted to establish how much exactly she'd found out before incriminating himself. He knew her well enough to realise she wouldn't stay away too long.

"I've been back to the fairground, but it wasn't there – as you know. And then I went to see Garrin. I knew he'd have Izzy's address and I felt I owed them an apology. For not going to Nanna Kane's funeral. Why didn't you tell me she was dead?"

Ignoring her question he stepped closer and reached out to touch her face. "Did he do this to you?"

"Don't. It hurts. And no of course not, what do you take him for, some sort of savage?"

He dropped his hand. "No – no, of course not."

"Why didn't you tell me about Nanna Kane?"

"Vanessa – sweetheart – we can talk about that later. God, it's so good to see you. Come here."

"Please, I want to know. I can't talk about anything else until I know." She was aware her voice was rising and that he looked faintly shocked, as if she'd never shouted at him before. She realised she hadn't. How had she managed it?

"You're upset. That's perfectly understandable, come downstairs, and I'll fix us a drink. We can talk all you want."

"I don't want a drink," she said, but it wasn't true. Five minutes back in this house and she did want one. She'd spent five years being comfortably numb and now she'd had a shot of reality she couldn't bear it. She needed an anaesthetic to numb the pain.

"Come on." His voice was quietly reasonable as if he was calming a child in a tantrum. "Let's go and sit downstairs."

So they went and she stood watching him at the bar, pouring himself another scotch and mixing her a gin and tonic, cutting up lemon from the small fridge below it, taking out two cubes of ice, his movements slow and

71

deliberate.

He handed it to her and she gulped it down, aware that once again she'd shocked him. She hardly ever drank.

"I want a divorce," she said before she'd put down the glass.

"No, you don't. You don't know what you're saying."

"Stop treating me like a child. Is that why you didn't tell me what was going on? Because you thought it was better to protect me? Or were you really trying to protect yourself?"

He looked at her. "Yes, okay, I did think it was best you didn't know. And maybe you're right. I didn't want you to go back to him. It was still early days for us and you were so hurt. I was scared, I admit it." He broke off, went to the bar, picked up a packet of cigarettes and lit one with fingers that weren't steady. He took a deep draw on it and turned back to her. "I love you. I've never loved anyone so much in my life. Is that so wrong?"

In a minute he'd bring up his mother, who'd never approved of their marriage and who made her feelings very clear on the few occasions they'd visited. He'd start telling her she wasn't the only one who'd given things up, who'd had to compromise. He'd done it once before when he'd caught her sending Izzy a birthday card. In the end he'd talked her round to his way of thinking and the card never was sent.

"I saw you with Tara," she said quietly. "On the day I left. I saw you kiss her in the car park."

He frowned, as if trying to remember some trivial detail and when he spoke he sounded puzzled. "We had a business lunch. We often do. I didn't kiss her."

"I saw you," she repeated, already feeling as if the situation was sliding out of her control.

"I may have pecked her on the cheek." Richard's voice was dismissive.

72

"You did more than peck her on the cheek. Then you lied to me about being in the office. How long has it been going on?"

"Nothing's going on, Vanessa. I swear. I'd never do anything to risk losing you. You're all I've ever wanted. Surely you know that. It's not a one-way thing. I've given up a lot for you." He abandoned the cigarette and took hold of her hands. His felt slightly damp and she could smell smoke and scotch on his breath. Yet his eyes were totally sincere and she began to feel the first threads of doubt.

Deciding to abandon this line of conversation for now, Vanessa went back to what he couldn't deny.

"I missed Nanna Kane's funeral."

"Yes, I know, but what good would it have done if you'd been there? It would have meant more upset, more grief. You couldn't have coped with that. You were in pieces."

"You should have let me be the judge of that!"

"With hindsight, maybe I should. But it's over now, past tense, ancient history."

"Not for me," Vanessa snapped. "I've only just found out – and what about the rest – what about the fairground? Why didn't you tell me about that? Did you think that would upset me too?"

His face was flushed – from drink or from shame – she couldn't tell. He put his hands on her shoulders and looked into her eyes. "Have you – been with him?"

"No."

"Truth?"

She shook her head, unable to repeat the lie, but knowing she'd break him if she told him she had; she couldn't bring herself to do it. Despite what he'd done – despite Tara.

"Then we can start again. This could be a good thing, getting everything out in the open. It's been haunting me for years. I've had nightmare after nightmare about it. I know I should have told you, but it got harder as time went on. I'm so sorry, sweetheart, but I know we can put this behind us." He was surer of himself now, his voice softly persuasive.

He strode back to the bar and mixed her another gin and tonic and, as she took it Jennifer's face flashed before her.

"I don't think I can, Richard. You've lied to me. How many more lies have you told?"

"White lies, that's all they were – to protect you. It'll take time, I realise that. But we can do it. We love each other."

The alcohol was soporific and his voice like a hypnotist's, soft and insistent. She could feel herself slipping back into her old life imperceptibly, moment by moment, fragmenting beneath his steady reassurance. It was what she'd run to, she thought, pressing her hand to her head: Richard's constancy and his calm because, when they'd met, that was what he'd offered her, a sea of steadiness amidst all the turmoil. The one thing that Garrin, too tangled in his own pain, hadn't been able to give.

And now they were face-to-face her resolve was weakening. Discovering she still loved Garrin, and that he despised her enough to sleep with her and throw her out like rubbish, hurt terribly. How easy it would be to let Richard take charge. How tempting to pretend the last four days had never happened. But even as the thought flashed into her head she knew she couldn't forget. She couldn't lie to herself about what she felt. Not this time.

Again she pressed her fingers to her face, and Richard, misinterpreting the gesture, took her drink from her hands. "Christ, what have you done to your wrist? It looks broken, have you been to hospital?"

Her skin was violet and blue, she noticed distractedly, but it didn't hurt any more. "There was no need. It's just a sprain."

"It doesn't look like one. Come on, I'll drive you there."

"You've been drinking."

"Then I'll call David. He'll come out. He owes me a favour."

"No, Richard. My wrist's fine." It was her head that felt muzzy. She shouldn't have drunk anything. It had taken all the fight out of her, and she needed a clear head or he'd tie her in knots.

She tried again. "I saw you kissing Tara. It wasn't a peck on the cheek. You had your arms around her. I didn't imagine that."

He sighed and with a small sigh he settled on the sofa and gestured for her to join him. "All right, I'll tell you what happened, but you must keep this to yourself. Tara's got problems. She and her husband have been trying for a baby. They've been trying for ten years."

She stared at him. "I didn't know that."

"No – well, that's because she didn't want anyone to know. She's very proud. She only told me because I caught her in tears a couple of weeks ago."

Vanessa frowned and tried to conjure up an image of Richard's hard-headed, ruthlessly-ambitious business partner crying because she couldn't have babies. It was impossible.

It was also the only thing he could have said that would get him off the hook.

"Tara had her first IVF treatment a few weeks ago and she'd just found out it hadn't worked." Richard sighed and met her steady gaze. "What you saw in the car park was me comforting her. That's why I had my arms around her."

Vanessa didn't answer. It could have been true. Before she'd found out about the fairground she'd have believed him without question. Now, she wasn't so sure. There was a long pause and finally she broke it, saying the first thing that came to mind. "Will she have more IVF, do you think?"

75

"Yes, I expect she will. I've been thinking. Maybe we could try that, too. I know how much you want a baby."

"Another baby," Vanessa said automatically, hating the thought of Jennifer being dismissed.

"Another baby," he went on, not missing a beat. "I know I said I wasn't keen on it, but if it would make you happy, I'm prepared to reconsider?"

She could hardly believe what she was hearing. The subject had come up before, but Richard had always been totally against the idea, insisting it would make him feel less of a man if she had IVF – particularly as it was probably his fault she couldn't conceive.

"I don't think we should be talking about this now," she murmured, getting up. "I've just told you I want a divorce."

"We can talk tomorrow then," he said, ignoring the rest of her sentence and following her into the kitchen. "I'm so glad you're home."

Chapter Ten

VANESSA KNEW SHE MIGHT have been a coward in the past, but seeing Garrin again – and more importantly, Izzy – had made her realise she'd no intention of making the same mistakes again. Okay, it wasn't possible to change what had happened, but she wasn't running away this time. Izzy was right, she needed to get things sorted out properly with Richard, which was more difficult than she'd expected, because he refused point blank to talk about divorce.

Over the next few days, every time she mentioned it he changed the subject. He left early for work in the mornings and he got back late and went straight to bed. Vanessa had been sleeping in the spare room since she'd returned and he didn't question this.

Perhaps he thought she'd change her mind if he ignored her for long enough.

"The atmosphere's terrible," she told Izzy, whom she'd taken to calling regularly. It was good to have Izzy back in her life. Izzy was part of her past, part of the good bit, without Izzy she wouldn't have had any stability at all while she was growing up. "I don't know what to do. He won't talk to me and I can't just walk out on him."

"I don't see why not. He's playing mind games with you, Nessa. He probably thinks he'll wear you down if he can keep you there long enough. Why don't you come and stay with me?"

"I don't want to impose."

"Don't be so silly. You're welcome any time. You know you are."

But although Vanessa knew Izzy meant it and was touched beyond belief that she still cared, she knew stopping with the old lady wasn't a long-term solution. She was ill – probably more seriously than she was making out – she needed peace and quiet, not more hassle.

Then one Friday, three weeks after her visit to Knollsey, things came to a head.

Richard got home before nine for a change and Vanessa waited until he'd showered, had poured his first scotch and was about to switch on the television – another handy little ploy he'd taken to using so he didn't have to speak to her – before confronting him. She switched it off at the mains and said quietly. "This isn't going away, Richard. Our marriage is a sham. I want out."

He stood up abruptly.

"I'll never agree to a divorce, Vanessa. In my family, marriage is for ever – 'til death us do part. You'd do well to remember that." He looked down at her, his blue eyes cold, and she felt a small shiver run down her back.

"Are you threatening me?"

He smiled without warmth. "I doubt very much it would ever come to that." Bending, he rested his hands on her shoulders and when he spoke again his voice was softer. "Besides, where will you go, Vanessa? Think about it – your old life is gone. It doesn't exist any more. You have no parents, no real friends. You're not qualified to do anything – well you might be qualified, but you don't have any work experience, except what you've done here – and I hardly think that's going to help."

Furious, but still holding his gaze, she stepped back a pace so he was forced to drop his hands. "Do you seriously think any of that is going to make me stay here? Don't kid yourself, Richard. I might have been naïve in the past, but I'm not that vulnerable little kid you married. You can't manipulate me like that. Not now. Not ever."

As if aware he'd pushed her too far, he put up a placating hand. "I'm sorry – I didn't mean it like that. I

78

don't want to lose you. Please, Vanessa, you have to give our marriage another chance. It hasn't been all bad, has it?"

"No," she acknowledged, surprised at how quickly he'd backed off. And he was right, it hadn't been all bad. She'd thought she was happy until she'd seen him with Tara. Or had it been until she'd seen Garrin and realised part of her had never stopped loving him?

She looked into Richard's eyes and caught a flicker of hope and knew he'd seen her indecision. But she couldn't let him think there was any chance of saving their marriage. It wasn't fair to mislead him. One thing had become crystal clear over the last few weeks. If she'd really loved Richard, she'd never have slept with Garrin.

What she'd said to Izzy was true. She'd been living a half-life since she'd been married and she owed it to herself to change it.

"Promise me you'll think about it. We could go away – have a second honeymoon."

That was the last thing she wanted. The thought of sleeping with him again – even being in the same bed as him – turned her stomach. Yet he was trying so hard.

"I need to go to Malaga anyway. There's a problem with the new villas. I thought we had it all wrapped up, but some bastard's crept out of the woodwork with a 'rights of access' claim." He sighed, stress creasing his forehead. "It's bad enough normally, but the whole damn country goes on holiday in August. I have to get it sorted before then. If I'm not there, it'll drag on and on and we can't afford it."

So that was what this was all about – his work – he wasn't thinking about her at all.

Vanessa shook her head in disbelief. "I don't want to go to Malaga. You go if you need to. When would you have to go?"

"Soon. Tomorrow if I want to salvage anything."

"How long will you be away?"

"A few days – a week tops."

She sighed. "I can't carry on pretending nothing's wrong, Richard. I'm not sure I'll be here when you get back."

"Where will you be?"

"I don't know. I'll be in touch."

His face hardened. Then he shrugged, turned abruptly and left the room. When she went upstairs he was packing a case in their bedroom – folding shirts neatly into it, his movements unhurried and controlled, as if he were going on any other routine business trip.

"I'm sorry," she said, standing in the doorway.

"Are you?" He glanced up, meeting her eyes fleetingly, but he didn't say any more. And she wondered if this was it – if he'd finally accepted she meant what she said – and their marriage was ending here, as quietly as it had begun.

In the morning when she came downstairs he'd gone and the house felt much lighter without him. But Vanessa didn't feel as relieved as she'd expected. She wandered around the tidy rooms, realising there was very little of her in this house. It was Richard's personality, not hers, that was reflected back at her from the modern kitchen and bachelor-style black and white lounge. The only colour in the lounge was the striking picture of a Spanish bullfight hanging over the mantelpiece. The matador, with his cold black eyes, stood over the stricken bull with a bloodied knife in his hands.

Vanessa had always hated that picture. It wouldn't be a wrench to leave this house. It would be a blessing.

It was as she was standing in the kitchen looking at the calendar on the notice board that something struck her. Her period had been due the previous weekend. Or was it this one? Perhaps PMT was partly responsible for the black cloud feeling that hung over her. Rummaging through her bag she found her pocket diary and checked the dates. The realisation that she was two weeks late knocked the breath out of her – she was always as regular as clockwork. It must be the stress. It had to be stress. No way could she be pregnant. They hadn't touched each other since she'd got back from Knollsey.

Her mind raced in frantic circles, but it always came back to the same fact – Garrin – how could she have forgotten Garrin? She felt a trickle of sweat run between her shoulder-blades despite the coolness of the kitchen. If she were pregnant and not just late, then she'd complicated things beyond belief.

On autopilot, she drove down to the chemist, filled her shopping basket with things she didn't need. Not that there could be any doubt about what she'd come in for, she thought wryly, as the girl serving rung up the three pregnancy testers she'd put in – all different brands – all promising ninety-nine per cent accuracy.

Chapter Eleven

"HE'S COMING ALONG BEAUTIFULLY," Izzy said.

"Yeah, isn't he?" They were watching Derry do a circuit of the school, Tracey on his back. Garrin never got tired of the horse's fluid movements. The way he dipped his head, perfectly balanced, his forelegs striking the peat as if they didn't really touch it at all.

"And how about you?"

"What?"

"Have you heard from Vanessa?"

"No. Why? Should I have done?"

"Garrin, don't be so difficult. It must have taken a lot of courage, getting in touch after all this time. Especially when she knew what sort of reception she was going to get."

"The bruises will have healed by now."

"The ones you gave her or those dratted birds?"

"Nobody asked her to come back. Okay, that's enough for now," he called to Tracey, walking away from Izzy and resting a hand on the horse's bridle. He looked up at Tracey's glowing face. "Not bad. A touch on the forehand."

"He bloody well was not."

"Do I pay you to argue?"

"You don't pay me anywhere near enough to take the crap you dish out." She dismounted incorrectly by swinging one leg forward over the horse's neck, and, ignoring his furious glare, she put an arm around Derry's neck and kissed him. "He's an absolute darling, unlike his owner."

Garrin gave up and went back to where Izzy stood giggling. "Well, at least that young lady knows how to handle you."

"Meaning?"

"Well, you are a bastard, darling. I'm surprised you've got any staff left."

"So, what about Vanessa?" she pressed him, when they were sitting on his patio, sipping white wine in the early evening sunshine and toasting Derry's future success.

"What about bloody Vanessa?" He turned, irritated. "Change the record, Izzy. I don't want to talk about her."

"She phoned me last night. She's leaving Richard, you know."

"So she said."

"I think you should talk to her."

"We said everything we needed to say, last time. Cleared up quite a bit from what I remember."

"And I think you have unfinished business."

"Well, I don't."

"Take it from me, you do. I've invited her round to my house tomorrow morning. And I would be eternally grateful if you'd be there."

Garrin sighed. "There's no point. I can't stand being anywhere near her."

"Hmm," Izzy said cryptically and turned her attention back to her wine.

He went, because he knew he'd never hear the end of it if he didn't. Vanessa was already there when he arrived, sitting on the chair next to Izzy. His damn chair. Why couldn't she stay out of his life? He'd spent the last month trying to get her out of his head and he'd almost succeeded. She stood up when she saw him, her face uneasy.

He nodded curtly. "Shall I put the coffee on, Izzy?"

"I've already done it. Sit down."

He pulled up a dining room chair and straddled it, resting his arms on the back. If he didn't look too comfortable, then maybe they'd get the message he wasn't staying.

No one spoke. He glanced at his watch pointedly. "What do you want, Vanessa?"

"I thought you might like to know I'm pregnant," she said quietly, her dark eyes on his.

"And why the hell would I want to know that?"

"Because it's your baby." She glanced at Izzy and stood up, shaking her head. "I knew this was a bad idea."

"What do you mean, MY baby?" He stood up too, knocking the chair over in his haste and stormed across the room.

"I surely don't have to spell it out for you." She looked up into his eyes and he saw her anger.

"No way. It can't be mine. You're married."

"That doesn't actually work as contraception." Sarcasm dripped from her voice. "Like it or not, it's your baby. I wasn't going to tell you, but Izzy thought you had a right to know. That's why I came." She picked up her bag from the arm of the chair. "But I'll go now, I think." She headed for the door and he grabbed her arm, impatience making him rougher than he'd intended. "Wait a minute. How do you know it's my baby?"

"Because Richard can't have children." She slapped away his hand and added coldly, "You could, of course, wait until it's born. Get a paternity test – if we get that far."

Pain stabbed through him, turning swiftly into anger. "No way, I don't believe this. Are you sure? I mean, are you sure you're pregnant? Not just late. Vanessa, are you certain?"

"I've done a test and I'm going to see my doctor this afternoon. But I've been sick a couple of mornings this week, so I'm pretty certain, yes."

"I'll come with you."

"You will not."

They were still glaring at each other when Izzy came back with a tray, her arrival announced by the clattering of saucers. Garrin hadn't realised she'd left the room, and he glanced at her.

"Just like old times," she remarked, putting the tray on the table and grimacing. "You two need your heads knocking together. Garrin, fetch the coffee, please. I'd hate to spill any on my nice carpet."

He went. In the kitchen he banged his fist hard on the table. This couldn't be happening. Why had he taken her to bed? Why hadn't he used a condom? There'd been a packet in his bedside table drawer.

He knew exactly why he hadn't. From the moment he'd touched her he'd known he couldn't let her leave without seeing if it was still the same between them. And it had been. Perfect, perfect sex. Stopping for a condom hadn't even crossed his mind.

Afterwards, she'd fallen asleep and he'd stayed up and watched her face, stunned by the strength of his emotions. He still loved her. For most of the night he'd lain awake, wondering what to do. He was pretty sure she'd regret sleeping with him in the morning and he couldn't bear to be rejected again.

So he'd got in first and told her to leave. For a split second there had been pain in her eyes, but when she'd gone without even a trace of a fight he'd known he'd done the right thing.

Now she was back and he didn't have a clue what to do. He shook his head, fixed a blank expression on his face and took the coffee-pot in.

Vanessa was sitting down again, but she didn't look at him.

"Well," Izzy said. "Are we going to talk sensibly now?"

Vanessa gave in and let him drive her to the doctor's in Chandlers Ford. She was tired of arguing and besides, Izzy was probably right. She was never going to win a battle like that with Garrin.

There were several women in the surgery with kids, but that didn't stop them stroking their hair and flicking flirtatious glances at Garrin.

Irritated, Vanessa tried not to look. She wondered if it was true what Tracey had said. Was she really one of a long line of women?

"You can wait out here," she told Garrin when her name was called. He looked as if he was going to argue about that too, but in the end he sat down again.

"Congratulations, Mrs Hamilton." She hadn't seen the GP before, he was new, but his eyes were warm, as if he were personally responsible for her condition. "We'll get you booked in for your first scan. I'm going to give you a leaflet on dos and don'ts in pregnancy, but you're in good health. I don't foresee any problems."

"I was in good health last time," she said quietly.

His eyes softened. He'd already been through her records. "There are no guarantees, but there's absolutely no reason why that should happen again. We'll keep an extra close eye on you."

Vanessa stood up. "Thanks."

Garrin was still sitting where she'd left him. He got up, reading her face. It was hard to tell what he was thinking. One night of revenge and this was what he'd ended up with. She almost felt sorry for him.

The feeling evaporated as soon as they got into his car. "You can move into my house," he said, putting the keys in the ignition, but not starting the engine.

"No thanks."

"Why not? You've left Richard, haven't you?"

"I'm twenty-seven, not ten. Just because I've left my husband, it doesn't mean I want to shack up with you."

"You were happy enough to jump into my bed."

She couldn't believe his arrogance. "From what I remember you were the one who did most of the jumping." She laid her hands deliberately over her stomach and stared him out. "This child and I will manage perfectly without you. I've already rented a flat."

This wasn't actually true. She'd looked at a few in the Purbecks and been jolted by how expensive they were. It would be cheaper to get somewhere in Southampton, but she wanted to be as far away from Richard as possible. She'd never really fitted in with Richard's friends. The women were wary of her because she wasn't one of them. The men ogled, while also managing to be patronising. It would be simpler to begin again and she wanted to be near Izzy. But renting somewhere expensive would eat up her savings very quickly. It was all very well for Izzy to insist she got a good settlement, but Richard hadn't agreed to a divorce. He might when he found out about this.

"Where is it then?"

"What?"

"The flat. I need to know so I can stay in touch."

"I don't want you to stay in touch."

"Vanessa, believe me, it isn't top of my wish list either, but what are you going to do? Think about it. You're pregnant, husbandless, and jobless – or are you planning on getting a job in a fair?" He glanced at her. "Thought not. How are you going to survive?"

"I'll manage."

"Bollocks. You're not taking risks with my baby."

His words cut deeply and for a few moments she couldn't speak. She closed her eyes. Her jaw was clamped with tension – she would not break down in front of him. She would not.

"I'm sorry." His voice was very soft. "That was a shit thing to say."

Still without looking at him, she nodded in

acknowledgment. "Although it's not as though I don't deserve it."

He neither contradicted nor agreed with her, but when he spoke again, his voice was still gentle. "I'll take you to your flat if you tell me where it is and we can talk there. I want to be part of my child's life. I've a right to be."

"I'm not saying you can't be when it's born," she murmured. "We'll make some arrangements then."

"But what are you going to do? I don't believe you've got a flat and Richard won't have you back in that condition. I doubt you'll get much of a settlement out of him now either."

Vanessa shivered. There was a lot of truth in what he said, but she would have died rather than admit it. "If the worst comes to the worst, I'll stay with Izzy."

"Over my dead body."

"Just take me back to Izzy's, Garrin. I'm not fighting with you."

He ignored her and took her to Fair Winds. "I'll take you to your flat when I believe you've got one," he said, screeching to a halt on the gravel outside the house.

She was so furious she could hardly speak. She got out of the car and glared at the churned up gravel beneath his tyres.

"Go in," he said. "I've got things to do."

And unless she wanted to walk back to Izzy's, where her car was parked, in the skirt and strappy uncomfortable shoes she'd put on for her doctor's appointment, she had very little choice but to do what he said.

Tracey was sitting on a patio seat, smoking a cigarette and drinking tea. "Oh, is he back? Better get going," she said with a grin. "Bloody slave-driver. Are you all right? you look a bit pale."

"I'm fine," Vanessa said, slipping into the seat beside her. "I don't suppose you know of any cheap local flats, do

88

you? I need a job as well."

"The free paper's on the coffee table, you might find something in there. I'll get it for you."

When Tracey had gone back to work, Vanessa scanned through it. There was bar work, which she'd never done, and a temporary cleaning job. Well, she could do that if she got stuck. There was nothing resembling an office job. Besides she wasn't sure if working as Richard's PA qualified her to be anyone else's. He was hardly going to give her a reference.

There was also a cottage for rent in the village for about three times the amount she could hope to earn. She sighed and put down the paper and wondered if Izzy had meant it when she said it wasn't up to Garrin who she had in the bungalow. She didn't want to cause trouble between them.

She called a taxi, walked slowly down to the end of the lane to meet it and asked to be taken to the nearest Nat West.

"Just a balance, please," she said to the cashier, hoping it wouldn't take too long. She didn't have money to waste on taxis.

The cashier handed her a slip of paper and Vanessa glanced at it. Enough for a deposit and a month's rent. She supposed she could do that for starters.

"How about this one?" she asked, giving the details of her joint account with Richard. Pride had stopped her from withdrawing money from it since she'd decided to leave him, but she was running out of options.

Vanessa stared at the second balance slip in horror. Richard had obviously anticipated she'd do this and there was next to nothing left in it. Well that was that then. Crumpling the pieces of paper and stuffing them in her bag, she went back to the waiting taxi and gave him Izzy's address.

*　　　*　　　*

89

"Of course you can stay here, Nessa, love, but wouldn't you be better off with Garrin?"

"I'd rather sleep rough."

"That wouldn't be very sensible, would it?" Izzy sighed. "Come in, love."

"He's not going to be pleased when he finds out."

"Don't worry about that. I'll deal with him, but honestly, Nessa, you are going to need something more permanent eventually. This place isn't really big enough for a little one, much as I'd love it."

"I'll be long gone by then," Vanessa said confidently. "I'll get a job and rent a flat."

"You can't work when the baby comes. How did it go with Richard?"

They settled in Izzy's beautiful lounge, the sea beyond the window sparkling and vibrant today. It was impossible to stay depressed for long with a view like that. Vanessa looked at Izzy and decided it was probably why she loved this place so much.

"It didn't go all that well, to be honest. He doesn't want a divorce. He asked me to stay and try again and I almost did, but it wouldn't have been right. I should never have married Richard in the first place. I kidded myself I was in love with him, but I'm not so sure I ever was. I think I was just running away."

"Have you told him you're pregnant?"

"No. He's gone to Spain and I can't tell him something like that on the phone. He asked me before, you see, if Garrin and I had been – well, together – and I lied. Christ, it was only the once. Garrin's idea of revenge, I think, I didn't expect this to be the result. I've made a mess of things, haven't I?"

"Nothing's ever as bad as it seems," Izzy said slowly, leaning back in her chair, but she wasn't quick enough to hide the tremor that went through her.

"Are you all right?"

"Yes, I'm fine. I'm on new medication, that's all. The hospital keeps changing it around, but nothing much seems to suit me. Right pair, aren't we?"

Vanessa nodded. Izzy's illness was another reason she didn't want to go too far away. So much that she'd thought was solid had been proved not to be so. She wanted to stay as close as possible to Izzy, although she was beginning to realise that living with her might not be the ideal solution, even for a short while. Izzy was too independent to accept help on her good days and too proud to want a witness to her bad ones.

They were both asleep when the doorbell rang. Izzy was on her bed, having her usual afternoon nap and Vanessa was dozing on the sofa, drowsy in the sun that flooded through the window. She'd been intending to phone up about a job, but she was exhausted and Izzy had insisted it could wait until tomorrow.

Knowing the old lady was asleep and who it probably was, Vanessa went to answer it.

"Don't you listen to anything I say?" Garrin said, staring at her. "It'll be too much for Izzy to have you here. She's ill – or hadn't you noticed?"

Vanessa nodded, too tired for another argument. Not that he looked particularly argumentative. He was wearing jodhpurs and smelled of horses. She stood back so he could come in and he walked over to the window and then turned to face her.

"I can't force you to stay with me, I just think it would be best, that's all." His eyes were troubled and she knew he was worried about something going wrong. You couldn't lose a child without being terrified it would happen again. Even though this time she'd be ultra careful – if necessary, she'd stay in bed for the last month of her pregnancy. Every time she thought about the baby inside her she felt a mixture of fear and slow-growing joy.

"All right," she said.

He stared at her.

"Just temporarily," she added. "I'll move out as soon as I find somewhere and get myself a job."

"If you're worried about earning your keep, you can work for me."

"I don't know anything about horses."

"I wasn't expecting you to muck out stables," he said dryly. "There are plenty of other things you can do. I've got a batch of A.I.s coming on Monday and they're full board. I usually get a woman from the village to do the cooking, but if you could do that it would save paying her. It would only be part-time – I wouldn't expect you to do anything strenuous – obviously."

Vanessa knew it was the baby's welfare, not hers, that had sparked this note of concern.

"Where do they stay?"

"In living wagons at the back of the stables." He smiled at her expression. "I brought one or two from the fair. Besides, I don't want them in my house, do I? Might cramp my style."

Chapter Twelve

IZZY HAD NEVER CONSIDERED herself psychic; she'd met too many people over the years who read palms and gave Tarot and crystal readings, regardless of the fact they were about as psychic as house-bricks. Izzy didn't believe in making money out of other people's desperation to be told the future held better things. Despite this, she'd always been very empathetic and she was deeply worried about Vanessa. Vanessa's pregnancy should be a joyous event, but Izzy had the feeling it was going to drive an even deeper wedge between her and Garrin.

After they'd left, she got up and went shakily into the kitchen to get her tablets. It hadn't been a good day. Parkinson's was like that, unpredictable and erratic. She hadn't been completely truthful to Vanessa about it being painless. Now and again, she did get odd pains, but they didn't last long and were nothing she couldn't deal with. Her illness did, however, stop her doing a great many things she'd once have done with ease and today it had left her with tissue-paper legs.

She sat in her lounge and tried to pinpoint what was bothering her and came to the conclusion it was Richard Hamilton. When Nanna Kane had died, he'd been the first developer to call by, his face drawn into fake lines of compassion. Garrin had been hell bent on flattening him, but Izzy had insisted they talk to him because she wanted news of Vanessa.

The three of them had sat in Izzy's living wagon, Garrin, his face dark and angry, every line of his body tense, Richard, apparently at ease, but Izzy had known his blandness covered something almost as dangerous as

Garrin's anger.

"How's Vanessa?" she'd asked easily. "I haven't heard from her lately." She hadn't, in fact, heard from her at all, but she didn't know if Richard knew this. It was immediately obvious from his reaction that he did.

"She sends her regards," he said. "She's so sorry she couldn't come with me today, but she's rather busy at the moment. She's abroad."

He was lying. Vanessa would have sent her love not her regards, and Izzy was sure she'd have been in touch if she'd known Nanna Kane was dead, wherever she was. Suppressing her anger, she said tightly, "Do give her our love, won't you. Will we be seeing her if we do sell to you, Mr Hamilton? Would she be involved in the development at all?"

"I doubt it. She doesn't get involved in my smaller projects."

Garrin had been unable to contain himself a second longer. "Get out," he snarled, standing up and brushing Izzy's hand from his arm.

"I'll make you a very good offer," Richard said, unfazed. "In view of my wife's previous involvement with the place."

"If you were the last developer on earth I wouldn't sell to you."

Izzy had been afraid Garrin would hit him and some instinct told her that was what Richard wanted. Not necessarily a fight, but an opportunity to do more damage – as if he hadn't done enough already – an opportunity to sue this man from whom he'd already stolen so much.

"Sit down," she said sharply, and then to Richard. "I think you can see we're not interested, Mr Hamilton. Please go."

"You won't get a better offer." Richard smiled benignly and took out a business card. "Call me when you change your mind."

When he'd gone, Garrin had stormed around the confined space, slamming his fists into Izzy's cupboards. "Bastard, fucking, fucking bastard."

"Yes," Izzy had agreed quietly. "Please don't take it out on my home, Garrin."

He'd sat eventually, still trembling with anger.

She'd leaned forward and touched him gently. "I don't think Vanessa knows about this. I'm sure she doesn't. You know she'd be here if she did."

"I don't want to hear her name. I never want to hear her name again. Anyone who could live with a bastard like that is…" He shuddered and tailed off, obviously unable to think of a cutting enough insult. Or maybe he couldn't bring himself to badmouth the woman he'd once adored.

Izzy wished she could pick him up like she had when he was a child, sit him on her lap and stroke away his pain, but she knew she'd never be able to do that for him. There was no way of undoing the damage Richard Hamilton had done. No way at all. And Izzy, who had always seen the best in people – who had never hated anyone in her life – had hated Vanessa's husband with a passion for tearing apart the two people she loved most in the world.

Now, she leaned back in her chair and closed her eyes. She was a day-to-day person and she didn't often think about the past, but Vanessa coming back had unsettled her. Unlike Garrin, Izzy had always expected her to come back one day. You didn't bring up a child without knowing what she was like, without always being able to see the nugget of the child within, even when they'd grown up and wore several different masks for the world. And Izzy had had a hand in bringing up both Vanessa and Garrin. She'd been pleased when the closeness between them had evolved naturally into love and even more so when they'd announced they were having a baby.

It still grieved Izzy when she thought about how tragically wrong things had gone for them. If only Vanessa had paid more heed to her gentle warnings that she couldn't carry on working in the same way she'd done before she was pregnant. Vanessa, who'd always been as agile as a cat, had refused to listen when Izzy had suggested that dancing from dodgem to dodgem collecting fares from punters probably wasn't the best way for a pregnant woman to behave.

"Don't nag me, I'm perfectly fine," Vanessa had scoffed. "I'm pregnant, not ill."

It was the only time Izzy had ever seen echoes of Vanessa's beautiful reckless mother in her. But she'd ignored her instincts and held her tongue and stopped nagging, as Vanessa had put it. If she had one regret in her life – then this was it. She'd have given everything she owned to have been able to go back and reverse what had happened on that dreadful summer's day.

It still broke her heart when she remembered Garrin's stricken face as he'd come to her wagon. "Vanessa's had an accident. Will you come?"

"What's happened? What's wrong?" Izzy could hardly keep up with him as they'd raced across the scrubby grass to where Vanessa was lying on her side, her face scrunched up with pain.

"Oh my love, my darling, what happened? Have you called an ambulance, Garrin?"

"It's on its way."

As Izzy knelt beside the young woman she loved with every fibre of her being, she'd felt a terrible shadow of foreboding. She knew very little about childbirth, but she knew that falling – even a short distance – at this late stage of pregnancy was incredibly dangerous.

"I'm really sorry," Vanessa had sobbed. "I wasn't doing anything stupid, I swear. My foot slipped."

It wasn't the time to point out that Vanessa's shoes were hopelessly impractical for a woman in her condition. So Izzy just held her hand and prayed.

But her prayers hadn't been answered. She'd been as devastated as Garrin and Vanessa when they'd lost Jennifer, but she'd hoped they'd eventually come through it. They were made for each other, anyone could see that.

Bloody Richard Hamilton. He'd come along at just the wrong time. Vanessa had been so vulnerable, unable to talk to Garrin, who'd locked his emotions away. All Richard Hamilton had had to do was offer a sympathetic ear and wait.

Izzy had hoped the relationship wouldn't progress, but when Vanessa had come in one day and announced that she loved him, Izzy had broken one of her unwritten rules and tried to talk her out of it. The more she'd pleaded with her, the more adamant Vanessa had been that she wanted a fresh start and that Richard was the one to give it to her.

Izzy had expected the marriage to fall apart a great deal sooner than it had. But then Richard had done a pretty good hatchet job on Vanessa's roots. She shuddered. She hadn't told Vanessa that she'd tried to get in touch with her several times over the years, but her letters had always come back, opened and resealed with, 'not at this address' scrawled on the envelopes. Perhaps she should have told her. Perhaps it would give her the strength to get away from the man because Izzy knew he wasn't going to let her go that easily. He was the type that didn't give up.

Garrin had sold to Blake Anderson in the end and Izzy had been horrified to learn they'd sold the site straight on to Hamilton's. Her last memory of Richard Hamilton's face was as he strolled across the fairground, one morning, looking around him with satisfaction as his diggers began to tear up the dusty earth. To her very great relief Garrin hadn't been around to see it. And although she hadn't been able to keep the news from him for long, she'd kept him away from the site after that, slowly channelling his anger into more positive emotions, focusing him on horses, making him look towards a future without Vanessa.

Dusk was drawing across the room, shadowing the walls, but Izzy couldn't be bothered to put the lights on or to make herself any tea. She couldn't be bothered to do anything. Her thoughts were too disturbing.

Richard wasn't going to let Vanessa leave him. Not when he'd gone to such lengths to wipe out her previous life. Vanessa and her child were going to be the losers in all this and Garrin was going to be hurt again and Izzy was deeply concerned that the worst was yet to come.

Chapter Thirteen

"DO YOU STILL PLAY the guitar, Garrin?"

It was late one evening and Garrin was sitting at the dining room table going through some paperwork, a glass of brandy beside him. Vanessa was on the settee, flicking through a copy of *Horse and Hound* and trying to work out how she could get some normality into the situation.

"Not much, I don't have time."

"How many staff do you actually have helping?"

He shot her an irritated glance.

"I'm only asking because I'd like to know how I fit into things if I'm going to be working for you."

Sighing, he put down his pen. "There's Tracey, who you've met, and the A.I.s are working pupils so they do quite a bit in the yard. You won't see much of them, I keep them pretty busy, and they've got studying to do."

"How many horses do you have here?"

"It varies, I've got two liveries at the moment and one of the A.I.s has her own horse. Then there are three school horses and Derry and some youngsters. I'll take you down there tomorrow and show you round properly."

"Thanks." She smiled at him and got a half smile back.

"Are you still crap at crosswords?" he asked idly.

"Is that all you can remember about me? Charming."

"There's a lot I remember," he said, narrowing his eyes. "But I try not to think about it much. I hope you can cook better these days. Not that they'll want anything fancy. Sandwiches will do at lunchtime and whatever you can knock up for tea."

"I'm sure I can manage," she said, deciding to ignore his goading. She went across the room and leant on the back of a dining room chair. "There's a lot I remember about you too, Garrin Tate. You used to be lovely."

"I used to be young and stupid," he said, meeting her eyes. "I'm not any more."

"No, I don't suppose you are," she murmured, feeling a jolt of pain because he'd never been stupid, just trusting. And he should have been able to trust her. "I won't stay here longer than I have to. I'll get another job. It's just going to take a bit of time."

"There's no rush." He hesitated. "I know I've given you a hard time lately, but I'm not a complete bastard. I think I'm still in shock."

It was the nearest to an apology she was going to get, Vanessa thought, but before she could say anything else, he went on quietly, "You had bad morning sickness last time, didn't you. Is it the same?"

Caught off guard, she nodded.

"I'll make you something for it. I've got a recipe for ginger tea somewhere. And don't bother about getting up too early. The girls can do their own breakfasts for a couple of months – that should see you through the worst of it."

"Thanks," she said, touched.

"Like I said, I'm not a complete bastard. You can stay as long as you want, but if you are going to leave me in the lurch, a week's notice would be handy."

"Of course," she said, wondering if that was a reference to her walking out without telling him where she was going last time.

He smiled and she saw in his eyes that it was. Well, she supposed she couldn't blame him for that.

"As long as we both know what the score is, I think we'll get along fine," he said.

"Oh, I think we know that." Weary of this conversation and feeling slightly unnerved he could still read her so easily, she left the room. A lot might have changed, but one thing certainly hadn't. Living with Garrin was going to be just as much of an emotional roller-coaster as it had been the first time round.

Particularly as this house was full of memories, Vanessa thought, as she got ready for bed. It was where she'd lost her virginity. Well, not in the house exactly. But not too far away from it.

She lay beneath the duvet, her mind drifting back to that first time. She and Garrin had talked about it, planned where it would happen. Neither of them wanted it to be some fumbled affair in the back of a car, which was what a lot of the other kids did. They'd both wanted it to be special.

"Leave it to me," Garrin had told her, grinning. "I've got an idea." When he'd borrowed a car from Jimmy, who worked on the dodgems, she'd felt her heart sink. Garrin had taken one look at her face and shaken his head in exasperation. "This is the transport, not the venue, you plonker."

"So where are we going?"

"Wait and see."

When he turned into Uncle Bert's drive, she frowned at him.

"He's not lending us a room, is he? How did you wrangle that?"

"No, he's not," Garrin said, parking the car out of sight of the house and grabbing her hand. "He doesn't know we're here."

"Are you sure he won't catch us?"

"Not a chance." He reached into the back and pulled out a rucksack. "We're going to borrow his barn."

"Garrin, we can't, what if he comes in and finds us?"

"He won't. It's full of hay. He had a delivery last week. I came over and helped him stack it. Only I was thinking ahead. Look, it's easier if I just show you."

Vanessa held back. "I'm not sure about this, Garrin."

"Is it the barn you're not sure about, or what we're thinking of doing there?" His voice was gentle and he held out his hand. "I'm not going to pressurize you. I told you I was happy to wait."

"It's not that."

"Well, let's just have a look then. We don't have to do anything. We can look upon it as a recce for the future."

Vanessa took his hand.

"There won't be any mice in here, will there?" she said, as they stood inside the barn a few moments later.

"I doubt it."

"Can we put the light on and check?"

"No, we don't want to risk Uncle Bert spotting it."

"Doesn't sound like much of a romantic evening," she said, disappointed. She'd wanted to see his face, his eyes, his nakedness, savour the moment, not just have a quick fumble about in the dark.

"Oh, ye of little faith," Garrin muttered, climbing up on to the first level of the haystack. He lifted a tarpaulin and pulled out a bale of hay. Then he pulled her up beside him so she could see the place he'd removed the bale from wasn't solid, a dark tunnel led into the centre of the haystack.

"After you," he said, handing her a small torch. "It's really cosy in the middle. I'll close the door behind us."

Vanessa crawled in and lit the torch. Only Garrin could have come up with something like this, but he was right. It was cosy and sweet-scented. She wondered how big the middle was.

Big enough for both of them to lie outstretched, she discovered. The tunnel was about six bales long and led into a hollowed out area with a tartan blanket and two cushions set out in the middle – she recognised the blanket and cushions as Nanna Kane's.

"I brought them over last night," Garrin said, "but I brought another blanket in case they'd got damp. I also brought more light and some bubbly." He produced three more penlight torches and stuck them in between various bales around them. Then he lifted out a small bottle of Moët and two paper cups.

She smiled. It was like sitting in a room of gold, fragranced with the sweet smell of hay and it was utterly private. From the outside the haystack looked solid.

Garrin knelt in front of her, his eyes sparklier than champagne. "Fancy a glass of bubbly? Or we can just talk? Hay's a pretty good insulator. Bert wouldn't hear us, even if he came right in."

"Or we could do what we came for," she murmured, stroking his face with the palm of her hand and feeling the slight stubble against her skin.

"Is that what you want?" he said, his eyes suddenly serious and in answer she kissed him.

They'd been kissing for a while, but this was different. When their lips met she felt the charge bolting through her body and she knew from the sudden tension in him that he felt it too. She'd put on a blouse and a front-fastening bra, to save any fumbling about, but he didn't bother undoing any buttons, he just slipped his hands beneath the thin material, caressing her skin and sending sparks flaring from every place he touched.

Vanessa was more impatient. She unzipped his flies and discovered he wasn't wearing anything beneath his cut-off jeans. Her fingers closed around warm hardness and then he gave a soft moan and pushed her away.

"What's the matter?"

"Not yet." He pushed her gently onto her back, undid her blouse and slipped it from her shoulders. The penlight torches threw shadows across the lean lines of his face and she watched him trying to fathom out the front-fastener, wanting his touch on her breasts, but suddenly shy of him seeing them. They weren't very big. What if he was disappointed?

Just as she was deciding maybe the dark would have been better he mastered the front-fastener and released her breasts. And then he took one of her nipples into his mouth, teasing her with his teeth, and she forgot all about worrying and moaned. It was ecstatic. He was amazing. He must have had plenty of practice, she decided, arching her back.

The rest of their clothes came off with some urgency. Neither of them bothering with finesse any more. They just tugged away the fabric with urgent little cries, desperate to feel skin against skin, to explore each other's bodies, until finally he was full length on top of her, his eyes full of need. He stroked her hair and cupped her face with his hands and groaned. "I can't wait any longer."

"Me neither. Have you got a condom?"

Nodding, he reached for it, and she sat up and helped him put it on. When they were both satisfied it wasn't going to come off, he rolled back on top of her. This time it was for real, she thought, looking up into his eyes. It was really going to happen.

She parted her legs for him and he guided himself against her with his fingers.

"I don't want to hurt you."

"You won't," she said, not sure this was true, it was amazing how big he was.

"You're ever so wet."

"Is that bad?"

"No, I don't think so. It feels…" He finished the sentence with a groan, but she couldn't have spoken either.

It felt so weird – like she was being stretched, part painful, part exquisite. Mostly exquisite, she decided, as he began to move inside her.

She'd just decided they should have done this ages ago

when she felt him tense, his body arching above her, and she knew it was over for him. It always seemed to go on longer on telly, but she supposed it took a bit of practice to perfect the timing.

He collapsed against her, his head against her breasts. She stroked his hair, uncertain of how he was feeling. "Was that okay, Garrin?"

"It was fucking amazing," he said, lifting his head and grinning at her. "How about you?"

"Same," she said, caught up in the warmth and the smell and the closeness of him, and hearing her voice come out a little husky. "I think I'm in love with you."

And his eyes were soft as he cleared his throat and gazed down at her. "I've been in love with you all my life."

He'd loved her for the next four years, too, Vanessa thought with an ache of regret. If she hadn't left him, perhaps he still would have done.

The following day Garrin showed her round the yard properly, as he'd promised. The hay barn was still there, she saw, as Garrin headed purposefully towards it, but it looked different. It was bigger and had a new roof.

Garrin swung open the double doors and gestured her ahead of him and she went, feeling a jolt of unease, which turned instantly to surprise. It was no longer a hay barn, but an indoor riding area. It had a peat floor that felt soft beneath her feet and was set up with brightly painted jumps.

"This was the first thing I had built when I bought the place," Garrin explained. "It's an indoor school so I can still work with the horses even if it's no good outside. It cost a small fortune. What do you think?"

"It's great. Very professional," she said, not sure what he expected her to say.

He grinned. "That's what I thought." Then he turned, folded his arms across his chest, and gave her a direct look.

"I'll tell you something, Vanessa, it's a damn sight more useful than the crummy hay barn that was here before."

Chapter Fourteen

TWO WEEKS LATER, VANESSA decided she'd been wrong about the emotional roller-coaster. Garrin made no more references to their past. He treated her like a distant cousin, which was what he'd told the A.I.s she was. Tracey was the only one who knew the truth – and Tracey – Garrin had said glibly – would get the sack if she didn't keep her mouth shut.

Vanessa stooped to pick up the bundle of dirty sheets she'd just stripped from the A.I.s' beds. Garrin had insisted he pay a small wage as well as giving her full board. In return, she'd insisted on doing the cleaning as well as the cooking – at least for as long as she could manage it. She felt less beholden to him that way, not that she saw a lot of him. He was gone before she got out of bed, which was just as well, as she tended to hog the bathroom once she was up. The morning sickness was better with the ginger tea, but it still bothered her.

The students were lovely – all young girls, who were bright and chatty. She mainly saw them at mealtimes, which they had in what had once been Nanna Kane's living wagon, but was now set up permanently with table and chairs. They chatted about their day and often about Garrin – a mixture of complaints and compliments. But more of the latter, Vanessa had realised, as time went on. If she'd told any of them she was carrying his baby, they probably wouldn't have believed her. In fact, they probably saw a lot more of him than she did, which suited her fine. She still wasn't sure what she was going to do long-term, although she'd thought about nothing else.

As Garrin had said, she didn't have a lot of options.

She'd be okay for a while. She planned to sell the Mercedes and get something cheaper and more practical. She needed the car's documentation, but she hadn't been able to find it when she'd popped back to the house. It hadn't been in its usual place in the filing cabinet in Richard's office.

The place had felt empty. There was no sign Richard had been back from Spain. She wasn't surprised – his trips often took longer than he expected. He'd always told her the paperwork would take even longer if he wasn't around to chivvy up the Spaniards, who had no sense of urgency whatsoever. He was probably right.

On impulse, while she'd been in his home-office, she'd phoned Tara. Half of her expected Tara to be out of the country, too, but she'd answered the phone. Vanessa apologised, explained she'd misdialled, and hung up. Perhaps Richard hadn't been lying about Tara. She still wasn't sure. A part of her wished he'd come back – she needed to tell him about the baby. She was dreading it, but at least it would bring things to a head. No way would he want anything to do with her once he knew she was carrying Garrin's child.

Vanessa took the laundry back to the house, put on the washing machine and was in the process of making sandwiches for the students when Garrin came in.

"How are you feeling?"

"Fine, thanks," she said, surprised.

"Ginger tea's working then. Good. The girls like you. Suzy said you make a pretty mean hotpot."

She blushed, sudden tears springing to her eyes, hormones, memories, or just the fact that Garrin was harder to deal with when he was being nice to her. He was still looking at her, his eyes thoughtful. "Have you thought any more about what you're going to do when the baby's born?"

So that was what it was about. "I'll get a job, like I said

before."

"And get some stranger to look after our baby – I'm not keen on that idea."

"Well, I can't be in two places at once, can I? I don't know. Maybe I can work from home or something."

"Vanessa." He came across and took her hands and she jumped, fire sparking through her at his touch. "You can both stay here as long as you like. You don't have to go all independent on me."

She looked at him suspiciously. "You've changed your tune. I thought you couldn't bear to be near me."

He grinned and squeezed her fingers. "I'm getting used to having you around."

"Well, don't get too used to it," she snapped, sure he had some angle. She drew her hands from his. "Are you stopping for a sandwich or do you want to take something back with you?"

"I'll stop."

To Vanessa's relief he didn't say anything more about her future plans, but as she was reaching for his empty plate, he said, "I've entered Derry in a show-jumping class over at Lakeside on Sunday. Do you fancy coming to watch? Izzy will be there."

Vanessa was so surprised she didn't answer him at first.

"Think about it," he said easily, getting up and taking the plates from her. "I'll do these. It's not a big show, but it'll be the first time I've ridden him myself. I thought you might enjoy it."

Lakeside was near Lulworth, only a few miles up the road, but there was still quite a bit of preparation to be done, Vanessa discovered, finding Garrin in the stable yard on Sunday grooming an already gleaming bay horse. She'd seen Derry before – once or twice she'd watched Garrin riding him in the indoor school in the evenings – but she'd never seen them jumping. He was right, it would be interesting, especially as Izzy could tell her what was going on.

"This show is just experience for him," Garrin said, as he plaited the horse's mane. "He's been doing well with Tracey, but I want to start riding him a bit more seriously. Get him into the swing of things because he's going to be pretty busy over the next year or two."

"Will you be taking him eventing?" Vanessa asked. She hadn't been around the A.I.s for a fortnight without taking something in.

"I hope to qualify him to jump at The Horse Of The Year show eventually," Garrin said smiling at her. "That's the plan, isn't it, boy?" He stroked Derry's neck with the back of his hand and the horse flicked his ears good-naturedly.

"What do you have to do for that?"

"A lot of work." Garrin sewed up the last plait, his fingers moving deftly. "And it won't be cheap, but he's going to be worth it. Anyway, there's no rush. He's only six, still a baby."

Vanessa had never been to a horse show before. At ten-thirty they were bumping across a rutted field, dry from a week or so of no rain, past roped-off rings of jumps, and people leading horses in bright rugs out of their boxes.

"I hope the ground's not too hard," Izzy said, as Garrin jumped down from the driving seat and went round to lower the tailboard.

"What difference does that make?" Vanessa asked.

"It means it's harder on their legs and they're more likely to hurt themselves. But this is affiliated show-jumping, which means they'll have prepared the ground. Affiliated means that the competition is run under BSJA rules – The British Show Jumping Association – so certain standards have to be met. Anyway, Garrin won't jump him if it's too hard."

Having tied Derry to the side of the box with a hay-net, Garrin came round to where they stood watching the bustle of other people tacking up horses, putting on jackets and tying numbers around their waists. "Our class doesn't start 'til twelve, so there's plenty of time before we need to warm up. Do you two fancy a coffee?"

"He's nervous," Vanessa said to Izzy in surprise, when Garrin had headed away across the field.

"It's their first time out, he's bound to be. They'll be fine when they get going."

Garrin seemed to know everyone, Vanessa noticed. Loads of people stopped him and smiled and chatted as he came back with their coffee, which was only just still hot enough to drink.

"He's done a lot in five years," she murmured to Izzy. "I feel as though he's become part of a world I know nothing about."

"Well, I guess he has in a way. He's moved on," Izzy said gently. "He had to – and you know what Garrin's like, he never does anything by halves."

Vanessa nodded.

"Do you think they'll win?" she asked later, as they watched Garrin circling Derry in a corner of the field.

"He's aiming for a double clear, but first time out if they jump one clear round he'll be more than happy."

Garrin concentrated on reading his horse's mind, as he always did when he first mounted. It was part of the warming-up process. He wasn't sure exactly how the telepathy worked; it was a combination of senses, part touch, part listening, part looking and something that transcended all of these so he could get clear messages from the horse's mind. *I am happy: I am afraid: I am dreaming.*

Usually one of them would be predominant. *I am excited*, Derry told him today, as he danced around the field, *I am also a little clumsy*. Damn, that didn't bode well. Concentrate, Garrin told him, firming his hands on the reins and squeezing his legs closer to the horse's sides, feeling the power surge as Derry decided to canter on the spot.

No, no, no. Trot now, we're just trotting. Just trotting, and Derry gave a head toss of displeasure and broke into a clumsy trot that was all over the place. Pack it in, mad horse; it's only a silly little show, nothing to get excited about. Nothing at all. Garrin wondered if he was transmitting his own nervousness. Was that what this was all about?

He made an effort to still his mind and felt Derry instantly respond. They changed rein, cantered in a circle, popped over the practice jump with ease, and then rode back towards Izzy and Vanessa.

Izzy patted the horse's neck. "He's full of himself."

"He'll be all right when he gets in the ring. He could do that course with his eyes closed." He smiled, wondering if the reassurance was for them or himself. There were two more riders to go and then they were on. Knowing that Derry would get too excited if he was waiting with the other horses, Garrin walked him around until the steward beckoned him over.

"Garrin Tate riding Sorrento's Boy," said the commentator and then they were in a beautifully balanced canter.

I'm looking forward to this, Derry told him.

Me too, Garrin answered, as they cantered towards the first fence. They cleared it with a foot to spare.

Stop showing off.

I'm happy.

Concentrate.

They took the double perfectly and didn't put a foot

wrong until the gate, which Derry rapped. Cursing, Garrin didn't risk looking back.

Bloody concentrate.

Sorry.

The rest of the round was perfect.

"And a clear round for Garrin Tate and Sorrento's Boy," the commentator called, as Garrin rode out to where Izzy and Vanessa were waiting.

"You were lucky with that gate," Izzy said, as he dismounted.

"He won't do it again. He's into his stride now, aren't you, my beauty?"

"I didn't know you could ride like that." Vanessa was smiling, but there was something else behind the smile, sadness, why would she look sad? Garrin dismissed the thought as his imagination.

"Be a while before the jump off, there's a few more to go yet. I'm going to take him for a walk about."

Vanessa and Izzy sat on the grass to watch the jump off. Izzy wouldn't admit it, but it was obvious she was tired, her face pale, her eyes heavy.

"It's all this fresh air." Izzy suppressed a yawn. "But I wouldn't miss it for the world."

It was exciting, Vanessa decided. She'd watched show-jumping on television a few times, but you couldn't beat the real thing: the thud of the horse's hooves; the creaking of saddles; the expressions on the riders' faces. She'd half expected Garrin to swear when Derry had hit the gate, but his face had been serene. It was as if he were on a different plane when he was riding. No temper, no histrionics, just him and Derry moving as if they were part of each other, almost musical, and Vanessa was reminded painfully of how they'd once been in bed.

As they watched the other contestants, Izzy told her bits

and pieces about the riders. "That chap there is Lloyd Battersby-Smythe, Garrin teaches his daughter, Amanda."

"Can't he teach her himself?"

"Garrin's one of the best instructors in the area. He's a BHSI, which is highly qualified, one step up from an Assistant Instructor. He's also very intuitive, knows exactly what people need to do to improve. Lloyd wouldn't be doing Amanda any favours if he taught her to ride like he does. He's got a seat like a sack of potatoes."

"Has he?" Vanessa stared. The man did seem to be bumping around a bit.

"If he carries on like that his horse will run out," Izzy continued.

"Out of the ring?"

"He'll stop at a jump." Horse and rider were approaching the gate as she spoke and they didn't seem to be quite lined up, Vanessa saw, wondering if that was what Izzy meant. Lloyd's horse cleared the gate, but stopped dead at the next fence, the poles, so Lloyd only stayed on by the skin of his teeth.

He belted his horse with his crop, jerking it round for another attempt.

"That's not helping matters," Izzy said, shaking her head. "He ought to try riding it instead of bullying it."

The horse refused the poles again and Vanessa frowned. "If I was that horse I'd buck him off and trample on his head."

"He's disqualified now anyway."

"For beating his horse up?"

"For two refusals. Anyway, forget about them, Garrin's on now. Got your fingers crossed?"

"I've got everything crossed," Vanessa said, watching Garrin canter Derry around the ring. There was no bouncing with Garrin. He seemed to be glued to the saddle, his body moving in perfect time with the horse's. As they cleared jump after jump, she felt her heart speed up.

"They're doing well, aren't they?"

"They're fast, too," Izzy said. "Wow, I think they've done it, Nessa love. No one's going to beat that very easily."

Garrin rode back to them, his face flushed. "Wasn't he brilliant? Little star." He dismounted. "I think there are only a couple left to go, we were fast, weren't we?"

"You were ten seconds faster than anyone else," Izzy said, as they watched the next competitor canter round the ring.

"She's going for it," Garrin said with interest, as the rider cleared the first fence and hurtled towards the double.

"Too fast," Izzy said, and was proved right a moment later when the last part of the double fell. "Tracey's going to be pleased if you come back with another red rosette."

"Don't tempt bloody fate."

But Izzy was right about this, too. The last rider jumped clear, but a good five seconds slower than Garrin.

Vanessa smiled at Garrin's delight as he accepted his red rosette and cantered around the ring with Derry putting in a little celebration buck, which neither unseated nor seemed to bother Garrin in the slightest.

"He really loves it, doesn't he?"

"That horse will go a long way."

"As far as he wants him to?"

"I hope so," Izzy's eyes were serious. "They've certainly got the potential, they just need a bit of luck on their side."

They dropped Izzy off on the way home, as she'd finally admitted she was exhausted. Vanessa felt tired too, but Garrin was in an excellent mood. "Are you doing anything later on or do you fancy a celebration drink when I've finished evening stables?"

Vanessa resisted the temptation to say she never did

anything in the evenings, or hadn't he noticed, and nodded. It seemed churlish to upset him when he was in such a good mood, and besides she had enjoyed the day.

They sat outside – Garrin with a glass of champagne, her with a pink grapefruit juice – and toasted Derry. Garrin's face was so relaxed, so happy, that Vanessa felt an ache of loss inside her. Once in another lifetime they'd always been like this – but it was in another lifetime she was starting to realise. Garrin had carved out a new future for himself, in more ways than one.

"What's on your mind?" he asked, standing up and coming round the table to top up her glass. "Are you sure you don't want half a glass of champagne?"

"I don't want to take any risks," she said, her voice sharper than she'd intended.

Garrin's face instantly sobered. "Course you don't. I'm sorry." He was all contrition now. Then he bent and kissed her forehead. She was so surprised she didn't move. His face was very close to hers and there was tenderness in his eyes – a softness she hadn't seen for a long time.

"It'll be okay, Nessa. Don't worry. Last time was a terrible accident. It wasn't your fault. Don't ever think it was."

It was what she'd needed him to say six years ago. Even if it hadn't been true – she'd so badly needed him to say it. She'd spent night after night torturing herself with what might have been if she hadn't fallen.

But Garrin had said hardly anything when they'd lost Jennifer. Izzy was right – he'd been too locked in his own grief.

"This is supposed to be a celebration," she whispered, feeling her throat closing with regret and pain.

His eyes clouded and Vanessa wished she'd acknowledged his reassurance instead of pushing him away. He sat again, gulped back his champagne and in silence they watched the sun slide beyond the distant sea.

Chapter Fifteen

VANESSA WAS BEING SICK a couple of days later when the doorbell rang. She straightened, washed her face and looked at her reflection in the mirror. She looked like a ghost – bloody morning sickness. It hadn't been too bad lately, and, lulled into a false sense of security, she'd told Garrin not to bother making up any more ginger tea. She should have known better. The sickness hadn't stopped until the thirteenth week when she'd been pregnant with Jennifer, so if she followed the same pattern, there was another month of this to go.

She answered the door, expecting to see the feed-merchant, who Garrin had mentioned might call that morning, and was stunned to see Richard standing there.

"Vanessa, we need to talk. Good grief, are you all right? You look ill."

"I'm fine, just a bit tired. Why didn't you phone and say you were coming?" Why were they talking such trivia? She'd walked out on him. He should be furious – not calmly asking after her welfare.

"I tried this morning, but your phone's switched off." He wore jeans and white tee shirt which emphasised his deep tan and his hair was bleached from the sun. His eyes were cold.

Knowing suddenly she was going to be sick again, she clamped a hand over her mouth and fled along the hallway to the downstairs loo. Pain bumped along her temples as she flushed the chain and stood up slowly. Christ – Richard wasn't stupid, he was going to put two and two together pretty quickly and she felt too ill for a confrontation.

He was still on the doorstep when she went back, his

hands clasped behind him, studying her car, which he'd parked alongside. "I'm not stopping here." He looked at her gravely. "Let's go somewhere we can talk – that's if you're not going to be sick again."

She blushed and shook her head and went with him to his car. It was unnerving sitting beside him; he was very tense, but he didn't speak, just drove down to the village and pulled into the car park of the White Heather.

"I need a drink," he said, striding ahead of her.

She followed him inside and sat at a table, glad of the shadows. It was dim in the pub, compared to the bright sun outside.

He got a scotch for himself and a mineral water for her with a slice of lemon floating in the top. Vanessa sipped it warily and waited for the onslaught. He surely must know she was living at Garrin's. He must have had the address all along.

"You're pregnant, aren't you?"

She nodded and he sighed heavily and put his head in his hands. "Why didn't you tell me?"

"On the phone? How could I?"

"You could have asked me to come back."

"I assumed it was impossible for you to get away," she said carefully. "You said you'd only be gone a week or so. I'd have thought talking about the end of our marriage was pretty important. Why should me being pregnant make any difference?"

"Of course it makes a difference. I'd have flown back straight away." Now he did look at her. "How far gone are you?"

She told him and he frowned. There was a pulse beating in his cheek, but his eyes were unreadable. Vanessa wished he would shout and rave at her, but that wasn't his style. In her lap, her hands were sweating. "It only happened once. It was a mistake – his idea of revenge."

119

"He forced you, did he? Is that where you really got those bruises?"

"No." She had never felt such a shit in her life. "No, he didn't force me."

"I see." His voice was still quiet – such a contrast from Garrin's – so controlled, so reasonable, even when he was faced with the worst type of evidence of her betrayal.

The air filled up with silence and she wished he would speak. Say something, anything to give her some clue as to what he thought.

"If it was just the once," he said at last, "then it might be my baby."

"But I thought…"

"Don't say it, Vanessa. Don't make me feel any bloody worse than I already do. I said it was unlikely I could father children. I didn't say it was impossible. And the dates tie in too – or don't you remember?"

She stared into her drink. The last time they'd made love was indelibly printed on her mind because it was the night before she'd seen him with Tara. She'd lain beneath him, thinking of Garrin and four days later she'd been in Garrin's bed. How ironic if she'd already conceived. If the baby she was carrying was actually her husband's, after all.

"We'll get a paternity test when it's born," Richard said, his voice bleak. "Are you coming home?"

"No, I'm not. I told you. I want a divorce."

"Do you still love him, is that it? Is that why you're here?"

"I don't love Garrin. It was a mistake."

"Then why are you shacked up with him? You could have stayed in the house, waited for me to come back. Talked things through. I thought that's what we agreed."

It was pointless reminding him that wasn't what they'd agreed at all – sometimes Vanessa thought he must live in an alternative reality, seeing only what he wanted to see,

120

and ignoring anything that didn't fit in with his plans. She sighed. "We can't sort this out by talking. Not now. It's too late. I'm here because I had to get away – besides I didn't think you'd want me in the house – like this."

"I don't want you living with him. You're my wife, Vanessa. I want you back."

"But I'm pregnant, Richard, I've been unfaithful to you. This baby is very likely not yours."

"That remains to be seen. And besides I don't care. I want you home."

"But I don't want to carry on living with you."

"I can't allow you to live here."

"You can't stop me."

He looked at her and there was an expression in his eyes she'd never seen before. Hatred – or was it love twisted in upon itself? It was gone so quickly she wasn't even sure it had ever been there.

A little shaken, she carried on quietly, "This isn't about Garrin. It's about me. You've lied to me since the day we were married. I don't trust you any more."

"That's ridiculous. All I've ever done is try and protect you. You've had everything you wanted. I thought you were happy. I didn't think you were still hankering over some dirty little gypsy."

"Don't, Richard, please. This is difficult enough for me."

"And you think it's easy for me, do you? Finding out my wife has been unfaithful." His eyes dropped to her stomach. "In some countries you'd be stoned to death for less." He sounded like he approved and Vanessa shivered.

"Izzy is the reason I'm here. She's ill, she's been ill for the past five years and I haven't been in touch and I feel terrible about that."

"Well, that's one thing you can't blame me for. I didn't know she was ill. Anyway, you can stay in touch with her. You can come and see her whenever you like. I won't stop you. If I'd known it meant so much to you I'd have suggested it before."

Vanessa didn't bother to comment on this blatant lie. She met his eyes steadily. "If you knew for sure it was Garrin's baby you wouldn't want me back, would you?"

He hesitated and when he spoke again, some of the emotion had gone from his voice and he was once more the reasonable man she'd always thought him to be. "If you knew for sure the baby was mine, would you come home?"

"I don't know," she said quietly. "That's the truth, Richard. I just don't know."

"I'm not agreeing to a divorce," he said again, steepling his hands and looking at her. "I'm prepared to accept you've been unfaithful to me. I'm also prepared to give you another chance if you promise me you'll never see Garrin again. You can still see Izzy. I understand why you'd want to do that. When the baby's born I'll bring it up as my own, which may well be the case anyway. I can't say fairer than that."

He sounded like he was offering her a formal contract, which she supposed in a way he was. Vanessa bit her lip, thinking once more that she didn't know him at all.

"What if I want to bring up this baby on my own?"

"What with? You'll get no money from me unless you're living as my wife. And if the baby does turn out to be mine, I guarantee gypsy boy won't want you. Why take the chance?" He still sounded perfectly reasonable; blackmail cloaked as an option, she realised, feeling anger rising.

He got up. "I don't expect you to decide now. I'll take you back and I'll phone you later."

They drove in silence and he parked beside her car on the gravel.

As she leaned to open the door, he turned and gave her a crooked little smile. "For my sins, I still love you. And life would be fuller for you, wouldn't it, with a baby. Our child

122

would want for nothing. Think about it, Vanessa."

She watched him turn the car, the sun picking out the highlights in his fair hair. He didn't look back as he went down the drive. She could hardly believe what he'd just said. She'd been so sure he wouldn't want anything to do with her when she'd told him about Garrin. She'd expected him to be furious, to agree to a divorce readily, not come out with something like this.

There was a *New Mother* magazine on the back seat of her car, she noticed, as she walked past it. So maybe Richard had known she was pregnant before he'd even rung the bell.

She told Garrin about the visit, later that evening, as he was flicking through some show schedules at the dining room table.

"Good job I didn't see him. I'd have broken both his legs. What did he want?"

"Me to go home with him."

"Did you tell him you were pregnant?"

"He guessed."

"Then, he's even more of a tosser than I thought." Garrin's eyes were blacker than usual. "Or is there something you're not telling me?"

Vanessa shook her head. Richard's news that he might, after all, be able to father a child – when he'd always told her it was impossible – had thrown her. She wasn't even sure he was telling the truth. Would he really demand a paternity test when the baby was born, or had he meant what he said about bringing up the child as his own?

"So what are you going to do?" Garrin asked, and his voice was casual, even though his eyes weren't.

"Would you take on another man's child?"

"Nope."

"You wouldn't have me here either, if I wasn't carrying

123

your baby, would you?"

Garrin dropped the schedules on the table. "I don't like rhetorical questions. You're here because you are – that's all there is to it as far as I'm concerned."

Vanessa nodded and closed her eyes. Garrin wasn't easy, but then he never had been. Since she'd been here, he'd swung between aloofness and warmth, anger and tenderness, passion and indifference, she never knew where she was with him, but she still felt complete in his company. And although she'd told Richard she didn't love Garrin, she wasn't sure it was true.

She didn't hear him move but she felt the seat dip as he sat beside her and when she opened her eyes he was looking at her, his face serious.

"I don't want you to go," he muttered, moving a little closer.

Vanessa stared at him, afraid he would touch her. She could kid herself she didn't want him, as long as he didn't touch her. When he was close, her body ached for him, as it always had – needed him like it needed food and water.

"It's not just because of the baby that I want you to stay." He was reading her face, his proximity quickening her heart and her breath. She tried to snap her thoughts away from sex, not very successfully. Think of pickled onions, eggs, gherkins – Christ, no not gherkins – how did he still manage to do this to her?

Before she could gather herself enough to move, he smiled, cupped her face in his hands and kissed her, confident of his welcome.

One of them moaned, Vanessa thought it was probably her, and, needing no more encouragement, Garrin drew her down onto the settee and kissed her some more.

Hesitant, because of the baby, she wrapped her legs around him, then rolled carefully on top of him, twining her hands in his hair, feeling his response. And all the while a voice hammered away in her head. He's using you, he'll hurt you, but she didn't care. She could use him just as easily; women could do that, these days. It wasn't just about love any more. Besides, she couldn't stop. She wanted him too badly and he knew it.

But in the end it was Garrin who stopped. She was still straddling him, but sitting up now. He'd undone the top few buttons of her blouse while they'd been kissing, and he was now stroking the exposed skin, skimming the tops of her breasts with his fingertips. Vanessa's eyes were closed; she ached for him to touch her nipples.

"I don't want you to leave me, Vanessa."

Her eyes snapped open and she knew he'd been reading her face. Knew exactly how much she wanted him.

"Why not?"

"Because I couldn't do this, then, could I?"

His flippancy struck a chord of unease. "You really are a complete bastard, aren't you?"

"Through and through." He grinned, and in one swift movement, he freed her breasts, which were swollen and tender with pregnancy, leaned forward and took one nipple into his mouth.

She gasped, passion overriding unease.

"Or this." Garrin released her for long enough to speak, before turning his attention to the other breast and tracing little circles with his tongue.

"Is that all I mean to you?" She'd meant to sound as flippant as he did, but the words came out as a breathless whisper. What had happened to equality? Why did she need him to love her as well as desire her? Perhaps it was her hormones making her long for security.

Sadness swept through her. What would have happened if she'd stayed? Would they have still been like this, but without the bitterness? Would they have half a dozen kids? She drew away from him and he glanced up in surprise.

"I was enjoying that."

"It's late. I think we should go to bed."

"Good idea."

"Not together." Not bothering to refasten her bra, she buttoned her blouse and stood up. Garrin rolled on to his side and looked at her.

"Why not?"

"Because I don't want to be your sex toy. That's not why I'm here."

For a moment she thought he was going to ask why she was here and she knew she might actually tell him she stayed because she couldn't bear to be too far away from him, even if he was a complete shit. But he didn't ask her why. He just stood up, adjusted his jeans, stretched languidly like a panther, and said, "Night, night, Vanessa."

She nodded and stayed where she was in the lounge. She could still feel his touch on her skin. Her nipples were hard, aching for him. How dare he make her feel like that and then disappear without a backward glance? Torn between wishing she hadn't stopped him and feeling relieved she had, she stood for a moment cupping her breasts and wishing he'd come back. It wasn't going to happen. Upstairs she heard the slam of his bedroom door.

Hugging her arms around herself and still breathing heavily, she went across the room. As she passed the coffee table she noticed her mobile, switched off, as it had been all evening, and wondered if Richard had tried to phone. She thought again about what he'd said. What if the baby was his? He could demand a paternity test and he'd delight in telling Garrin and that would be the end of it.

In all the years of their marriage Richard had never forced her to do anything – he'd never had to. She'd always gone along with what he'd wanted. There had been no reason not to because she'd loved him, or at least she thought she had until she'd seen Garrin again. Despite tonight, or maybe because of it, she knew she'd rather live with Garrin being the bastard he could be, than live with Richard at his most charming. At least she felt alive.

Richard left her alone for three days before he called. He didn't bother with small talk, just said briskly, "Have you decided yet?"

"I haven't changed my mind."

"Neither have I. There'll be no divorce."

"There will eventually. You can't force me to stay married to you. We're living in the 21st century."

"You'd better hope the baby's not mine then. Where are you planning on having it?"

She told him, knowing he could find out anyway if he put his mind to it. There was only one maternity hospital near by.

"We'll catch up there then," Richard said softly. "This isn't over, Vanessa. Don't think you can just walk away from me." He disconnected and she felt a wave of nausea that had nothing to do with her pregnancy. She couldn't believe he was the same man she'd lived with all this time. But then she couldn't believe he'd kept the secrets he had either. She wondered if he really could force a test and what she could do to stop it. Maybe she should see a solicitor and find out.

Garrin came into the kitchen, his face streaked with dirt. "Problems?"

"Nothing I can't deal with." She forced a smile.

"Good, I've got enough of my own." He grinned at her. "Let me know if you change your mind about being my sex toy, won't you?"

Chapter Sixteen

"WHAT WAS IT LIKE living in a fair?" Tracey asked Vanessa one Sunday when they were eating sandwiches, and Garrin was away at an end-of-season tack sale. "Bet it was bloody cold at this time of year with nothing but a Calor-gas fire to warm your hands over."

Vanessa smiled. "A lot cosier than living in a house, actually. Not so much space to heat."

Tracey glanced out of the lounge window to where frost still shimmered on the wooden patio table and shivered. "Chilblain city. You won't believe how cold it gets in this place. I can't get my hands to thaw out before ten. Want to swap jobs?"

"No thanks."

"What was it like the rest of the time?"

"All right. Same as living in a house really because we were on a fixed site. We had satellite television – double-glazing, all the mod cons," she said, enjoying Tracey's surprise.

"What did your parents do?"

"They were fire eaters and they were dancers. They had this act that combined the two."

"Bloody hell – no wonder your living wagon was warm. Did they practise in there when you were getting ready for bed?"

"I don't think so. To be honest, I can't really remember them. I was too little and they worked away in Europe a lot. One day they never came back."

Tracey's eyes widened. "Weren't you upset?"

"No, not really. I'd always lived with Izzy anyway. She was more of a mum to me than my real mother."

"What did Izzy do at the fair?"

"All sorts. She had a coconut shy and a juvenile ride. And for a long time, she had the helter-skelter. Me and Garrin used to drive her mad. We used to pour cooking oil down the slide so we could get a bit of speed up. In those days we used to go down it on those old woven mats. Garrin used to carve bits off them to make them more aerodynamic."

Vanessa smiled at the memory. She'd loved the helter-skelter when she was small: the creaky old stairs, with gaps where you could look through and see the grass far below; the rhythmic beat of the music and the smell of fried onions and burgers; then the stomach crunching moment when you pushed off the top and the breathless slide downwards. More often than not, Garrin would be waiting for her at the bottom, arms outstretched so they tumbled onto the ground together laughing.

For a moment she ached for the simple pleasures of times gone by. It was an effort to pull herself together and continue the story.

"One of Izzy's husbands had the paratrooper."

"How many did she have?"

"Three, but I only knew the last one. He left when I was about six, he didn't like being stuck in one place, but Izzy stayed. She loves the sea."

"Strange she didn't have any children of her own," Tracey said thoughtfully.

"I think she was too busy looking after everyone else's. She looked after me, and she looked after Garrin a lot, too, when he lost his mum. It was Izzy who taught him to ride – well, her and Uncle Bert between them. We used to spend winters here quite often."

"Weren't you interested in learning to ride?"

"Not really. I was always falling off. Garrin was a natural. He fell off a fair bit too, but he always bounced."

"No change there. He still does – jammy sod. I don't know how he gets away with it. I've broken my arm twice and my collarbone. I spent a week in hospital for that."

"Garrin wouldn't last five minutes in a hospital. He'd be climbing the walls, he hates being cooped up."

"Yes, he'd be a nightmare patient, wouldn't he?"

They both smiled and there was a pause.

"If it's not too personal, why did you and Garrin split up?" Tracey asked curiously. "Apart from the obvious reasons like him being bad-tempered and moody and completely unpredictable. Don't tell me if you don't want to. I'm just being nosey."

"I met someone else and I left him," Vanessa said quietly. "We'd been having a bad time and it seemed easier to make a clean break."

"The guy you married?"

"Yeah, that's right. It was the biggest mistake I ever made."

"Leaving Garrin or marrying someone else?"

"Both, I think," Vanessa said, surprised she was being so candid, but it was easy to talk to Tracey and she knew it wouldn't go any further.

"You seem to be getting on all right now, though."

"On the surface, we get on okay. We don't share a bedroom." Vanessa sighed, and sensing her change of mood, Tracey's eyes softened.

"I'm sorry. You don't want to rake up the past. So, what are you going to do when the baby's born? Are you still going to move out and get another job?"

"I don't know." Vanessa frowned because she was worried that she still didn't know, especially as the birth was only three months away. "I suppose I should have done something about it by now. Time's sort of slipped away from me. I doubt I'd get a job now anyway." She patted her bump gently. "No one's going to take me on in this

130

condition."

"I don't know why you don't stay here. I'm sure Garrin doesn't want you to go. I think he's looking forward to being a dad."

Vanessa nodded, not wanting to admit she was worried about that too. Garrin had been extraordinarily nice to her lately. The other night, as they'd sat on the settee, he'd leaned across and slid up the baggy T-shirt, which she'd been living in.

"I thought I'd told you I'm not interested," she snapped, slapping away his hands.

"I'm not after your body – lovely though it is. I want to feel the baby." He'd laid his head very gently against her stomach. "Is that indigestion or baby heartbeats I can hear?"

"I expect it's indigestion," she said dryly, but she'd felt a deep sense of tenderness as he lay lightly against her, his hair soft against her skin.

He'd stayed like that for ages, the darkness pressing against the windows, the fire crackling in the grate, the room peaceful and cosy. And when he'd finally raised his head he was smiling. "Shall I rub your back for you?"

"Yes please."

His hands, so skilled at arousing every part of her, had slid languidly across her skin, finding and relieving every ache until she'd wanted to purr in ecstasy. Afterwards, she'd fallen asleep in his arms.

"Perhaps I will stay here," she told Tracey now, wishing it were as simple as that. She had visions of Richard turning up at the hospital and a punch-up breaking out in Maternity, not that she either expected or wanted Garrin to come with her. She had a feeling she was going to have to fight him on that one, though. "What are you doing for Christmas?" she said, changing the subject. "Will you go home to your parents?"

"It'll be expected. Although, to be honest, I'd rather stay

here and work. Garrin's going to need someone to look after the horses. The working pupils are all going home and he can't do everything on his own."

"Well if you do stay, you can have dinner with us. Izzy's coming and I'm cooking a goose. I shall enjoy that."

Tracey laughed. "I bet you will. Vicious buggers, aren't they?"

On Christmas Eve a card arrived for Vanessa. The first to come by post – testimony to just how alone she really was. She glanced at the handwriting and saw it was Richard's.

Inside was an expensive Christmas card with the words, *To My Darling Wife* emblazoned across the top. Below was a nativity scene, Mary looking serenely at the child, while Joseph rested a protective arm around her. Vanessa shuddered and opened it and something fell out onto the floor. She bent with difficulty and saw it was a cheque made out to her. It was for forty thousand pounds and it wasn't signed.

Come round and see me and I'll sign it for you, Richard had written inside the card. Plenty more where that came from. Is it such a hard decision, Vanessa? He hadn't signed the card either. Perhaps he thought she would somehow transfer the signature. He was obviously ignorant of the fact she could forge his signature perfectly if she wanted to. She'd seen it on enough documents over the years. She ripped the cheque into shreds and decided to set the card on fire in the sink.

This was easier said than done. It was made of some sort of fabric that wouldn't burn. Annoyed, she decided to help things along a bit by pouring brandy over it – well it worked for puddings, didn't it?

Engrossed, she didn't hear Garrin come in.

"What the hell are you doing?"

"Nothing." She turned round guiltily and stood with her

back to the sink.

He picked up the bottle of brandy from the draining board and frowned. "Why are you pouring my best brandy down the sink? Have I been drinking too much, or something?"

"I was trying to set something on fire."

"Well obviously – what else would you be doing? What is it?" He leaned across her and retrieved bits of blackened card. The word wife was still visible. "Stupid prat. Doesn't he know when to stop?"

"I guess not." Vanessa could feel her face burning, but Garrin said no more about it, just retrieved his brandy and put it back in its place.

"Is there anything you want me to do for tomorrow? Or are we all set?"

"All set. The goose is well and truly stuffed and the veg are done. There are some shop-bought mince pies. I was going to make some, but I didn't have the energy."

"I'm not surprised. Stop pissing about with that. I want to talk to you."

"What about?"

"Come and sit down and you'll find out, won't you."

Vanessa sat, feeling inexplicably nervous. Garrin sat beside her, "I thought I might do up the spare room as a nursery. How do you feel about that?"

"Does it mean you want me to stay?"

"Yeah – I want you to stay. I thought we'd already got that sorted."

She looked at him. "It's really kind of you, Garrin, but I don't know whether I can stay here indefinitely."

"Why not?"

She thought of Richard and the time bomb of the paternity test. She wanted more than anything to stay here with Garrin, but she wanted him to love her, not just feel

133

obliged because of the baby.

"You wouldn't want me here if things hadn't turned out – well, like they have. That first day I came, you couldn't wait to see the back of me."

"I was hurt. I didn't want to get involved with you again." He laid his arm along the back of the settee and stroked her hair. "You can't blame me for that. But we are involved now – one way or another we're always going to be involved."

He glanced at her bump. His voice was tender, but it wasn't what she wanted to hear. She had an urge to just pour it all out to him, tell him she loved him desperately, that she'd do anything to turn the clock back. They should have tried harder. She should never have walked out on him, however difficult he'd made it.

"I'm scared," she said quietly.

"Well, that's natural, isn't it, but it'll be all right this time. You're being really careful. You're getting plenty of rest. And I'm giving you maternity leave from now on."

"You're what?"

"You heard." He grinned. "I've already organised cover for the next six months – so you can put your feet up. Nothing's going to go wrong. I won't let it."

She smiled, wishing she could tell him that wasn't what she meant. But maybe it was better if she didn't. Better to wait until the baby was born because whatever he said, he couldn't guarantee it would be all right. Neither of them could.

"Don't go to too much trouble with the nursery."

He raised his eyebrows. "I'll go to as much trouble as I want. This is my child we're talking about. I've ordered a cot – a pine one from a place in Lulworth. I've also got the catalogue from the New Mum shop. I thought you might want to have a look at it. Choose some stuff. Shall I get it?"

She nodded. "What a way to spend Christmas Eve."

134

"Would you rather do something else?"

"No," she said softly, laying her head against his chest and wondering if they would be together this time next year. Or would everything have changed again? She didn't think she could bear it if it did.

Garrin had arranged to collect Izzy as soon as he'd done morning stables, which wasn't going to take as long as he'd feared as Tracey had decided she couldn't face going to her parents and was helping.

"Are you sure your parents don't mind?" Vanessa asked her when Garrin had left and Tracey came in, blowing on her hands and stamping her feet.

"My sister's going so they're happy. She's got three kids, that'll keep them entertained for the day. And it's my idea of a nightmare." She clapped her hands over her mouth. "Not that I don't like kids or anything. It's just that my sister's kids are spoilt brats. Also, we have this tradition of going to Auntie Laura's after the Queen's speech. She's got a rest home. Mum always wraps up some extra presents and takes them over for the old biddies."

"How sweet of her."

"Sweet, but boring. It's her Christmas good turn. We never go near the place the rest of the year. Is it all right if I leave my boots here?"

"Yeah, sure, go through. You know where the shower is. Help yourself."

Tracey reappeared wearing a long skirt, cream blouse and lipstick.

"Bloody hell," Vanessa remarked. "I didn't know we were dressing for dinner."

"When you spend most of your time looking like a scragbag and stinking of horses it's nice to dress up." Tracey grinned. "Is there anything you want doing? Sprouts to peel, carrots to scrape. I can be pretty domesticated you

135

know."

"All done, I think."

"Well, are you getting changed then?"

"What – into another pair of leggings and a different coloured T-shirt?. Doesn't seem much point."

"No. Well, you've got your man, haven't you." Tracey grinned wickedly. "I know you keep saying there's nothing going on, but Garrin hasn't had a single girlfriend since you've been here. So, I have to say, I don't believe you. I think it's really romantic – getting back together after all this time. Garrin never shuts up about being a dad. He's got the whole future mapped out. I hope your little one likes riding."

Vanessa was saved from having to comment on any of this by the sound of the front door slamming. Izzy came in, looking beautiful in a blue dress that brought out the colour of her eyes. Behind her Garrin was carrying a bag of presents.

"Someone's been busy," Vanessa remarked.

"I love Christmas," she said, "And this one's going to be extra special because I'm spending it with my favourite people." She kissed Vanessa, smiled at Tracey and said, "There are some bottles in there too, my love, and some ginger beer for anyone not partaking of the more traditional drinks."

"Thank you. What would you like?"

"A small brandy will do nicely, if it's not too early."

"It's Christmas," Garrin said. "It can't be too early. Same for you, Tracey?"

When their guests were settled in the lounge beside the fir tree that Garrin had dug up from somewhere and decorated with red and silver tinsel, Vanessa wandered into the kitchen to check the goose.

Garrin followed her and she watched him pouring their drinks and longed to be in his arms. The latter stages of

136

pregnancy had done nothing to dampen her desire for him – if anything, it had had the opposite effect. He was wearing jeans – his smart ones, he'd pointed out, when Vanessa had commented, and a black shirt. He looked amazing.

Catching her watching him, he glanced up. "What?"

"Nothing."

He grinned and came across the kitchen. "How's baby? Does she know what day it is?"

"What makes you think it's a she?"

"Instinct." He spread his hands across her stomach. "And how's Mum?"

"Fine," she said, wondering why her voice came out a little husky.

"Then stop looking so bloody sad. And leave the oven alone – it can cook fine without you standing over it. Come and be sociable."

Izzy watched Vanessa and wished she could shake off the feeling of foreboding that wouldn't seem to leave her. It was obvious Vanessa loved Garrin desperately; she wasn't going to walk away from him, so why did she still have such a strong sense of impending disaster? Maybe it was the Parkinson's. Had it not been Christmas Day she'd have stayed in bed. It had been difficult to get out of it and a mammoth effort to get across the landing to the bathroom because the dyskinesia, which usually left off until after lunch, had kicked in early. Cleaning her teeth had been a nightmare with her hands not under her control and her legs as wobbly as marshmallows. In an attempt to improve things she had rearranged the timing of her tablets this week, but it didn't seem to be working. Getting dressed had taken almost an hour and she'd only just been ready by the time Garrin had come to pick her up.

"Is that all you're going to eat?" Garrin's voice cut across her musings.

"I'm saving myself for Christmas pudding," Izzy said, smiling at him. "This bird's delicious. One of yours?"

"Hand picked by Vanessa," Garrin said, raising his eyebrows. "Revenge is a dish best served hot, wouldn't you say, Nessa?"

Izzy frowned. His voice was light, but there was an edge there, or perhaps she was imagining that too. His attitude to Vanessa had been solicitous all day; he couldn't be planning anything nasty. And he was thrilled about the baby – that much was obvious, he'd never jeopardise that. She decided to have a quiet word with Vanessa after dinner while Garrin and Tracey did the washing up.

"So, my love," she began when they were installed on the settee. "Do you want to watch the Queen's speech, or shall we just talk?"

Vanessa looked wary. "I can live without the Queen's speech. How are you feeling?"

"I want to talk about you, not me. Has Richard been in touch? You haven't mentioned him lately."

"He sent a card. I burnt it."

"Good for you. So has he come round to the idea of a divorce yet? He must know you're not going back."

"I think he does – yes."

Izzy was sure Vanessa wasn't telling her the whole story. Her eyes were guarded. She tried a different tack. "And are you okay with that? Are you happy with the way things have turned out?"

"I'll be glad when this little one comes," Vanessa said. "I'm scared, to be honest. Everyone keeps telling me not to be. But I can't help it."

"It's only natural you should feel like that." Izzy reached for Vanessa's hand, knowing the young woman would always blame herself for Jennifer's death – no matter what anyone said. Vanessa needed to forgive herself, but Izzy was sharply aware she never would.

138

"What has the midwife said?"

"That everything's fine and I shouldn't worry."

"Then you should try taking her advice."

Vanessa nodded, but her eyes were haunted. The same look Izzy had seen before. Vanessa was going inside herself – and, whatever was really worrying her, she obviously hadn't told Garrin about it.

"If you ever want to talk to me, about anything – you know you can, don't you. I'd do anything to help. Just ask."

"Thanks, but I'm fine, Izzy, really."

Izzy nodded, knowing she would get no further. Vanessa looked far from fine. She'd wondered a couple of times what their sleeping arrangements were. Something told her they didn't share a bed, despite how they felt towards each other. Every so often she caught Garrin looking at Vanessa, hunger in his eyes. Perhaps she was more comfortable in her own bed. Perhaps they were worried about hurting the baby if they made love. Perhaps that was at the root of the tension between them.

Tracey came back into the lounge, with a tea towel in her hands. "Garrin wants to know what you two want to drink."

"I've had enough, thanks," Izzy said.

"I'm fine too." Vanessa looked from one to the other. "I hope you won't think I'm being unsociable, but I'd really like a lie down."

"Course we don't mind," Izzy said, although she had a feeling that Vanessa was more interested in escaping than lying down.

Chapter Seventeen

IT WAS A BRIGHT BLUE day in February and Garrin was giving Amanda Battersby-Smythe a lesson on her new horse, Shadowman, which he'd just sold her. He was pleased with his pupil. She'd come a long way since that day Nero had dumped her.

"Great," he said, as she pulled to a breathless halt. "He's going well, isn't he? A bit more work and you'll have a good season. Have you had any more thoughts on where you're taking him first?"

"I wouldn't mind going to a few small shows, but Daddy wants to go straight into affiliated classes. He says the courses are better built and he wants us to jump under BSJA rules straight away."

"Yeah, well he's got a point. Not nervous about it, are you?"

"Terrified." Her eyes sparkled as she dismounted. "I was wondering, Garrin, if we paid you for your time, whether you might come along to the first one. I'd feel so much more confident if you were there."

"I might make you more nervous," he said, grinning.

"No, you wouldn't." She touched his arm. "Please think about it. You've helped me so much. I wouldn't have got this far without you."

"Yeah, you would." He was pleased despite himself. "You've got a lot of guts. And this boy's a good'un. You'll be fine."

"Daddy wondered if you might come round for dinner one evening," she went on, running up her stirrups as she spoke. "He wants to say thank you – you could discuss terms – you know – if you did come to a show."

"He doesn't need to thank me, he pays me," Garrin said distractedly, glancing at her bum – she'd definitely got fitter – and wondering if he'd have taken her to bed if Vanessa hadn't turned up again. Not that Lloyd would have been inviting him round for dinner if he had. So maybe it was just as well.

"So, shall I tell him you'll come?" Amanda said, smiling at him, and he knew she'd been aware of his gaze.

She'd dropped the little girl act now and gave as good as she got, which he liked. He dragged his thoughts away from the possibility of taking her to bed and smiled.

"Yeah, why not." It wouldn't do any harm to keep on Lloyd Battersby-Smythe's good side – the man had plenty of money. After this season he might well buy another horse from him. And it wouldn't be a great hardship to spend an evening with Amanda.

He'd just helped her load her horse into the box, when he had a sudden powerful feeling that Vanessa needed him. She wasn't due for another week, but the feeling was growing stronger by the second. Saying a hasty goodbye to Amanda he hurried back to the house and found Vanessa lying on her bed, her hands across her stomach. "Has it started?"

She nodded, wincing a little.

"Why didn't you call me on the mobile? I was only in the yard."

"Because it'll be hours yet. Sod off, Garrin, and get me a book or something. I don't need an audience."

"I'll phone the hospital and tell them we're on our way. We're not taking any chances."

"They'll tell you to sod off, too."

But they didn't – not that they had much choice about it, as Garrin told them in no uncertain terms that he was worried because they'd lost their first baby and they sure as hell weren't taking any risks with this one.

Vanessa looked at him in irritation, but didn't protest when he told her they were going, and he knew she was scared too. He could see it in her eyes, a fear deeper than her pain. At the hospital, he found a wheelchair and held her hand as they went down to Maternity despite her protests that she was perfectly capable of walking.

"I'll be with you the whole time, don't worry."

"You bloody well will not," Vanessa told him. "You can go back to the stables. I don't want you here."

"Why not? You wanted me with you last time."

"That was different."

"I don't see why."

"Get lost," she hissed, as another pain crumpled her face.

"No way. How quick are they coming? I think you might be further along than you think."

"You know nothing about it. Just leave me alone."

Ignoring her, he went into the delivery room, but the midwife chucked him out at Vanessa's request while she checked how things were progressing.

He waited, tapping his foot, until the midwife came out again, her face calm.

"It'll be a little while yet. Why don't you go and get yourself a coffee."

"I don't want coffee. I want to be with Vanessa."

"She's not too keen on that idea."

"She doesn't know what she's saying," Garrin snapped. "Look, we lost our last baby, she was stillborn. Vanessa's terrified of it happening again. I have to be there."

The midwife, knowing this was true, looked at him doubtfully. "She said…."

"Bollocks to what she said. I'm coming, darling," he called, dodging around the midwife and going back into the delivery room.

"I thought I told you to get lost," Vanessa said. "If you come anywhere near me, I'm going to kill you."

"Turn on your side and I'll rub your back."

"I want him out," Vanessa began, her voice turning into a shout as another contraction staccato'd through her.

"Please let me stay. I don't want you to be on your own. I can't bear the thought of not knowing what's happening."

"Out," the midwife said. "Unless you want me to call security."

"Oh, let him stay," Vanessa relented. "It'll give me someone to punch when it gets really painful."

Garrin grinned. "You can punch me all you like."

The midwife shook her head, and left them to it.

As soon as she'd gone, Vanessa sat up. "I'm scared."

"It's going to be fine. You're in the right place – nothing's going to go wrong, I promise."

She looked at him, suddenly glad she hadn't made him leave. She hadn't wanted him to see her vulnerability, scared of giving herself away to him. But it was pointless trying to hide from Garrin. He was the one person who knew the depths of her fear, how terribly scared she was of things going wrong. It didn't matter how they felt about each other, it was only right they should share this.

Time, punctuated by visits from the midwife, passed slowly. The sky outside the windows darkened and Vanessa concentrated on dealing with each pain as it came.

It was different from how it had been with Jennifer, because last time she'd gone into labour very prematurely. Last time she'd been racked with guilt and terrified out of her wits that she'd harmed her unborn child – a fear that had become tragic reality when Jennifer had been stillborn.

And even though the doctors had said it could have happened if she hadn't fallen – that Jennifer's heart had stopped during labour and her death wasn't a direct consequence of her fall – she hadn't believed them. She hadn't believed anyone who'd tried to relieve the terrible burden of her guilt.

This time she felt more in control. Or at least she did for a while. Unlike the first time she'd been pregnant, she'd attended every antenatal appointment, and for the last eight weeks she'd hardly done a thing, but she was still scared.

What if she wasn't meant to be a mother? What if she didn't deserve to be one? What if she lost this baby too? As the pains increased so did this irrational fear and she took it out on Garrin, swearing at him as he tried his best to make her more comfortable.

The contractions grew and grew in intensity until Vanessa decided she'd rather die than carry on any longer.

Then, finally the midwife said, "Okay, lovie, we're just about there. Another few moments and you can start to push."

Vanessa screwed up her face and rolled away from Garrin on to her hands and knees. Her world had narrowed into one long tunnel of pain, the contractions all blurring into one. Sweat ran into her eyes as she gripped hold of the metal bedstead and fleetingly she was reminded of the gates of the remembrance garden, her fingers slip-sliding downwards. And Jennifer's face – Jennifer's still and perfect face.

"Okay, now push," the midwife instructed, her voice the only calm thing in the world.

Vanessa pushed. She'd lost sight of Garrin now, lost sight of everything, there was just her and the pain, and the fear swamping through her like a great black shroud.

"That's it, love, you're doing brilliantly. Baby's crowning. One more push for me."

It was over. That moment she'd longed for and dreaded so much had arrived and time was frozen into stillness, into memory, into déjà vu. She was still on her knees, but the baby was here, she tilted her head round to see, frantic with fear, and found she was looking into Garrin's eyes.

"It's all right, everything's fine, it's okay." His eyes were gentle, acknowledging and reassuring in the same look, and then she heard the midwife's voice.

"You have a beautiful baby girl. An absolutely perfect baby girl."

Vanessa swivelled round. "Is she all right? Are you sure she's all right? Why isn't she crying?"

"She's perfect. Stop wriggling and keep still a minute and you can hold her."

Vanessa took the baby, oblivious now to what the midwife was doing. "Hello, darling. Hello, beautiful."

"You're getting her wet," Garrin observed, and she glanced at him.

"What?"

He smiled and wiped her face with gentle fingers and then he wiped his own. "I'm not much better."

And she saw without surprise that he was crying too, the tears pouring down his face as he bent his head over their daughter.

The midwife pulled the sheet over Vanessa's legs. "I'll get her cleaned up for you properly in a minute," she said, smiling. "You enjoy her for a little while. I'll be back in a sec."

"Isn't she beautiful, isn't she gorgeous."

"Stunning," Garrin said. "She's got your ears."

"And she's got your nose," Vanessa said. "And your mouth." It was true; the baby was the image of Garrin. She had the same dark hair. She looked uncannily like Jennifer, too, except she was moving, stretching out her tiny hands, wonderfully, gloriously alive. Neither of them could stop crying.

"She'll think we're not pleased to see her," Vanessa whispered. "Crying all over her like this. She's the one who's supposed to do the bawling."

"No, she won't. She'll know she's the most wanted baby ever born. She'll be able to feel it. Can I hold her?"

Vanessa watched him take the baby, his movements reverent, his face still wet with tears. "Hello, angel. Hello, my darling. Welcome to the world."

Neither of them was aware the midwife was back until she spoke. "Can I borrow her for a second? I'm not taking her out of the room."

Vanessa tensed as Garrin handed her over. "Oh, please, don't be long."

The midwife smiled. "In a couple of weeks you'll be begging someone to take her away for a night – you wait and see."

"No, I won't. I never want to let her out of my sight."

"Me neither," Garrin said, taking her hand. "Thanks for letting me stay."

"Did I have a choice?" She could feel warmth spreading through her, partly because there was such tenderness in his eyes, but mostly because there was no way their daughter could possibly have anything to do with Richard.

He'd see it instantly. He couldn't fail to. There was nothing of Richard in that tiny perfect face. Nothing at all. It was going to be all right. She sighed and squeezed Garrin's hand and he smiled at her. The midwife brought their daughter back, wrapped in white, and now Vanessa held her, and Garrin put his arms around both of them, and the perfect, perfect moment stretched on for ever.

The following afternoon, a nurse came in, frowning, "A man's just turned up claiming to be your husband," she told Vanessa. "I thought I'd better check with you. He seemed agitated and we get all sorts of odd people coming in here."

"He is my husband." Vanessa decided not to enlighten the nurse any further. "Yes, you can let him in. Thanks for asking."

"Why didn't you tell me?" Richard said, storming over to the cot and looking down at the baby. "I could have been here."

"I didn't want you here," Vanessa said warily. The sharpness of his voice worried her, but not as much as his appearance. He'd lost weight since she'd last seen him – his face looked haggard and there were new deep lines around his eyes. Normally immaculately dressed, he looked as though he'd been sleeping in his clothes.

Richard left the cot and came across to her. "She looks just like you."

"Yes."

"It's still not too late. You can both come home with me. I've got everything ready. I've had the back room decorated and I've got the best cot money can buy, with mobiles hanging over it. It's beautiful; you'll love it, Vanessa. And I've got a baby changing station and some Harry Potter books, first editions, all signed." He knelt down by the bed. "Please come home, I can't live without you."

His breath smelt sour, black coffee and cigarettes. Involuntarily, she drew away from him, even more worried by his words than his appearance.

"We don't even need to do the paternity test – it's obvious she's got nothing to do with that – with him. We'll put the last few months behind us." He drew a hand through his fair hair, which looked greasy. "Can I hold her?"

"She's asleep," Vanessa said. "She's only just gone down."

Ignoring her, Richard went to the cot. "She wants to meet her daddy, don't you, sweetheart?"

The baby began to cry as he lifted her, and Vanessa felt pain tear through her. "Don't, Richard, please." She started to get out of bed. "Give her to me."

"She's all right with her daddy, aren't you, my sweetheart." He held the baby tighter. "I thought we could call her Julie-Anne after my mother, she'll be thrilled. She's always wanted a grandchild."

He'd definitely lost the plot. Julie-Anne Hamilton had never got over the fact her precious son had married beneath him. Vanessa had imagined she'd be out celebrating now they'd split up.

"Please – just give her to me."

His eyes glittered. "Get back into bed, she's fine. Look, she's stopped crying now."

Vanessa hesitated, torn between wanting to take her daughter and doing as he said for fear of antagonising him further. She'd never seen him like this. There was a trace of madness in his eyes, all the calm rationality gone.

"If you get back into bed," he repeated. "And talk to me sensibly, then I'll put her down."

She did as he said and to her huge relief he kept his word and came back to the bed. "What's the matter? Did you think I was going to hurt my own daughter?"

"She's not your daughter."

"Don't say that. Of course she's mine. She's got Hamilton stamped all over her. She looks exactly like I did when I was born."

Vanessa shook her head, wondering whether it might be safer to just go along with him. She'd never thought of Richard being dangerous, but in this mood there was no telling what he would do.

"I'm very tired," she said.

"Of course you are. Well, don't worry; you won't have to do a thing. I've hired a nanny to look after Julie-Anne, she's Spanish, nice girl. You'll like her."

"You've what?" Vanessa stared at him. God, no, she couldn't play along with him. He was starting to scare her. Surely he couldn't really think she'd go back to him.

He stroked her forehead and she saw his fingers shaking. "I'll come and pick you both up tomorrow. I'll check with the nurse to see when you can come home."

"No."

"Don't be silly, darling. It's all sorted. I'll go and fetch your things from the stables in a minute – and then we'll be all fixed, won't we?"

"No!" Vanessa could hear the fear in her voice now and Richard obviously heard it too. He turned and smiled at her. "Don't worry. I'm not going to hurt him. I'll just get your belongings, that's all, and tell him what's happening. I'm a civilised man and after all he has been putting you up all this time."

Then he was gone, striding out of the room. Vanessa got out of bed, trembling, and stood by the cot. She wasn't worried about Richard hurting Garrin – more the other way round. Perhaps he was bluffing. He must know he couldn't just go round and demand her things. He'd be flattened before he could get out of his car.

The nurse came back into the room, her face anxious. "Is everything all right, Vanessa?"

"Can you get me the trolley phone, please? I need to call someone urgently."

"I'll see if it's free."

Vanessa waited, impatience and fear flooding her body with adrenaline, all sorts of scenarios flashing through her head. What if Richard told Garrin it was his baby? Garrin wouldn't believe him. It was so obviously untrue. Richard must have lied when he said he could have children. No wonder he didn't want a paternity test. He must have been bluffing about that too – so sure she'd change her mind. And now that she hadn't, he was determined to force her to go back. And if he couldn't get her to agree, then the obvious solution was to make sure Garrin wouldn't let her back in the house. Make sure she had nowhere to go, except to him.

The nurse came back with the phone. "There you go,

love. I did a bit of queue jumping for you."

"Thank you."

She phoned Garrin's mobile and got no answer. Shit, where was he? He'd said he'd keep it on – although there were parts of the stables where it was difficult to get a signal. She tried the landline and hung up in frustration when the answer machine kicked in. Then she tried Izzy and got another answer machine. This time she left a message apologising and telling Izzy Richard was on his way round to Garrin's. As soon as she'd done it she regretted it. What could Izzy do about it? Just worry probably – as she was going to worry – until she knew what was happening.

Chapter Eighteen

GARRIN WAS JUST LEAVING to get Izzy so he could take her to see Vanessa and the baby when he saw a black BMW coming up the drive.

He waited impatiently, not recognising the driver through the tinted windows until the car pulled up and Richard got out. What the hell was he doing here?

"I've come to collect my wife's things," Richard called cheerfully. "I've just been to see them and I'm taking them home tomorrow. Vanessa asked me to collect her bits and pieces."

Garrin looked at him steadily. The man was clearly unhinged. "I'm in a hurry," he said, deciding that punching Richard's lights out, tempting as it was, probably wasn't the best plan.

"It won't take a minute." Richard strolled towards him, still smiling.

Garrin bent to unlock his car. "Get off my property before I call the police."

"There's no need for that. I can understand you being upset – but you must have known she'd come back to me eventually."

Feeling Richard's hand on his arm, Garrin swung round in annoyance, and deciding he'd been restrained enough, he punched him. Not as hard as he'd have liked, he was too close, but hard enough to send him reeling back a couple of paces.

Richard didn't even try to retaliate. He stood up slowly, rubbed at his chin as if he wasn't quite sure what had just happened, and said, "After all, it is my baby."

"And I'm the fucking pope. Now piss off."

"It's true, I'm afraid. The dates tie in – exactly – I expect Vanessa told you the baby wasn't due until next week, didn't she? I expect she also told you I can't have children." He carried on rubbing his chin and said idly. "Not true, I'm afraid. But of course you don't have to take my word for it. One little test will easily prove it."

"You're lying," Garrin snapped, wanting dearly to hit him again. Not just hit him, but run him over in the car – several times to make sure he was dead. That would have been very satisfying – almost worth a life sentence or two.

"Why don't you go and ask her? Get her to look you in the eyes and tell you there's no chance this could possibly be my baby. She won't be able to do it, I promise you."

Garrin got in his car. He'd had enough of this. He screeched away from where Richard stood and hurtled down the drive. The bloke was a nutcase, but his words had sparked a nugget of unease – especially the bit about the dates. How had Richard known exactly when she was due?

He picked up his mobile, saw there was a missed call from a local number and dialled Izzy.

"I'm going to be a bit late picking you up," he started to say into her answer phone. And then she picked up the phone.

"Garrin, I'm so glad you've rung. I had an odd phone call from Vanessa just now. She said Richard was on his way round to you."

"I've just seen him."

"Are you all right?"

"I am – he's got a sore chin."

"Garrin, you should be careful. That man's dangerous, I've told you before."

"It's only my word against his. Anyway, don't worry about him. I've got to sort something out – half an hour should do it. I'll be round after that."

He parked in the hospital car park and made his way

towards Maternity, adrenaline flooding his system. Was he really going to ask her? Once he'd have trusted Vanessa with his life, but not now. When she'd left him, she'd hurt him more than he'd thought possible. Gouged out a part of his soul, or at least that's what it had felt like at the time. He strode past reception, gave the nurse a brief nod and went into Vanessa's room.

She was breastfeeding the baby. He stopped in his tracks, his throat raw with tenderness. That bastard had to be lying. There was no way this beautiful little girl could be Richard's.

Vanessa glanced up. "Oh, Garrin, thank God you're here. Richard's just been in. He was acting really strangely. I think he might be having a breakdown or something. He scared me."

"I doubt he'll bother us again," he said, stroking the baby's head. "She looks like she's grown since yesterday. Is that possible?"

"I doubt it." She smiled at him, but her eyes were worried. "What did he say?"

"That he'd come to get your stuff because you were going home with him. That I should have known you'd go back to him." He hesitated, and hating himself, but knowing he'd never feel easy unless he knew, he went on softly. "And he said this little one was his, not mine. Is that possible?"

Vanessa didn't reply. The baby had finished feeding and she put a pad over her nipple and re-buttoned the long blouse she was wearing.

"Vanessa, I need to know."

"She's yours. Can't you tell?"

"That's not what I'm asking. Richard says you were sleeping together the week before you came and found me. Is that true?" He touched her face and she glanced at him. Her eyes were tormented. "Jesus Christ, it is, isn't it?

153

Fucking hell, I don't believe this."

"He's just trying to cause trouble. Please stop shouting, you're frightening her."

"Christ," Garrin muttered, turning away. "Is that why you asked me if I'd take in another man's baby? Because you thought it was his, all along?"

"I didn't ask you to take us in. I didn't want to live with you at all."

"So, are you planning to go back with him? Was that bit true as well?"

"No, of course not."

He looked at her and at the baby in her arms and thought about everything that had happened yesterday and suddenly he couldn't bear to stay in the room. He thought she called after him, but he didn't stop. He just kept walking along the corridor until he was outside again, sweating despite the crisp February cold.

At first Garrin drove aimlessly, his thoughts a jumbled mess of past and present until he realised he was heading, not in the direction of home, but towards Knollsey, towards Jennifer's grave. On autopilot, he stopped at a petrol station and bought flowers, he never went empty handed. And then, calmer now he had a purpose, he continued his journey.

It was a beautiful blue day and the cemetery was scattered with people. He passed a teenager wearing a Manchester United scarf, and an old woman, standing at a headstone, shiny with newness, her sobs puffing out into the bitter air, but he avoided their eyes and kept going until he was at Jennifer's grave. Only when he was there did some of the tension start to ebb out of his body because this was the past and, however terrible it was, it couldn't be changed, couldn't be rewritten by some maniac with madness in his eyes.

154

He knelt, his shadow falling over the marble, and traced the outline of her name with his fingers.

"You've got a sister," he murmured, because that much was true, whatever else Vanessa had lied about. "She's beautiful – she looks a lot like you."

And then he did something he had never done in all the times he had come here. He cried – great empty gulps that did nothing to ease the grief of the past or the grief of now. He cried noisily and without embarrassment, and he didn't move until his legs were cramped and stiff with kneeling and his hands were white with the cold and some of his body's numbness had seeped into his mind.

He laid the flowers on Jennifer's grave, left the remembrance garden and went to visit Nanna Kane. She was buried in a different part of the cemetery in a plot long reserved for her, alongside her husband, his grandfather, who he'd never met. It had worried him at first that Nanna and Jennifer were so far apart. As if space or time mattered where death was concerned. As if they wouldn't find each other anyway in that vast universe of souls. It was the only thing that had given him any comfort when his grandmother had died. That there'd be someone to look after Jennifer now, someone he trusted to hug his little girl, to tell her all the stuff she'd never have the chance to learn about her parents, because her entrance to the world had also been her exit from it – her right to know her family snatched away, like the life from her body. Nanna Kane had always loved babies; Nanna Kane would keep her warm wherever they were.

He'd never believed in God, seeing religion as the crutch of the weak, but just thinking of his grandmother and his daughter together had helped him get through those first hell-laden days. When the worst of his grief had passed, he'd forced all such thoughts from his mind. Dismissed them as nonsense. But last night, watching Vanessa push her second daughter into the world, emotions long buried had exploded inside him. He'd known they were back where they'd begun and this time nothing would part them.

And then Richard fucking Hamilton had come along just when he was at his most vulnerable and had tried for the second time to destroy him.

Garrin thought about Vanessa and fresh bitterness rose in him. She'd been so close to smashing through his barriers – love and hate, such a hair's breadth between them. Like birth and death, all part of the same circle. He put his hands in his pockets and retraced his steps to his car. He wasn't going to let her do it again. He'd wasted far too much of his life already on Vanessa.

Chapter Nineteen

"I DON'T WANT ANOTHER bloke's child in my house. I need proof she's mine."

Vanessa glared at Garrin, anger rising. He'd hardly spoken to her for three days and now he'd started she wished he hadn't bothered.

"I'm not proving anything to you. I'm not having her messed about with. And we're not staying anyway. We're moving out."

"Where to?"

"It doesn't matter, does it, seeing as we're not going to be keeping in touch?" She glanced at her daughter, who was asleep in her Moses basket, oblivious to the argument raging above her head. At least Garrin wasn't shouting, but his quiet bitterness was worse somehow. And she felt ragged enough already.

"I want the truth. You owe me that, Vanessa. It's not like I'm accusing you of something you haven't done. You were sleeping with the bastard the day before you came to find me."

"He was my husband. What did you expect me to be doing with him?"

"Still is your husband. Is that where you're going now? Running back to him because we've hit a rough patch – typical."

"That's bloody unfair and you know it. I didn't leave you because we'd hit a rough patch. I left because it was over. You weren't talking to me. You shut me out."

He paced across the room and she stormed after him.

"You're doing it now, Garrin. You're so choked up with anger you're not even listening to me. You know damn well she's yours."

"I don't know anything." He looked back at her, his eyes unreadable. "I'm going out. I've got to see someone."

"Now who's running away? Where are you going?"

"To find some better company." He paused, his hand on the door handle and she realised for the first time that he was dressed for going out. Black jeans, white shirt, open at the neck. He smelt of something expensive, he never wore cologne, and suddenly she was sure he was going to see some woman.

"What company?"

"I'm going to see Amanda – she's a student. Her father has asked me to dinner." He turned, as if wanting to see the effect of his words. "It's business, but I'm planning on enjoying myself. I've been looking forward to it."

Stunned, Vanessa stood back a pace to let him go. An image of Amanda, smoothly blonde, and thin and perfect, flashed into her head and she was uncomfortably aware of the contrast she must make. She was wearing tatty leggings and an old T-shirt and there were damp patches where her milk had leaked through the front.

"Bastard," she muttered as the door slammed behind him.

The baby began to cry and she went across to her. "It's all right, my darling, my sweetheart. Everything's fine."

But everything was far from fine, she thought, as she took Isobel upstairs to the nursery and laid her on the baby mat to change her, the routine still unfamiliar, still bitter-sweet.

These first days with Isobel – her name was the only thing they'd agreed on since she'd brought her home – should have been the happiest of her life. But they weren't. There was so much she didn't understand. When she held her daughter, her emotions were contradictory. There was tenderness, awe that she was so beautiful and an ache of love so intense it brought tears, but there was also a deep sense of unease threaded through the love. She was so like Jennifer. Why had Isobel lived when Jennifer hadn't? All the guilt that had overwhelmed her when Jennifer died had come flooding back. If she'd paid attention to Izzy and Nanna Kane and the rest of the fairground crew, then Jennifer might still be alive.

Vanessa swung between overwhelming gratitude and fear that something was going to go wrong. That she didn't deserve to have a healthy baby. Was it normal to feel like this?

She knew she would never be over Jennifer completely – how did you ever get over losing a child – but she thought she'd come to terms with it. Neither had she imagined that having another baby would in any way assuage the dull ache of grief, which never permanently left her, but she hadn't thought it would renew the pain of her loss either. Every time she looked at Isobel, she saw Jennifer. In the night she got up and stood by her cot, watching for movement, panic-stricken that she was going to find Isobel lifeless, too, and the panic would only ebb away when she'd touched the baby's cheek and felt her warmth or saw her tiny fingers move.

Vanessa wanted to tell Garrin about this, see if he felt the same, because if anyone could understand, surely he could. But now he'd finally decided to talk to her, all he was interested in was practicalities. She hated him for that. And she hated him for going to Amanda's when she needed him so badly.

The Battersby-Smythes lived in an impressive gabled house, which couldn't be seen from the road and had stone lions on either side of the gates. Garrin had lied when he'd said he was looking forward to going. He was dreading it, but it had been worth it to see the look on Vanessa's face.

The thought of her with Richard had tormented him for years and the knowledge that Isobel might not be his twisted the knife deeper. It was about time Vanessa had a taste of what she'd put him through. Her reaction had brought a brief surge of satisfaction, but that was gone now and he felt worn out and nervous as he drove up the rhododendron-lined drive and parked his car beside a new Mercedes.

He wished he hadn't agreed to this – dinner parties weren't his thing. He was far more comfortable in a pub. He didn't even like restaurants – at least not the kind where you had choices of cutlery and glasses and some waiter laying a serviette across your knees – the whole set-up made him self-conscious.

Still, if he got another sale out of it, he supposed it would be worth it. At least they'd talk horses all night. He stood on the doorstep, clutching a bottle of wine, which Izzy had told him would go down well in any company, and clinging to the desperate hope they might have forgotten he was coming and gone out.

Amanda opened the door, smiling and pausing for a moment so he could take in the details of her dress, which was midnight blue and fitted and low cut. He almost expected her to do a twirl. Keeping his eyes carefully on her face he smiled back. "I've got the right night, then?"

"You certainly have. It's great to see you, Garrin. Come through, we're having drinks in the conservatory."

She wiggled along a hallway lined with pictures of horses, individually lit and probably worth a fortune. Her bum looked better in a dress than it did in jodhpurs, Garrin decided. The material clung and moulded and either she was wearing a G-string or no knickers at all. Realising he was actually interested in finding out, he dragged his gaze away and concentrated on horses.

Amanda led him into a conservatory that was larger than

160

his entire ground floor and easily accommodated several palm trees and a dining table that looked as though it could seat twelve and was set up with crystal glasses, polished cutlery and white linen. He felt his stomach muscles clench. Shit, this was going to be a nightmare.

As they entered, Lloyd Battersby-Smythe and a woman who looked like a slightly older version of Amanda turned to greet them. Either Lloyd had married someone fifteen years younger or she'd had a lot of surgery, Garrin thought, as he looked into a replica of Amanda's face.

"Garrin, good to see you," Lloyd said in his heartiest voice. "Let me introduce my wife, Katherine. She's been longing to meet you."

"Oh, I have. You've done wonders with Amanda." Her voice didn't match her looks. Husky and attractive, but not put-on, the result of years of smoking, he thought, taking her outstretched hand and wondering if he was supposed to kiss it. In the end he just dipped his head and she looked amused.

First faux pas of the night – oh well – they hadn't asked him here for his etiquette skills.

"What are you drinking, dear fellow? Brandy, scotch?" Lloyd hooked his thumbs into the waistband of his trousers and thrust out his stomach.

"Something soft, I'm driving." Remembering suddenly that he was still holding the wine, he looked round for a place to put it, and Amanda stepped forward.

"Thank you so much, Garrin, I'll take that while Daddy does the drinks. You don't really have to drive, do you? If you like, you can leave your car in our garage and we can get Melbourne to run you home later. Be a shame not to have some of your lovely wine."

"I don't drink much."

"Nonsense, you must do as Amanda says, no sense in having a chauffeur and letting your guests drive home. I

161

absolutely insist. He can run your car back in the morning."

"That's kind, but…"

"No buts," Katherine interrupted smoothly. "It'll be our pleasure, won't it, Amanda?"

There was no getting out of it without offending them. Garrin nodded stiffly. "A small brandy, then, ta."

He and Lloyd obviously had different definitions of the word small. Garrin glanced around, wondering if he could get away with tipping half of it into one of the plants.

"So tell us about your dear cousin's baby," Katherine said. "How are they? Is your cousin coping?"

"She's fine," he said, wishing he hadn't come. "The baby's great."

"Her first, is it?"

He nodded, hating himself for denying Jennifer, but there was no way he could discuss her with these people.

"Are you one of these new men, Garrin? Would you like a family of your own?"

"Oh, Mummy, stop it, you're embarrassing him. He came round to discuss horses not babies." Amanda came back at just the right moment and he shot her a grateful smile.

"My specialist subject. So how's Shadowman doing? You must be pleased with the way he's turned out."

They were on safer ground now and he breathed an inward sigh of relief. At least they wouldn't expect him to stay late. They'd understand he had to be up early.

Vanessa fed Isobel, sitting in the chair Garrin had bought for the nursery. It was a cross between a rocking chair and a swivel chair and was gloriously relaxing, the perfect place to bond. The nursery was perfect too. Garrin had painted the bottom of the walls orange and the tops yellow and a frieze of giraffes, elephants and tigers ran around the middle. There was a horse mobile hanging over the cot.

162

Show-jumpers. God knows where he'd got that. A pine cupboard held shelves of nappies, babygros and teddy bears, and there was a baby bath and a changing mat and a buggy. Everything Isobel would need for the first months of her life. Everything, except parents who loved each other, Vanessa thought, her anger turning slowly into sadness.

After she'd fed the baby she stayed where she was, the rhythm of the chair gentle and soothing, and she found herself drifting back to the days when she and Garrin had been happy and then further back in the past when they'd been growing up.

The old days, Izzy would have called them, before mobile phones and foreign holidays, when people flocked to the fair in their hundreds. Vanessa's favourite times were just before the season started when they were still taking off dustcovers and re-stocking the stalls, not yet open to the public. Waking up the rides, which in Vanessa's mind were like great beasts that had been hibernating all winter. She learnt afterwards that not all the rides even stayed all winter, they were packed up and serviced and maintained, but in Vanessa's mind, they were always there. The people, like the rides, would come slowly to the season, pasty-faced from their winter jobs indoors.

As Isobel fell asleep on her lap, Vanessa's mind drifted back to a long-ago evening. She'd been about ten and Garrin fourteen. They'd just had their tea and a group of seven or eight people were sitting on a blanket at the far edge of the fair, near the cliff-top with the sea spread out in the bay like a great slab of glass, stained pink and orange by the setting sun. Someone got out a guitar and someone else a bodhran and they began to play, the twang of the acoustic guitar blending with the earthier beat of the drum and in the background the ever-present rhythm of the sea.

The guitarist played folk songs while stars began to come out like fireflies in the slowly darkening sky and the air chilled around them. They would all sing, joining with the guitarist's gravelly voice. Vanessa didn't remember there being anyone at the fairground who couldn't sing, but Izzy was the best. When Izzy began to sing, everyone else stopped and listened. She sang haunting Scottish melodies, her pure voice needing only the lightest accompaniment, standing barefoot on the grass, her eyes half closed, her face moving in passion, pale hair white in the shadows, looking like some stray spirit who'd drifted in on a sea mist.

And Vanessa would watch, entranced, wondering how Izzy, so practical, so down to earth, could suddenly become someone else, with a voice so beautiful it seemed even the sea stopped to listen. Something would shift in her heart while Izzy sang, as if there was a little part of her that was torn out by the music. And sometimes her throat would fill up with tears and she didn't know why – but when she looked round the faces, she'd see that they'd all be the same, tears anonymous in the falling dusk. Even Nanna Kane cried sometimes and Nanna Kane never cried. Not about big things anyway, like losing her daughter to a drunken driver, but Izzy's voice had the power to crumble her.

Garrin could sing too, although not like Izzy. He also played the guitar. And it was through the guitar that their childhood closeness had matured into something else. Garrin had always been her self-appointed protector and her teacher and the person who got her into the most trouble, not that Vanessa needed much leading astray. She loved him unconditionally and she also hated him because they were so alike that they clashed, often and passionately. She remembered the night when everything changed between them.

It was an autumn evening, soon after her seventeenth birthday. Seagulls were calling and circling in the blue air above them, and they were walking, Garrin with his guitar slung around his shoulder, Vanessa with a blanket rolled up under her arm. Garrin had been giving her guitar lessons for a while and they were on their way to their favourite spot, a field a little higher up than the fairground, somewhere they could get away from the crowds.

Vanessa set the blanket out on the grass and Garrin tuned the guitar, played a few warm-up chords and then handed it to her. He always made it look so easy, but Vanessa found the finger positions unnatural and tricky to maintain for long.

"You're trying too hard, that's the trouble," he murmured, "I think you're probably too tense." He knelt on the grass behind her and began to massage her shoulders, his fingers finding the knotted muscles and easing them. Vanessa sighed in pleasure and leaned back against his hands.

"Hey, don't get too relaxed. This is a means to an end. It's not for your enjoyment."

"Pity," she said, tipping back her head and looking up into his eyes and he grinned, showing white teeth and kissed her forehead. It was something he'd done a thousand times before. He'd always been a touchy-feely kind of person, but as he raised his head again, their eyes met and suddenly he was kissing her lips. She kissed him back and the kiss took them into new territory. Moments later, they were lying beside each other on the rug, the guitar forgotten, as they explored each other's mouths and Vanessa felt the first sparks of the fire that would end as a white-hot inferno.

It hadn't felt odd to be kissing, but as if they'd always been meant to do it, an inevitable progression. It was on that night that they'd decided to take their relationship one step further. The night that Garrin had said he'd arrange something – the night that had led to Uncle Bert's hay barn.

Not much had changed after all this time, Vanessa

thought, shifting her arm, which was beginning to cramp and waking Isobel, who stared up at her, eyes wide in her sleep-crumpled face.

"Maybe you'll be able to sing one day, my sweetheart," Vanessa murmured. "Have the kind of voice that will bring people to their knees. You're certainly going to be beautiful, the most beautiful girl in the world and clever – oh, so clever! – you'll go to university and maybe you'll be a doctor or a teacher. And everyone will love you, everyone will always love you." And Vanessa crooned on, talking rubbish, her voice gentle until Isobel fell asleep again. Then she got up and put her in her cot and leaned her elbows on the wooden sides and just watched her.

And she tried not to think about Garrin with Amanda – tried not to hate him for the way that he'd looked at her, wanting her reaction. But it didn't work and eventually she left the room and went to bed because she was exhausted and it was the only room in the house that didn't remind her of Garrin.

Garrin was a lot drunker than he'd planned to get. He didn't have the slightest clue how much he'd drunk because his glass had been topped up before it had even got to the halfway mark despite his protests.

The evening hadn't been as bad as he'd thought. Both Katherine and Amanda had flirted with him shamelessly, and Lloyd, far from seeming to mind, had been encouraging them. Flirting was something he felt at home doing. It hadn't even mattered about the knives and forks. They'd all been very kind, but it was definitely time to go. It was gone midnight and in the bit of his brain that still had some grip on reality, he knew he'd got to get up early.

"It's been a great night," he said. "And I really 'ppreciate your hospitality," – Christ, he was slurring his words – "but I should be making tracks. Is it still okay for a lift?"

He wasn't drunk enough to miss the glance that Amanda exchanged with her mother.

"Oh, Melbourne will be asleep by now." Amanda's voice was silky. "Seems a shame to wake him, doesn't it, Mummy. Garrin can stay in the guest room, can't he?"

"You'd be most welcome," Katherine said. "It's the least we can do after all your help."

"I can get a taxi."

"Taxi!" Lloyd guffawed, as if he'd cracked a joke. "No chance, dear fellow. It would cost them double the fare to get here. No, you must stay. It's really no trouble at all."

Why did you always feel drunker when you stood up? Garrin felt his head spin. Not that it mattered because Amanda was holding his arm. She smelled of something spicy and exotic. She smelled gorgeous and he had a sudden urge to press his face into her cleavage. Only he'd probably have grazed himself on the bloody great diamond thing she had round her neck.

He concentrated on walking straight as they went across the room and he didn't think he'd made a bad job of it. Amanda led him along a corridor, which had several doors. The house was a lot bigger than he'd realised.

"It's just up these steps," she said, slightly too late, and he felt himself stumble. The room – a very impressive room – spun around him and he found himself on the floor, nose pressed into the carpet. Amanda knelt beside him. "Naughty boy, there's a bed just here."

"Fuck," he said, turning his head and seeing her come in and out of focus.

"Oh, yes please, but let me get my dress off first." She giggled. "And unless you've got a particular preference, the bed is so much more comfortable than the floor."

That was the last thing he remembered before he passed out.

*   *   *

When he woke up it was daylight and he was in a giant double bed. He shut his eyes against the glare – Christ, he felt awful – it took a few moments for him to remember what had happened. Too much to drink, he hadn't had a hangover like this in years. He had a vague memory of Amanda taking off her dress, or had she just said she was going to do that? He didn't remember getting undressed himself, but he was naked – completely naked, he realised, pushing back the duvet and sitting up. Bad move – pain hammered across his head and a wave of sickness washed through him. He was going to be useless today – total bloody crap – at least it was still early. His body clock had somehow worked despite the booze.

Now, what was the etiquette of leaving a house before its owners were up, particularly if you'd spent the night shagging their daughter? Had he shagged her? He got up carefully – he'd certainly fancied the idea, he could remember that much. His jeans and shirt were folded on a chair beside the bed. Not by him, he thought wryly. He couldn't remember taking his clothes off in the first place; perhaps she'd undressed him too. Well, that cleared that up, if he'd been too drunk to take his own clothes off, then he'd certainly been too drunk to shag her.

He was just letting himself out of the back door when he heard someone coming downstairs.

"Garrin? Going before breakfast?" Amanda wore a pale silk robe, which didn't leave much to the imagination and she didn't look in the slightest bit hung-over. She came across the kitchen, sweeping her hair back off her face.

"How are you feeling?"

"Like shit."

"Daddy's got some wonderful hangover cures somewhere. Little sachets." She opened a cupboard. "At least have one of these before you go, you'll feel much

168

better." She came across the room and smiled at him. "Not that I've any complaints about how you feel."

He blinked, not sure how to answer this, but Amanda didn't seem to want an answer. She handed him a glass. "There you go. It'll take the edge off it. Half an hour and you'll be as good as new."

"Ta." The drink tasted foul and he was aware of her watching him. "And thanks for last night. I had a good time."

"The pleasure is all mine," she said, glancing at his groin and then back at his face and smiling. "It was very nice to be the one doing the bossing about for a change. Riding lessons will never be quite the same again."

Christ, he wished he could remember what had happened. He took the empty glass back to the sink. "I'd better get going. Thank your parents for me, won't you?"

"I will. And, Garrin, don't look so worried, you were wonderful. The best."

He got into his car still frowning. Perhaps the whole thing had been a set up – perhaps they'd got him drunk on purpose so he'd stay the night. No – he'd got himself drunk – unused to so much – besides, what could they possibly have to gain from making him think he'd shagged Amanda? He'd already agreed he'd go to the show with her. He shook his head, started the car, and aware that he probably shouldn't be driving it, he headed back to Fair Winds.

Chapter Twenty

SO HE'D SPENT THE night with her, had he? Vanessa couldn't believe the pain. He must have slept with dozens of women over the last few years – from what Tracey had said he'd never been short of female company, but she'd managed to put this out of her mind, partly because she'd never seen him with a woman and partly because it was nothing to do with her. She'd given up the right to care what he did when she'd married Richard. But there was nothing logical about what she was feeling now. All night she'd lain awake, listening out for Isobel, and for the sound of Garrin's key in the front door, and tormenting herself with pictures of what Amanda and Garrin might be doing, her stomach crippled with jealousy.

Once, after she'd been in to see to Isobel, she'd gone and listened outside his bedroom door, perhaps she was torturing herself for nothing. Perhaps he'd come back and she'd somehow missed him and he was in bed, sleeping peacefully – sleeping alone. And even though she knew this wasn't true, she'd pushed open the door and saw that his bed was neatly made, the duvet flat, the room shadowed and empty. The air smelt of him, part maleness with something sweeter overlaying it, the cologne he'd put on for another woman – for Amanda.

And Vanessa's stomach cramped tighter and she heard herself moan and she'd only just made it to the bathroom. She retched over the toilet bowl, sickness spilling out of her, and afterwards she'd wiped her mouth and looked at her reflection in the mirror, pale and empty and exhausted. This was madness, how had she let herself get to this? This couldn't be love. Love didn't tear you into pieces and leave you empty of everything but despair.

Eventually, her body had given way to exhaustion, but she didn't really sleep because the pictures had carried on through her dreams. Distorted fragments playing across the blackness. Garrin on top of Amanda, his darkness against her pale, young body. Images of them writhing together against an ever-changing background. Once it had been the fairground. Amanda and Garrin, naked astride a galloper, smiling at her as the ride turned, the flashing lights turning their bodies different colours, red, green and garish purple.

At dawn Vanessa gave up trying to sleep. She went out to the landing window and saw that his car still wasn't back. There was just hers, a dark isolated shape, the windows frosted with ice. She knelt on the carpet, looking out at the fields on either side of the long drive and watching as the sky slowly lightened into day. And she knew it was over. She would never be able to forgive him for this endless night.

But at last, finally, she was calm, her survival instincts kicking in, giving her a strange detachment. He was never going to make her feel like this again. She fought down the urge to pack up Isobel's things and drive away. She would do it properly this time. Get herself a job, find somewhere for them to live, be self-sufficient, she would focus all of her energies on that. One day, Garrin Tate would be a distant memory. Until then she would keep out of his way and she would never, never let him see how much he'd hurt her.

She didn't know what time he did come home, because she went back to bed and finally she slept until Isobel's cries woke her again just before eight. His car was back, but he wasn't in the house, which was just as well because she didn't want to face him until she was composed and ready, with nothing of the night on her face.

171

It was lunchtime when the back door slammed and she heard him whistling in the kitchen. She was in the lounge with Isobel on her lap when he came in.

"Are you all right, Vanessa, you don't look well." He stood in the middle of the room, his eyes speculative. "Everything okay?"

"Fine, thanks." She glanced up, knowing her voice was as icy as her face. "You?"

"I've got a hangover." He grinned. "Serves me right. I had far too much to drink last night."

"Perhaps you should take something for it." Cyanide would be good; a nice little pot-full should do it. She'd enjoy seeing him writhing about on the floor, his face screwed up in agony, fighting for his final breaths.

He came across the room and stroked Isobel's head. "Had any more thoughts about what I said last night?"

"We will be moving out, yes, but I'll need a bit of time to get a job organised. I take it we can stay here until I do?"

"I meant about the paternity test." He was so close she could smell him – shower gel mixed with horse – and was that a trace of Amanda on his skin? Reminding herself she didn't care, she bowed her head and said coldly. "I've not thought any more about that, no."

"I expect Richard will want to know the score, too. After all, one of us will need to support you."

"We don't need your support. We'll be fine by ourselves, won't we, sweetheart." She kissed Isobel's hair, sniffing in her baby sweetness, which blotted out the smell of him.

He sighed. "Of course you can stay until you find a job. I'm not kicking you out on the streets. But I need to know about Isobel."

Vanessa didn't reply and eventually he got up and left the room. She was surprised Richard hadn't been in touch. She'd discharged herself before he'd come back to the hospital and she hadn't heard from him since. She could understand why he wouldn't want to come round and risk getting another thumping, but she thought he might have phoned and demanded she go back. Or perhaps he'd realised his behaviour had been out of order and had finally decided to let her go.

Richard was in a better position to force her to arrange a paternity test, too. Maybe that was what he was up to. Consulting his solicitor – Richard would never do anything on impulse. He'd gather all the facts and then he'd come round, armed. He hadn't been very rational at the hospital though. A sliver of unease ran through her. All that stuff about calling the baby Julie-Anne after his mother and taking them both home with him. That hadn't been like Richard. Perhaps it would be better if she kept out of his way, too. It was amazing how strong she felt now she had a plan.

Tracey leant on her pitchfork and stared at Vanessa in amazement. "You're not serious, are you? I thought that things were okay between you, now."

"Well, they're not. Actually, I can't stand him."

"What's brought this on?"

"Nothing's brought it on. It was only ever going to be temporary – me staying here." She adjusted the baby sling and kissed Isobel's head. "It's time for us to move on and the sooner the better as far as I'm concerned. I need a job where I can take Isobel, preferably a live-in one. So if you hear of anything, let me know."

Tracey shrugged. "I will. Actually, I thought I might look for another job, too. I could do with working somewhere where I get less abuse and a lot more money."

"You wouldn't really leave, would you?"

"I might. Garrin's been a complete pain in the arse lately. The fact that he's sex on legs can only get him off

173

the hook for dishing out so much aggravation."

Vanessa stared at her, surprised. "I thought you said he was too moody for you to be interested."

"Oh, he is, he is – but it's nice having a pin-up for a boss. I might end up with some bitter old hag who hates me for being gorgeous." She swept her blonde hair back and pouted. "Or a tosser like Lloyd Battersby-Smythe – he's advertising for a groom at the moment, but he got an official warning the other day from the BSJA for beating up his horse in the ring. I don't think I could stomach that. At least Garrin's nice to his horses."

Vanessa didn't want to hear about Garrin's good side. She frowned. "I don't know how you've put up with him this long."

"Nor do I. He had Chloe in tears this morning. I spent ages talking her out of leaving. She's a nice girl. I don't know what his problem is."

"He had a hangover. And he was probably knackered. He stayed at Amanda's last night." She was amazed she could say it so casually, that the words didn't bring any new pain.

Tracey looked taken aback. "I didn't know he was seeing her. Is that why you're going?"

"No, I don't care what he does in his spare time. It's nothing to do with me."

"Well, I'm not surprised you're upset. That's not very responsible behaviour for a new daddy."

"As I said, it's up to him what he does. I'm only concerned about Isobel."

"Well, I'll ask around, but don't hold your breath. It's going to be tricky finding a job where you can take her, gorgeous though she is. What's it like, motherhood? Is it how you thought it would be?"

"It's brilliant," Vanessa said, wondering why such a question should bring tears stinging her eyes, when she

174

could discuss Garrin without a flicker. For a moment she had an urge to tell Tracey how she couldn't stop thinking about the baby she'd lost, how Isobel was a constant reminder of Jennifer. Then she remembered Tracey didn't know this was second time round for her and Garrin, and a loose-box was hardly the place for such confessions.

"What?" Tracey said, picking up some of this in her face.

"Nothing."

The clatter of hooves heralded Garrin's return and he came into the yard, riding Derry.

"I'm paying you to muck out that stable, not chat," he snapped, as he dismounted.

Vanessa screwed up her face. "Sorry, I'm getting you into trouble."

"Oh, just ignore him, I do."

"I'd better get back anyway, the midwife's due soon." She smiled at Tracey. "Don't forget what I said about the job." She hurried back up to the house. Maybe she should mention how she felt to the midwife. Perhaps she could give her some reassurance that in time she'd stop worrying, looking for problems where there weren't any. Perhaps it was only time that would let her heal.

The midwife hadn't been gone long, when the doorbell rang again. Vanessa, cradling Isobel in her arms, went to answer it and was startled to find Amanda, wearing a fake fur coat and expensive trousers – she obviously wasn't here for a riding lesson. Her car was parked behind Garrin's. Vanessa's stomach clenched – well at least she'd put on make up, and looked half decent, but she still couldn't compete with this girl, who obviously had nothing else to do but tart herself up.

"Yes," she said coldly.

"Hi, I don't think we've met officially. I'm Amanda, you

must be Vanessa, and this is little Isobel, isn't it? Garrin was telling us all about her. Is he in?"

"He's in the yard. Why don't you go down, I'm a bit busy at the moment."

Amanda looked taken aback and she realised she must have been sharper than the situation warranted. But the last thing she wanted was this woman in Garrin's house. Wandering around making herself comfortable. He could at least have the decency to wait until she'd moved out.

"I'll deal with this, ta, Vanessa." She jumped, aware of Garrin behind her. Where had he come from? Aware that Amanda was grinning and Garrin was waiting for her to move, she spun round and went back into the lounge. She was shaking, which was ridiculous; she could handle this. She must. Isobel, picking up on her tension, had started to cry. Well, hopefully that would put them off coming in here.

It didn't. Garrin loped into the room, bending to hear something Amanda said as they came in. He was smiling. Vanessa looked away, concentrated on rocking Isobel until she was finally quiet. Then she stood up.

"Oh, don't go on my account," Amanda said easily. "I like babies."

Vanessa brushed past her, aware that Garrin was watching her, but not wanting to see his expression. She was going to have to change her plans. There was no way she could stay here if he was going to bring Amanda round on a regular basis. It was all very well thinking she could be rational, but she couldn't, not if he was going to do this. She went upstairs and picked up her mobile phone. She'd asked the midwife about a paternity test earlier and she'd promised to phone her back. That was something else she needed to sort out because, despite what she'd told Garrin, if he wasn't Isobel's father, then it meant she'd never have to see him again, which was probably for the best.

There was no message from the midwife, but there was a missed call. She glanced at the familiar number and felt a little jolt. Richard. So he'd had enough of waiting too. She shut the bedroom door, aware of muted laughter coming from the kitchen. Then she sat on the bed and phoned him back.

"Vanessa, it's good to hear from you." He sounded perfectly normal. His voice was rational and calm and it struck her that perhaps he hadn't been as overwrought as he'd seemed at the hospital. Perhaps it had been her, still shattered and exhausted from labour. Perhaps she'd read more into his offer to take her home than there had been.

"How are you?" she said quietly.

"Very well. And you? How's the baby?"

"I've called her Isobel – after Izzy. She's great. We're both fine."

"I take it you still want a divorce. Is that why you called me back?"

Surprised at his directness, and not at all sure why she had called him, apart from the fact she'd have to speak to him sooner or later, she said, "Well, yes. I do think it's best."

"Then we'd better meet up and get things set in motion. I don't want to drag things out."

Taken aback at this complete turnaround, she heard herself agreeing. Had it always been this easy? Perhaps she'd just been seeing problems that weren't there. Seeing Richard as slightly deranged, seeing an affair between Garrin and Amanda where none existed. No, she definitely wasn't imagining that.

"Shall I pick you up?"

"No, it would be better if I met you."

They set a time and place and Vanessa put the phone down, puzzled. At least if he was going to be reasonable then she'd be able to move out of Garrin's.

177

                    *   *   *

By the time she arrived at the coffee bar Richard had specified she was beginning to feel the first flickers of optimism. He was sitting at a table near the entrance and when he saw her he came over and held the door so she could manoeuvre the buggy through it.

"Thanks."

"No problem." He smiled. He was clean-shaven and smartly dressed – work clothes, as if he was going on to a business meeting. There was no trace of the man who'd ranted at her in the hospital. "I owe you an apology," he said. "For my behaviour last time we met. I was overwrought, but that's no excuse, I know. I'm sorry."

She looked into his blue eyes and saw only sincerity. "It's all right. I'm not surprised you were upset. It was understandable in the circumstances."

"Which is why we're here," Richard said smoothly. "Now I'm sure you've got plenty to do and I've an appointment this afternoon, so we'll make this brief, shall we? Do you have any news about the paternity test? I take it I'll need to provide some sort of sample."

Vanessa nodded.

"We'll need to know whose daughter she is – it'll make a difference financially – naturally."

Aware that he didn't even glance at the buggy, Vanessa nodded again.

"Good. Well, let me know what you need me to do. In the meantime, I propose I let you have an advance payment in lieu of the final settlement. I'm sure you could do with it."

She was very tempted to say she didn't want his money, but then she thought about Garrin and Amanda and knew that she couldn't. "It would be helpful, Richard, thanks."

He took an envelope out of his pocket and handed it to her. "That should keep you going for a bit. It's a cheque –

twenty thousand pounds – I would have given you cash, but I didn't think you'd want to carry too much money around."

The waitress arrived with their drinks, coffee for him and Diet Coke for her, and spent some time cooing over Isobel. Richard smiled paternally and agreed she was utterly gorgeous and that they were both very proud of her.

Vanessa glanced at his face, which was animated, and felt a tug of guilt. She'd misjudged him, she'd treated him terribly and his only crime had been to love her – perhaps too much, but that was hardly his fault. For a second she was transported back to the early days of their marriage: the endless hours he'd spent listening to her talking about Jennifer, and it struck her with bitter-sweet irony that if anyone could understand the guilt she felt about Isobel living when her sister had not, it would be Richard. But she could never tell him.

"Are you all right?" he asked and she glanced at him and nodded, but he didn't look convinced.

"You don't look it," he said, half getting up and reaching across as if to take her hand. He jogged the table, which overbalanced her glass of Coke. The whole thing happened in a split second, and although she reacted instantly, pushing back her chair, most of the drink went over her lap.

"I'm so sorry." He looked stricken. "Did it get you?"

"Just a bit," she admitted, screwing up her face as she felt the drink's coldness seeping through her jeans. It had soaked the front of her blouse, too. Damn, there'd be no chance of getting that out. He must be nervous; it wasn't like him to be clumsy.

He handed her a paper serviette, but it wasn't enough. "I think I'd better rinse this out," she said. "I won't be a sec."

"I'll get you another one."

"No, you keep an eye on Isobel."

"But what if she cries?" He looked alarmed at the prospect and Vanessa felt a fleeting irritation.

"I'll be as quick as I can." She stood up. When she glanced back from the door of the Ladies, he was looking into the buggy, his face apprehensive.

The last time she'd seen him, he'd been hell bent on taking them both home, she thought. Just as well he hadn't, he looked absolutely terrified now.

She rinsed the Coke out of her blouse and sponged off her jeans. Then she dried herself as best she could on the hand dryer. When she stepped back into the warmth of the restaurant, the waitress was carrying plates down the aisle, temporarily obscuring her view of the table, so that she could see Isobel's buggy, but not Richard.

Vanessa waited for her to get out of the way and then, as the table came into view, she stopped, and her heart began to thump. Richard wasn't even there. What the hell was he playing at? She dodged round a family in winter coats and hurried towards the front of the restaurant. When she finally reached the buggy, she felt ice coursing through her. It was empty.

Chapter Twenty-One

SHE TORE OUTSIDE, PANIC tossing explanations into her mind. Maybe Isobel had got too hot, the restaurant was baking, and Richard had wanted to give her some fresh air. That would explain why he hadn't taken the buggy. But as she scanned the street and saw no sign of them, she knew it couldn't be that. Why had she left him alone with her? Guilt mixed with increasing panic. She would kill him if he hurt her. Her heart was thumping so violently it was impossible to think straight.

She clenched her fists. Calm down. There was no reason why Richard would hurt Isobel. He might be a control freak, but he wasn't a monster, he wouldn't hurt a baby. Tears were running down her face, she realised, swiping at them. She had never been so terrified.

Perhaps they were still in the restaurant. Yes, that was it. Richard had gone to order her another drink and hadn't wanted to leave Isobel unattended. She went back inside. He wasn't at the counter. She cornered the waitress who'd served them.

"Have you seen the man who was sitting here just now? Did you see where he took my baby? I just went to the loo and when I came back they weren't here."

The waitress shook her head. "I'm sorry, no, but I thought he was your husband."

"He is, but – oh, never mind…" Aware of the waitress's bemusement and the fact that people on the nearest tables were looking in her direction, Vanessa ran out of the restaurant again. She raced to the end of the street, even though she knew it was hopeless, they'd be long gone by now. She went back to her car, adrenaline clearing her head, crystallising her thoughts. He must know she would follow him. Perhaps that was what he wanted, but why didn't he just say? Why give her all that crap about being happy with the divorce? It made no sense at all.

His car was in the drive at Chandlers Ford and she rang the bell, feeling sick with fury and relief. He answered it instantly. He'd abandoned the suit jacket and taken off his tie. All pretence of normality gone. His eyes were cold.

"Oh, hello, Vanessa, I thought you might turn up. Come in."

"What the hell are you playing at? Where is she? Where's Isobel?"

"She's absolutely fine, stop shouting. Don't you trust me?"

"I trusted you to sit with her – not snatch her and bring her up here. What have you done with her?"

"She's upstairs."

Vanessa went up two at a time and he followed more slowly. When she reached the landing she remembered him saying he'd had the spare room converted into a nursery. She pushed open the door and gasped. The room, which had previously been used as a guest room, was now decked out with Jungle Book wallpaper and curtains and an impractical white carpet. Along one wall were a cot, a baby bath on a stand, a changing station, a buggy and a full-size pram, all with their Mothercare labels still attached.

Isobel was in a Moses basket identical to the one they had at home. Vanessa knelt beside it, a small sob escaping. Her baby looked as though she was sleeping, but swamped with familiar panic, she still had to touch her to check.

Richard came in behind her and shut the door. "She's fine. I don't know why you're making all this fuss. What do you think of the nursery? I got a firm in. They came highly recommended. I think they've done a good job."

182

She couldn't speak. How could he stand there so calmly, talking as if this was all perfectly normal when he'd just kidnapped her baby? She gently folded back the blankets, and Isobel opened her eyes and gave a little whimper.

"What are you doing?"

"I'm taking her home. What do you think I'm doing?"

"You're not going anywhere." There was an edge to his voice.

She glanced at him, feeling washed-out, the adrenaline all gone now, leaving a great weariness in its place.

"You can't stop me."

In answer, he turned his back on her and she realised he was locking the door. The spare room had never had a lock on before. He must have had it fitted especially. She felt the hairs lift on the back of her neck.

"Richard, don't be ridiculous, you can't keep us here. Open that door."

Ignoring her, he moved across the room, opened a cupboard and took out a pink all-in-one. "Do you like this? I know it's a bit big at the moment, but she'll soon grow into it, won't she?"

"Didn't you hear what I said? We're not staying. I don't live with you any more and whatever game you're playing you can stop it, right now. You're scaring me."

"It's no game, Vanessa. You're my wife and this is your home." He folded the babygro carefully and put it back in the cupboard. "It's where you and Isobel belong." When he turned round there was disappointment in his expression, as if she was a disobedient child and he the long-suffering parent.

He came across to where she was still kneeling by the Moses basket. "Get up. I want to talk to you."

"Just let us go home, Richard, please."

"I said, get up." He caught her by the armpits and dragged her to her feet with casual brutality, and, for the first time in her life, Vanessa was afraid of him. He must have seen it in her face, because she saw surprise in his eyes.

"I'm not going to hurt you. I just want to talk. And this is the only way I could think of to get you to listen."

"All right, I'm listening," she said, swallowing the urge to pick Isobel up and storm past him. "What exactly do you want to talk about?"

"I want to take you back to March 26th 2000."

She nodded uncomfortably. That was their wedding day.

"You promised to love and honour me until death us do part. Remember?"

Again Vanessa nodded, wondering where on earth this was going.

"I promised the same," Richard went on easily. "And I've kept my half of the bargain. You haven't."

"Things change. Marriages break down. It happens."

"Not to me it doesn't."

"It happens to everyone."

"I thought you were going to shut up and listen."

Chilled, she shut up and he began to talk. He started with their wedding day. He could remember every detail, from the photographer's name to the handed-down items they'd had on their wedding cake. Then he jumped forward to their anniversaries and she listened, dazed, as again he went through each precise detail. The four-day trip to Venice on their third anniversary, the eternity ring he'd bought her last year, which like her wedding ring, she no longer wore.

He wasn't just remembering, she realised, looking at the distance in his eyes. He was re-living.

Once she tried to interrupt. "You're torturing yourself, Richard, there's no need for this. It isn't going to change anything." But she didn't think he even heard her. He just carried on reeling off events and the light outside the windows faded slowly and she began to wonder if he

184

planned to keep them here all night. What would Garrin do if she didn't come home? He was hardly going to send out a search party. He might even think she was deliberately staying away because he'd spent the night with Amanda. Perhaps he was with her now and hadn't even noticed she was missing.

Her mobile was in her bag, but Richard wouldn't let her call Garrin, or even Izzy. It was crazy, this didn't happen in real life, but it was happening. The more Richard talked, the more she realised she didn't know this man she'd married and had believed herself in love with, at all. He might have her husband's face, and his mannerisms, but he was a stranger, and she didn't have the faintest idea how to deal with him.

Garrin took his time over evening stables because he didn't want to face Vanessa. He was beginning to regret winding her up over Amanda. It had been obvious by her coldness earlier that she was furious with him and he didn't want another argument. It would have been nice to just get in and relax for the evening.

Tracey was cold-shouldering him too, no doubt Vanessa had been mouthing off about him, and while he did feel a twinge of conscience about staying at Amanda's all night, it was no big deal. Why shouldn't he? He certainly didn't owe Vanessa anything – not when she was still refusing to tell him if Isobel was even his.

He couldn't stay outside indefinitely. Eventually, he ran out of things to do and headed back to the house. He was surprised to find the place in darkness. Odd – Vanessa should have been back hours ago and had Isobel settled for the night. He went round the house, feeling its emptiness and switching on lights, which didn't help. Then, trying not to think about Vanessa and how late it was getting, he showered and put on his dressing gown.

When he came down he noticed the message light on the answering machine. Maybe she'd called to say where she was. But there was only a message from Izzy, confirming some arrangement she'd made with Vanessa for the following day. The niggling worry that Vanessa might not be all right turned slowly into anger. He was tempted to phone Izzy and ask what their arrangements were, but then he'd have to admit he didn't know where Vanessa was and Izzy had obviously spoken to her. Damn bloody Vanessa – if she wanted to play silly buggers, then good luck to her. It wasn't his problem. He was shattered from the after-effects of yesterday's alcohol. He'd have an early night and put Vanessa out of his head.

Izzy phoned him on his mobile the next morning. He'd just finished a riding lesson and was in a foul mood. As the two subdued working pupils led their horses back to the yard, he felt a mixture of guilt and relief. At least Izzy would tell him what was going on.

"Is Vanessa all right?" she said, without bothering to ask after him.

"I haven't a clue. She didn't stay here last night."

"What do you mean she didn't stay there? Where is she then? Does she have the baby with her?"

"Yeah, she does, and how the hell do I know? I'm not her keeper." He regretted this as soon as he'd said it, hearing the reproof in Izzy's silence.

"I'm sorry. I didn't mean to snap at you. I didn't have a very good night."

"She said they were popping round this morning," Izzy went on icily. "But don't worry I'm sure I can track them down without your help."

"Perhaps she's on her way."

"That doesn't sound very likely if she hasn't been home. I doubt she'd stay out all night with a new baby unless she

186

had a very good reason. Do you?"

"No. No, I guess not."

There was another little silence and then Izzy continued more softly. "I had the most awful dream last night about Vanessa. It's probably nothing, but it does seem odd she should go missing. I'm worried."

"Well, wherever she went, she took her car. So she hasn't been abducted."

"I think she might have gone to Richard's."

"Yeah, I suppose it's possible. She certainly wasn't very happy with me." He was tempted to tell Izzy exactly why Vanessa was pissed off with him, and exactly why he was pissed off with her, but it was pointless getting into that sort of conversation on the phone.

"Garrin, you might not be concerned about Vanessa, but I think you should be concerned about your daughter. I've got the address in Chandlers Ford. Would you like it?"

"Yes," he said because he knew he'd get no peace if he said anything else.

"Call me when you've tracked them down. Second thoughts, Garrin, I'd like to come with you. I don't trust that man. Could you pick me up on your way through?"

Didn't trust him more like, Garrin thought savagely, as he hung up. Still, maybe she was right. If Richard had somehow bullied Vanessa into going back to him, then he might be tempted to punch the smug bastard. Perhaps it was best to have peace-keeping Izzy beside him.

Crosser than ever, he went to find Tracey. "I've got to nip out and I might be a while. Can you reschedule my afternoon lessons."

"Sure." She glanced at him curiously, but he didn't enlighten her. Had Izzy not mentioned the dream, he wouldn't even have contemplated chasing after Vanessa. But although Izzy never claimed to be psychic, her premonitions of disaster were notoriously accurate and he'd long since learned not to question them.

Izzy said very little as they drove to Chandlers Ford. She didn't even comment on his driving, just gripped her hands in her lap with a slightly pained expression as he braked to go through speed cameras. Her presence was calming, he had to admit.

The house was easy to find, it was exactly the sort of place he'd have expected Richard Hamilton to live in – pebble-dashed and double-glazed, a neat little piece of suburbia. Vanessa's car was parked behind Richard's black BMW in the driveway and even though he'd been half expecting to see it, he felt his stomach tying itself in knots. What the hell was he going to say? It was obvious what had happened. Vanessa had decided to go back to Richard. History was repeating itself. Perhaps he should take this as evidence that Isobel wasn't his and just turn around and go home. He didn't need all this crap.

Torn, he hesitated, and Izzy touched his knee. "Just make sure they're all right," she murmured. "I'm right here if you need me."

He nodded and left her sitting in the car while he went to ring the bell. If Vanessa answered it and told him she was happy with Richard, then that would be the end of it, once and for all. He had no idea what he'd do if Richard answered. Sweat trickled down the back of his neck. No one came.

Impatient now and fired up with adrenaline, he pushed open the letterbox and shouted through it. "Vanessa, what the hell are you playing at? I know you're in there. Come and answer this bloody door."

Nothing. No sign of movement, not a shadow on the other side of the glass. Frustrated, Garrin banged the letterbox again and then he thought he heard something. He paused to listen and it came again, faint, but unmistakeable

– a baby's thin cry. Adrenaline pounded through him as he glanced around the house – there was no way he'd be able to break in, mortise locks, a burglar alarm box on the wall, which was probably directly linked to the police station. If they didn't want to let him in, he was stuffed.

"I'm not going anywhere until you answer this door," he yelled through the letterbox. "Come on – be reasonable. Izzy's worried sick."

Upstairs, Richard looked at Vanessa. "Gypsy boy's turned up. I thought you said he didn't care."

"He doesn't. It's Isobel he's worried about. You should have let me phone him."

"Do you think I want to listen to you talking to that loser? It's his fault we're in this mess."

Knowing it was pointless arguing with him, she made to get up from the chair.

"Where are you going?"

"To see to Isobel." Anger tightened her voice. "I can hardly go anywhere else, seeing as you've still got the key. This is madness, Richard. You can't keep us locked up for ever."

"You're my wife."

"That doesn't give you the right to keep me prisoner. I've had enough of listening to you. It's all right, my darling." She bent over her daughter, knowing she wasn't hungry because she hadn't long ago fed her.

In the night she'd fed her several times, here in front of him because Richard hadn't let them leave the room. He'd sat and watched her and she'd felt repulsed by his gaze. She'd never dreamed she'd feel repulsed by her husband, angry with him yes, even sorry for him, but this night had changed her perception of him totally. She might have been under his control mentally all these years, but she hadn't known it and she hadn't minded it. Being under his control

189

physically sickened her. The memories of the past sixteen hours would override for ever the sweetness that had been in their marriage

Still with her back to him, she said quietly. "Anyway, he knows we're here – he's not just going to give up and go away."

"Well if it's Isobel he wants, then take her down there. She's getting on my nerves."

She turned to look at him. His eyes were glittering, his cheekbones flushed.

"What?"

"He can take her back with him and we can carry on talking in peace."

Vanessa was about to tell him no way was she being parted from Isobel when it struck her that her daughter would be far better off with Garrin. Every instinct she had urged her to get Isobel as far away as possible, even if it did mean they had to be temporarily separated. Feeling sick with worry, she kept her voice casual, "All right, I'll take her down to him." She was about to pick Isobel up when he said, "Wait."

Disappointed, she spun round to look at him. Now he'd put the idea in her head she was anxious to carry it through. Get Isobel out of this house, even though she hated the thought of letting her out of her sight. "Make up your mind. She's bound to start crying again."

He crossed to the window and drew the net curtain aside. "Gypsy boy's not going anywhere in a hurry. Come here."

Reluctantly, she walked to where he stood and he reached out and caressed her face. "You can take her downstairs on one condition."

It took all her self-control not to flinch from his touch. "What condition?"

"Get undressed."

Chapter Twenty-Two

VANESSA STARED AT HIM in disbelief. "What on earth for?"

He smiled at her and didn't answer. Then he strolled across the room, opened the cupboard, pulled something out and gave it to her.

A black negligee, she saw with a gasp of horror. One he'd bought for her when they were first married.

"Put it on."

"No way."

"Then you both stay here. It's up to you, Vanessa. But I wouldn't hang around too long. I don't suppose he'll wait for ever."

As he spoke, the letter box banged again and she heard Garrin's voice.

"For Christ's sake, Vanessa, at least tell me you're okay. Or I'll break this bloody door down."

"He won't," Richard said confidently. "It's a quality door. He'll get sick of shouting, sooner or later. If he keeps it up much longer one of the neighbours will probably call the police."

It was true. She was surprised someone hadn't already done it. She looked at him, sickened, and he raised his eyebrows. "It's a simple enough request. Don't go all shy on me. I've seen it all before."

Rage boiled in her. He had her over a barrel and he knew it. Turning her back on him, she pulled off her blouse, unclipped the white nursing bra and tugged the negligee over her head. She'd expected it to be too tight and it was. It stretched taut over her breasts and stomach. She must look like some cheap whore, dressed to titillate.

"It'll be a better fit if you take off your jeans," Richard

pointed out, a flash of lust in his eyes.

Shaking with anger, she kicked off her jeans, knowing this might all be for nothing because Garrin could get fed up at any moment. Patience had never been his strong point.

"Very fetching. He can't fail to be impressed." Richard stared at her breasts. His eyes darkened and she was aware of milk leaking through the thin material.

Dismayed, she half turned from his gaze. "I'm not going down there like this."

"It's your choice." Richard took a step towards Isobel, a cruel smile on his lips and Vanessa moved between them.

"All right. You win. I'll go. Don't you dare touch her."

He raised his hands. "I wasn't planning on it. I'm not a monster." He was so close she could smell the faint sweat of his body, mixed with the more civilised trace of cologne. A thin veneer of respectability – what a small step between an animal and a man.

He touched her right shoulder, running his fingers lightly across her collarbone towards the swell of her breast. A possessive touch, its message reflected in his eyes. You're mine. You'll always be mine.

Flinching, but afraid to challenge him in case he changed his mind, she dropped her gaze.

"You said I could take her. You'll need to unlock the door."

He gave the slightest of nods and took the key from his pocket. Shaking with relief, she scooped Isobel gently from the cot and stepped past him.

"And don't try going with him," Richard added. "Because I'll be right beside you. One false move and the deal's off. You both stay here for as long as I choose to keep you."

She glanced at him, trying to gauge what he meant. What was to stop her going with Isobel – that's assuming Garrin would take them?

She soon found out. Richard followed her down the stairs and even though Isobel was in her arms, her face pressed against the baby's soft sweetness, she could sense him behind her. When they were in sight of the front door, he stroked the nape of her neck.

"I think it might be more convincing if I wasn't fully dressed, don't you?"

Numbly, she waited, while he shrugged off his shirt and put his arm around her.

"Chop chop, Vanessa. Best not keep him waiting."

With fingers that hardly worked for trembling, she unbolted and unchained the front door.

"What the hell's going on, Vanessa? Izzy's worried sick..." Garrin tailed off, as he took in the little scene before him, and his face hardened.

She swallowed tears. More than anything, she wanted to tell him what had happened – tell him how scared she was of Richard – but she had an awful feeling he wouldn't listen. Anger tightened every muscle in his face and there was contempt in his eyes. She could feel Richard's fingers digging into her waist. A reminder, if she needed one, that she couldn't just walk away. Not without putting her daughter at risk.

"Garrin, please just hear me out. Have you got the baby seat in your car?"

He nodded, his eyes narrowing.

"I need you to take Isobel back with you. It's very important."

His eyebrows shot up in amazement. "Why? What's the matter? Had enough of motherhood already? Or doesn't your husband want a screaming baby affecting his sex life?"

What else was he supposed to think? It was what Richard wanted him to think. All things considered he was behaving with remarkable restraint. He hadn't so much as glanced in Richard's direction.

"There are things I have to sort out here." She stared at him, willing him to see that she was far from okay. That she wasn't dressed like this through choice. There had been such telepathy between them once. Surely he could see past what she was wearing. But his gaze dropped to her breasts once more and she knew with a surge of despair that he couldn't.

Terrified he'd refuse to take Isobel, she held her out to him. "Please, Garrin? Just do as I ask. I won't be long, I'll explain later."

For a moment he looked as if he would refuse and then she caught movement behind him and saw Izzy getting out of the car. So that was the reason for his restraint. Vanessa felt a rush of relief. Izzy would help. Izzy would know she wasn't here because she wanted to be.

"Please?" she said again, aware of the old lady's slow approach.

Still Garrin hesitated. Vanessa felt sick. Being so close to Richard, feeling his naked skin against hers repulsed her.

"What's going on, Nessa?" Izzy's voice was non-judgmental, but her eyes were cool.

"We need a bit of peace and quiet," Richard said, saccharine sweet. "We've things to discuss."

With a swift, almost angry movement, and another look at Vanessa that left her in no doubt of what he thought of her, Garrin took Isobel.

Unable to control herself a second longer, Vanessa gave a small sob, but before she could formulate a sentence, Richard slammed the front door shut and turned towards her. His expression was a mixture of triumph and satisfaction.

She dipped her head. Before yesterday she'd still felt that maybe she'd pushed him into this, that perhaps his reaction to her leaving – although extreme – was understandable. Now she hated him for forcing her to be separated from Isobel. It took every bit of self-control she had not to break down and beg him to let her go with her daughter.

"I've done what you asked. So let's finish this now. What is it you want?"

"I think we'll go back upstairs and discuss that – don't you?"

She went ahead of him, past caring what he planned to do next. All she wanted was to be back with her baby. The pain of separation was acute. Every part of her ached for her child.

In the farce of a nursery, she stared out of the window, but Garrin's car was already pulling away.

"Right at this moment he'll be torturing himself about what we've been up to all night," Richard remarked. "Like I've been doing for the past nine months."

"Garrin doesn't give a damn what I do."

"Enough of a damn to come tearing up here after you. Enough of a damn to want you to go back with him. I don't suppose he was best pleased to discover you were happy to stay here with me."

She stared at him and he went on softly. "Because that's what he'll think, sweetheart. I can't see him believing stories of kidnap and locked doors. He'll think you came here because you wanted to and then stayed with me – because you wanted to."

He jangled something in his hand – her car keys. He must have been through her bag. Then he tossed them on to the carpet by his feet. "Well, you can go now. See if you can talk your way out of that one."

"You bastard. You utter bastard."

His face tightened and she saw a flash of anger in his eyes. "I haven't even started yet. You don't just walk out on me and get away with it. I always win, Vanessa. I'd have thought you'd have worked that out by now. I always get what I want."

She bent to pick up her keys, tiredness and frustration stinging her eyes, and he put out his foot and deliberately trod on her hand.

When she tried to snatch it away, he increased the pressure. Trapped, she stared up at him. "Let me go."

"Say please, Vanessa."

No way would she beg. She closed her eyes. The pain in her crushed fingers was nothing to the pain of being separated from her baby.

"Say please. Or have you reverted to type? Sunk back into your dirty little fairground ways?" He was wearing leather brogues. Brown ones – freshly polished – she remembered when he'd bought them. Her subconscious supplied the details of the posh man's outfitters in Southampton.

For the first time in her life Vanessa wanted to kill. Wanted to sink a knife into his heart – that's if he had one.

"Say it," he repeated calmly.

"Fuck you," she said, her voice trembling with pain and anger, "I'll sue you for assault."

"What with, sweetheart?" He let her go and with a sob of frustration she stumbled to her feet and faced him.

"If you ever touch me again, I'll kill you."

"I've no intention of touching you – you're soiled goods. But then you always were, weren't you?"

Chapter Twenty-Three

IZZY SAT IN THE back of the car with Isobel on the way home. Garrin assumed she was as horrified by Vanessa's betrayal as he was, but all he could get out of her was a mumbled, "Things aren't always what they seem, my love. Don't judge her."

"I don't know how you can say that. It's obvious what's happened. The same bloody thing as happened last time – she's gone back to him. Did you see what she was wearing?"

"They didn't look the picture of wedded bliss, though, did they? I don't think things are quite as simple as Richard would like us to think."

"Of course they are. What is it with you?" Garrin thumped the steering wheel and Isobel started to cry and he had to give up on further conversation.

After he'd dropped Izzy off because the Parkinson's nurse was coming, Garrin headed back to Fair Winds, his mind a conflict of emotions.

It was very odd holding Isobel. He'd deliberately distanced himself since he'd found out that she might not be his, but it was impossible to be distant with her in his arms. She was so like Jennifer and she felt so fragile. Garrin couldn't believe how protective he felt over this tiny scrap of a baby. Tenderness overwhelmed him as he laid her on the changing mat and she looked up at him with her huge dark eyes.

How he felt about Vanessa was something else. How could she have gone back to Richard after all that she'd said? It was best not to think about it, he decided, because he'd get angry and babies were supposed to be good at picking up on stuff like that, weren't they? He didn't want Isobel to think he was angry with her.

He'd never changed a nappy before and it took him a while. Isobel started to cry as he undid the tapes.

"Hush, my angel." Weren't nappies supposed to be designed for idiots these days? He wished he'd paid more attention to Vanessa as the yelling Isobel kicked her legs and wriggled about. Screwing up his face as he remembered why he hadn't, he wiped her clean and laid out a fresh nappy. He'd almost got it on when it struck him that he should have put some cream on her. He'd definitely seen Vanessa doing that. He hunted around, found a pot that looked likely and removed Isobel's nappy again.

"It's okay, darling," he reassured, picking her up so that the nappy, half un-taped, swung round and fell off altogether. She'd stopped crying, but started again as soon as he put her down. Gritting his teeth, he carried on regardless. This was a lot harder work than it looked. Isobel was still crying. Perhaps she was hungry. He laid her on the lounge carpet while he rummaged through the fridge for the bottle of expressed milk Vanessa kept for emergencies.

Tracey came in while he was warming it up. "You found them then. Is Vanessa having a lie down?"

"Yeah – make yourself useful, will you? pick her up or something."

Tracey raised her eyebrows and crossed to the baby. "Come along, darling. Daddy's getting stressed, isn't he?"

Isobel quietened miraculously as soon as Tracey picked her up. "I'm glad to see you're getting involved at last, Garrin. I thought you were going to be one of these old-fashioned dads who doesn't join in until they start dating boys."

Resisting the temptation to tell her to mind her own business, Garrin tested the milk on his hand. "Did you cancel my lessons?"

"Yeah, of course. Garrin, shall I do that?"

"I can manage."

She watched amused while he sat on the settee beside her, Isobel cradled in one arm and the bottle in his hand.

"Yummy," he said. "Lovely yummy milk."

"Obviously not as yummy as Mummy," Tracey taunted, as Isobel spat out the teat and began to yell. "Are you sure it's not too hot?"

"Of course I'm bloody sure. Haven't you got anything to do?"

"You should watch your language in front of her – it's amazing what babies pick up. And no, I'm on my lunch break. I am entitled to a lunch break!"

"Can't you have it somewhere else?"

"Nah – Suzy and Chloe have both got faces like smacked arses – what did you say to them this morning?"

"Nothing they didn't deserve." He bent his head over Isobel, who'd finally consented to take the bottle and was sucking greedily.

"You should be more supportive. They've got exams in less than a month."

"Better they get flack from me than the BHS. Their whingeing won't get them very far with the examiner. If they had any sense they'd have worked that out by now."

"They're not whingers, they're nice girls. You don't have to be quite so nasty."

Half the bottle was gone. Isobel spat the teat out and Garrin glanced at Tracey. "Does that mean she's had enough?"

"I should think most people have had enough of you today," she said crisply. "You know you're going to have to wind her now."

"What does that involve?"

"You work it out," Tracey said, getting up gracefully and taking her empty mug back towards the kitchen.

Thirty seconds later, she relented and reappeared in the archway. "It means you're supposed to pick her up and gently pat her back," she called.

Garrin wiped a dribble of milk from Isobel's mouth with his sleeve. "We're managing fine, aren't we, sweetheart?" he murmured, propping her up on his lap. And Isobel stared back at him with her wide dark eyes, then burped and threw up all over him.

He'd just cleaned himself up and put Isobel in her Moses basket when the doorbell rang. Cursing, because he wasn't expecting anyone and there was no one in the world he wanted to see, he went to answer it.

"Hello, Garrin." Amanda pouted at him. "Do you fancy taking me for lunch?"

"I'm busy."

"You still need to eat. I'll make you a sandwich." She marched past him and by the time he caught up she was in the lounge, cooing over Isobel. "Oh, you're babysitting, are you? How sweet." She looked up at him through her eyelashes. "You have all sorts of hidden depths, don't you, Garrin. I'd never have had you down as a baby kind of man."

He was tempted to tell her any man worth his salt would be happy enough to look after his own child, but then he remembered she didn't know about him and Vanessa, which was the way he wanted to keep it.

"Where's her mummy? I expect the poor lamb's worn out. You are good. You must have quite enough to do without having someone else's child foisted on you as well."

"I don't mind," he said gruffly. He never knew how to take Amanda. There was no sign of the shy girl he'd first met, and he wasn't sure if this was good or bad. He liked strong women, but Amanda was a contradiction, a mixture

200

of vulnerability and bossiness.

"So shall I make you that sandwich then?"

"Yeah, okay, thanks."

She was in the kitchen when he heard the front door slam. It had to be Vanessa; she was the only one who had a key, although he hadn't been expecting her back so soon. He felt himself tensing, this was all he needed – for her to come in and see him getting cosy with Amanda. It had obviously been what had sent her running to Richard in the first place. Still, what did it matter? She was going to have to get used to seeing him with other women sooner or later because he sure as hell wasn't planning on staying celibate for another nine months. He glanced across at Isobel and hardened his face. No, he wasn't going to pussyfoot around Vanessa. Not any more.

Vanessa hesitated in the hallway. She ached to see Isobel, pick her up and hold her tightly, make sure she was okay. Irrational fears swirled in her heart. What if something had happened to her on the way back? She should never have let her out of her sight. She wouldn't have done had she not been so desperate to get her away from Richard.

She was dreading seeing Garrin. Richard was right – it was going to be pointless trying to explain what had happened. She'd run through the conversation a dozen times on her way back.

'Richard invited me for coffee to talk about the divorce, then he kidnapped Isobel and kept us hostage for the night just so he could cause trouble between you and me.' The whole thing sounded fantastical, even to her. Garrin wasn't going to believe it in a million years. She knew exactly how he'd react.

'Is that the best you can come up with? For God's sake, Vanessa, do you take me for a complete idiot?'

It would be far better to say nothing. Let him think what

he liked because he was going to think the worst of her anyway. She glanced at her reflection in the hall mirror. Lank black hair, shadows beneath her eyes – she looked as though she hadn't slept for a week, which was how she felt. She pushed open the lounge door and stood, swaying slightly. God, that was the last thing she needed, collapsing at Garrin's feet, he'd think she was going for the sympathy vote.

He was standing in the middle of the room and he didn't look in the least bit sympathetic. Isobel was in her Moses basket, gurgling contentedly and Vanessa dropped to her knees, bowing her head, shutting Garrin out.

But before either of them could speak, Amanda came out of the kitchen with a plate of sandwiches in her hand.

"Oh, hi, Vanessa, how's it going? I was just doing us some lunch."

Vanessa glanced up. Amanda looked totally at home. Her sleeves were rolled up, her hair slightly tousled, the bed-head effect, hairdressers called it. Or perhaps it was real. Maybe that was why Garrin had been so reluctant to take Isobel, because Amanda had been waiting for him.

All the anger Vanessa felt towards Richard and Garrin was suddenly focussed on Amanda. It was all she could do not to tear across the room and grab a handful of Amanda's hair and pull until it came out, pull until it hurt unbearably and Amanda's perfect face was red with pain. Vanessa didn't know she was capable of feeling such hatred.

Garrin took half a step towards her, whether to break her gaze, to protect Amanda, or prevent whatever she was going to do, Vanessa didn't have a clue.

But he was too late. Amanda was already stepping across the room. "If you don't mind me saying so, you look awfully tired. Would you like a sandwich?"

"No, I bloody wouldn't," Vanessa said, standing up and moving away from Isobel. "I bloody well would not." She brought her palm up sharply beneath the plate, knocking it from Amanda's hand and sending sandwiches up into the air. They fell onto the coffee table and the carpet and the settee, coming apart so that bits of cucumber and tomato and grated cheese spilled out of them. Time slowed and, in that moment before it sped up again, Vanessa was aware of Amanda's shock and Garrin's stillness and the utter quietness that encircled the three of them. Then with a small sob she snatched up Isobel and fled from the room.

As she stumbled upstairs she was aware of Amanda's tinny nervous giggle. "Oh, dear, what was that all about? Has she got post-natal depression, do you think? Mummy had that with me. It went on for months. I'm so sorry about the mess."

Garrin muttered something she couldn't hear and then Vanessa was in her bedroom and there were tears pouring down her face. "I'm so sorry, darling. Are you all right, my precious darling? Mummy's never going to leave you again. I'm so sorry."

Chapter Twenty-Four

"OH, MY LOVE, WHAT a situation. Life certainly gets complicated when you're around, I must say."

Vanessa wasn't sure how to take that. Was Izzy blaming her? She rocked Isobel in her arms. "I didn't want things to turn out like this. It's the last thing I wanted. These should be the happiest days of my life."

"And they're not. I can see that. Well, it isn't surprising. Look, let's concentrate on the good things for a moment. You have a beautiful daughter and you're on your way to getting rid of Richard."

"I'm not so sure about that. If he's capable of kidnapping my baby, he's capable of anything."

"Well, my advice to you is to have nothing more to do with him. You don't have to see him to file for divorce. It can all be done through solicitors. You should make that your priority. And I don't think he can cause any more trouble as far as Isobel's concerned. Not now you've named Garrin as the father."

"Yes," Vanessa said with satisfaction. That was one positive thing that had come out of the debacle with Richard. It had made her sure she never wanted him to have anything to do with Isobel. She would still get the paternity test done, but she didn't care what the results were. If Garrin's names were on the birth certificate then Richard would never have any claim over Isobel. If he ever dared to touch her again, she'd kill him. The other positive thing that had happened was that she'd told Izzy everything. She'd been amazed Izzy hadn't known there'd been any question over Isobel's father. But then Garrin had never been very good at communicating – at least not when it came to his

204

emotions – and she knew he was deeply upset about the chance Isobel might not be his daughter.

"I still think you should tell Garrin about what happened with Richard," Izzy said now, her eyes serious. "Or maybe it would make it easier if I told him?"

"No. I don't want him to know. I don't care what he thinks about me. He couldn't have been that bothered about me anyway, jumping into bed with Amanda three days after I gave birth."

"And of course you don't care about that either," Izzy said dryly.

Vanessa didn't answer. She knew it was pointless denying her feelings to Izzy, but if she said she didn't care about Garrin enough times she might end up believing it.

"I want you to promise me you won't tell him," she said quietly.

Izzy sighed and nodded. "I won't tell him anything, but I have to say, I don't approve. And I don't understand why you don't want him to know."

"Because he should know me better than that. Can we change the subject?"

"All right. What's happening with Richard's cheque?"

"My bank is re-presenting it, but it'll probably bounce again." Richard had never intended her to have that money, so it had been pretty pointless putting it in the bank in the first place. With hindsight, it was obvious he'd stage-managed the whole thing, pretending to be so reasonable, pretending to care about her so he could tip her drink over her. All so he could destroy anything that might be left between her and Garrin.

Izzy winced as she shifted in her chair and Vanessa was reminded of why she could never stay here.

"Are you all right? Are you in pain? Can I get you something?"

"No thank you, my love, I'm fine. Where are you going

to live? I could lend you some money to tide you over if it would help?"

"Thanks, for offering, Izzy, but no, we'll stay at Garrin's. It shouldn't be for long and I don't think I'm going to see much of Amanda. She thinks I've got post-natal depression, or that I'm a complete head-case. Either way, she's not going to want to come near me, it's hardly a conducive atmosphere for romance."

"No," Izzy said with a wry smile. "Well, if you're sure you can cope. I know how difficult he can be."

"He's not speaking to me, so yes, I can cope." Vanessa smiled, too, and put Isobel gently into her carrycot. "At least we both know where we stand now. Thanks, Izzy, for listening. It's really helped."

"Any time. And let me know if you change your mind about that money. I'd like to know the results of the paternity test, too, if you don't mind telling me."

"Of course I don't mind. I've got an appointment with my doctor to discuss things. I'll ring you when I know what the next step is."

When Vanessa had gone, Izzy pottered around the bungalow, not able to settle. She wouldn't interfere between Garrin and Vanessa. She was all too aware that Vanessa would take flight if she pressed her too much. But it was the hardest thing in the world to stand back and watch them shutting each other out.

Déjà vu. She had to keep reminding herself what had happened when she'd interfered before. This time they had to work things out between them. For Isobel's sake. Izzy didn't care who the father was, she loved the baby on sight. She'd wanted one so desperately when she'd been younger, but it had never happened and Izzy had decided that, as she'd been married to three different men, the problem was probably hers. She hadn't wanted to go to hospital to find out why. That way led to heartbreak and she wasn't keen on hospitals at the best of times. Ironic really that she'd ended up with a disease that meant she had to spend so much time in them.

She put it out of her head. Isobel was the closest to a grandchild she would ever have. And she adored Vanessa. She always had.

Vanessa had been one day old when she'd first set eyes on her. It was difficult to believe that nearly thirty years had passed since then.

Anna, Vanessa's mother, had hated being pregnant. Fortunately she hadn't realised she was until it was too late to do anything about it. Always a slender girl, she'd hardly showed until she was six months gone. She'd come into Izzy's living wagon, her face pale, her dark eyes troubled.

"I'm up the bloody spout, aren't I?" she said savagely. "Jack's going to kill me – we'll have to take a whole season off – maybe longer. He can't do the routine by himself. We're going to lose out big-time." As she spoke she pressed her fingers into her belly as if by flattening her bump she could somehow deny the evidence.

"You shouldn't have to take that long off," Izzy said gently. "You're very fit – you'll soon be back in shape."

"But who's going to look after the bloody sprog? We can't go carting it around with us, can we? It's not the right image, is it? The most sensual act you'll ever see, plus screaming brat in background."

Izzy winced. Anna had always been a contradiction. So beautiful to look at – her father had been half Spanish – but so ugly inside. Or perhaps she was being unfair. Anna was only nineteen – a young nineteen – and a child was a huge responsibility. All Anna had ever wanted was to dance. She and Jack had come to the fair the previous season. They'd run the duck stall, Anna hooking in the punters with her dark gypsy smile, and Jack fixing the hooks and weighting the ducks so it was more or less impossible to get them out of the water. They hadn't made much money despite this and had developed a dance routine as well that incorporated juggling and fire-eating.

"It's a fair, not a bloody circus," Nanna Kane had commented good-naturedly, but she'd let them carry on because they drew people in and because they were good. Their act was billed as *the most daring and sensual performance you'll ever see.*

"I could look after the baby for you," Izzy had offered. "On the nights that you're working. It would be a pleasure."

"You serious? You wouldn't want paying or nothing?"

Izzy shook her head. "I like little ones." She put her hands over Anna's slender brown ones and looked into her eyes. "Don't worry, it'll be fine."

The day after Vanessa was born, Anna had brought her over to Izzy's living wagon in a battered looking carrycot.

Izzy had hidden her shock and said calmly, "You're not working today, surely?"

"Jack's taking me out for a slap-up meal to get me strength up. Bloody hard work giving birth to her, I can tell you." She wrinkled up her face in distaste. "You did say, didn't you?"

"I did," Izzy agreed softly, looking at the tiny dark-haired baby and feeling a deep sadness at Anna's attitude. "Of course I'll look after her. You two go and enjoy yourselves."

And that had been the pattern of things pretty much from then on. Izzy had done everything she could think of to get the new parents interested in their daughter, but to no avail. One night, she'd refused to baby-sit. Around eleven she hadn't been able to resist going by Anna and Jack's, and she'd heard Vanessa screaming on and on. When she'd gone in she'd found her alone, wet and dirty-nappied and obviously hungry, and she'd taken her back to her own living wagon because she couldn't do anything else.

"We were only out for a bit," Anna said sulkily when she caught up with her the next morning. "She never lets up that one, always whingeing about something."

"She's a baby," Izzy had said coldly. "That's what they do." But Anna had just shrugged, her beautiful face dismissive, and Izzy hadn't dared refuse again.

She'd been half-relieved, half-worried, when Jack and Anna had been lured away from the fairground by promises of big money touring with a circus around Europe. They'd asked her if she'd baby-sit on a more permanent basis and for the first five years of their daughter's life they'd come back each winter to check up on her. Each time they'd marvelled at how much she'd grown and how happy she looked with Izzy. Rather like people returning to see a favourite dog, Izzy had thought sadly, as they cooed over Vanessa and stroked her long black hair, gradually growing more restless and asking if Izzy would take care of Vanessa for one more season.

Then one year they hadn't come back at all. She didn't think Vanessa was particularly upset at this abandonment. She barely knew them anyway. For the next ten years or so, Izzy had lived in dread of them turning up and reclaiming their daughter, but it had never happened. Jack and Anna had disappeared as completely as the fire they swallowed each night. For all Izzy knew they were living abroad somewhere, perhaps they'd made their fortune and settled down at last in some glitzy city. Or perhaps they were living rough, it was impossible to tell.

Izzy went into her bedroom and got out an old photo album. She had just one photograph of Vanessa's parents and it was a mockery of reality. Anna was holding the baby, a devoted expression on her beautiful face. Jack stood behind her, his hair as gold as late summer grass, one arm around Anna's shoulders. He looked a little like Richard

Hamilton, Izzy thought distractedly, yet Vanessa had inherited nothing of her father – she was the image of her mother. Just as Isobel was the image of Vanessa. So perhaps Richard Hamilton's genes would have been equally ignored by nature. Izzy was uncomfortably aware that he could just as easily have been Isobel's father as Garrin. She tucked the photograph back out of sight and prayed Vanessa got the news she was hoping for from the doctor.

Chapter Twenty-Five

GARRIN WAS FURIOUS WITH Vanessa. Furious she'd run to Richard to pay him back for Amanda; furious that Izzy had been so irritatingly patient with her, murmuring vague things about new motherhood being traumatic. But all this was trivial compared to the main reason for his anger. Vanessa had forced him to drop his guard where Isobel was concerned.

For a couple of hours he'd been responsible for this child he'd seen come into the world, this child who had resurrected all sorts of feelings from the past that both hurt and exhilarated him. Memories of Jennifer entwined with hopes for the future. He'd felt tenderness, pride, and protective instincts rising from deep within him. He'd fallen for the tiny helpless baby big-time and it was tearing him apart because he still didn't know if she was his. He would be devastated if he found out he wasn't her father and equally devastated if he found out he was, because the one certainty about all this was that Vanessa was going to take her away.

The only way he could deal with it was to bury himself in work, which was easy as there was plenty to do. Derry was going brilliantly. The horse was the only spark of light in Garrin's world at the moment. And while he knew it was dangerous to focus all of his hopes on one horse because anything could happen, he couldn't help himself. He'd already entered Derry in several qualifying events and at one of them he was sure they'd win a ticket for the Horse Of The Year Show. He was also accepting far more judging appointments than usual, which meant he could get away from the claustrophobia of the yard, and he didn't need to see so much of Vanessa.

He couldn't escape the nights, though. Often, when he knew Vanessa was asleep, he crept into the nursery and stood looking at the sleeping Isobel. It was sweet torture, watching her. Sometimes she woke and he'd pick her up and talk to her – tell her all his plans for the future. About the horse he would buy for her as soon as she was old enough, and she would listen, her dark eyes wide. The first time she smiled at him, he felt his heart turn over.

On the day Vanessa went to the doctors to talk about the paternity test, Garrin took Derry out up onto the bridle path that led across to the cliffs. What he really wanted to do was gallop flat-out for about five miles. Feel the wind on his face, the power of the horse beneath him, feel the aloneness of being just him and Derry on the cliffs. Anything to take his mind off what was happening at the surgery.

I'm game, Derry told him, dancing on the spot as he felt the grass track beneath his hooves. *What are we waiting for?*

Not yet, Garrin responded. Don't be so impatient. The ground was rutted with mud tracks, slippery and dangerous to go too fast on.

In a minute, he sent the message down to the horse's mouth, but even as he did this, he revelled in the bunched-up power, the sheer energy and exuberance beneath him. Derry was something else. The horse of his dreams and he never let him down, pure perfection, why couldn't the rest of his life be as simple?

As they got onto firmer ground he allowed Derry to canter, still controlled, still not too mad along the track, but about halfway along, when he could see ahead for a quarter of a mile or so, he gave Derry his head and they stretched into a gallop. Garrin leaning forward over his neck, light in the saddle, feeling nothing but the sheer exhilaration of speed, and, when they had both got it out of their system, all

212

he did was shift in the saddle and Derry came back to him easily.

I enjoyed that.

I enjoyed it too, thank you.

Derry tossed his head in acknowledgement and jogged for a bit and then slowly came back to a walk and Garrin's thoughts drifted to Vanessa. Soon he would know. Would it change the way he felt about Isobel? It wouldn't change the way he felt about Vanessa – that was for sure. Nothing ever would. He clenched his fists against the horse's neck, unaware of the tension until Derry shook his head impatiently and began to jog again.

Garrin let him, not bothering to rise to the trot, hardly moving in the saddle, his long legs almost motionless against the horse's sides. He shouldn't have let her back into his life. He shouldn't have given her the chance to hurt him again, allowed himself to be taken for a fool. Pain twisted inside him; he'd lost one child and he couldn't bear to lose another. Damn bloody Vanessa. He'd managed without her perfectly well for six years.

Derry shied at something in the hedge and he shifted in the saddle, his fingers tightening on the reins. He could do it again, he thought suddenly. He could manage fine without Vanessa in his life, but not without Isobel. Very soon he would know if she was his and if she was, then he would make sure she stayed in his life. He would fight Vanessa for custody.

Vanessa sat in the waiting room feeling curiously detached. She didn't know what she was going to do if Richard turned out to be Isobel's father. The only thing she was sure about was that she wouldn't tell him. But she'd have to tell Garrin. Not that it could make things any worse between them. The last month had been hell. Things couldn't get much worse.

213

"Mrs Hamilton."

Vanessa jumped. She was going to have to change her name. She hated it now. At least her daughter hadn't got it. Isobel was going to stay Isobel Tate whatever the outcome of the test.

A few moments later she was sitting opposite the doctor and he was talking about blood groups and genetics and the fact that it was easier to disprove paternity than it was to prove it.

"So there could be some doubt even if I did go ahead with the test?" she asked, wishing he'd just get on with it.

"We can prove pretty conclusively whether someone is or isn't the father. We'd need to take samples from all possible contenders and we need their permission."

"There are only two," Vanessa snapped, feeling her face flush, even though his tone wasn't judgemental.

"And then we'd inform all concerned parties of the outcome," he went on patiently. "Mrs Hamilton – we can offer you counselling in case the result is – unexpected."

"I don't want counselling." And the last thing she wanted was Richard finding out he was Isobel's father, after all. Thinking on her feet she went on swiftly, "Can you prove anything from blood groups? I know their blood groups – the two possible fathers – surely that would tell you something?"

He was already frowning and shaking his head. "And you know mine and Isobel's – it's on our records. Please."

He hesitated and she fumbled in her bag. "Humour me – just look at the blood groups? Certain combinations would prove it, wouldn't it?" She pushed the piece of paper across the desk to him. She knew Richard's because, like her, he regularly donated blood and their donor cards were kept together in a drawer in his office. And Garrin had told her his blood group the last time they'd had a civil conversation.

214

Still frowning, the doctor looked, and then he glanced up at her. "If this information is accurate, then I don't think there's any point in going ahead with the test at all."

"Why not?"

"Because according to these blood groups only one of these men could possibly be Isobel's father." He got out a chart with some letters on and laid it in front of her. "It's easier to explain if I show you."

Vanessa looked at the chart and he went on slowly. "Isobel's blood group is AB."

"That's right."

"It's impossible for a mother with blood group A and a father with a blood group A to produce an AB child. The father would have to be a blood group O. I think that answers your question, doesn't it?"

"Yes. Yes, thank you, it does."

Vanessa stared at the diagrams he'd drawn and felt numb. So much had rested on this and now she knew the answer she didn't feel any of the things she'd expected to feel. There was just this strange blankness. Perhaps it was shock because she'd expected to have to wait for this. She'd thought she'd have had more time to prepare herself, but now the truth was staring her in the face she didn't know what to think.

She thanked the doctor shakily and he sighed, "Mrs Hamilton, this wouldn't stand up in a court of law – you'd need a proper test and proper samples for that."

"This is for my peace of mind, that's all. I don't need it to stand up in a court of law."

And then she was out of the surgery, her heart thumping madly. She gazed at Isobel, who was sleeping peacefully in her buggy, unaware of the turmoil her mother was in. "Oh, darling, my beautiful darling," she murmured, bending over the buggy and rearranging the cover. "You are so beautiful, do you know that?"

Vanessa was tempted to drop into Izzy's on her way home, but that wouldn't be very fair on Garrin. He ought to be the first to know. It saddened her that she didn't have a clue how he'd react. The telepathy that had always existed between them had faded. All she knew was that he didn't want her in his house, and she didn't want to stay. She'd always thought the date of the test would be a cut-off point. The moment they'd both make a decision, but she knew in her heart they'd made the decision already.

When she got back she found Tracey rummaging through the kitchen cupboards.

"Oh, hi, Vanessa, you don't know where Garrin keeps the clean bandages, do you? I brought a load in for washing the other day."

"Try the laundry basket in the lounge. Why? Have you got a problem?"

"They're for wrapping round horse's tails. To stop them getting rubbed when they're travelling, I need a decent one for Derry and I can't find the bloody things." She disappeared into the lounge and came back with one. "Panic over. Thanks. By the way if you're still on the job market I think I might have some news for you."

"I certainly am. The sooner the better."

"You remember I told you about my Auntie Laura, the one with the rest home, well her live-in housekeeper's just left. Her brother's had a stroke or something and she's had to move out to look after him, which has left Auntie Laura in a bit of a hole."

"Have you told her about Isobel?"

"Yes, and it shouldn't be a problem. There's a self-contained flat that goes with the job. Look, I can't stop now, we'll catch up later."

"Thanks, I'd be really grateful. Where's Garrin?"

"He's out riding. He's been gone a while. I expect he'll be back any minute."

216

Vanessa made tea and sat, sipping it. So perhaps it was true what they said about one door closing and another door opening. A live-in job in a rest home sounded perfect. She wouldn't have to rely on Garrin, or on Richard's divorce settlement. She and Isobel could be independent. She picked Isobel up and hugged her. For the first time since she'd been born she felt as though there might be light at the end of the tunnel.

"We are free, my darling. Things are going to be just fine. We are going to be so happy, just you and me and no nasty men to worry about. I shall teach you to cook when you're older and we can go dancing and swimming and horse riding."

"And where do I fit into all this?"

She glanced up guiltily. She'd been so engrossed with her daughter she hadn't heard Garrin come in. He was standing in the archway between the lounge and kitchen, one hand resting on the wall. He was wearing jodhpurs and carrying a riding hat. Tracey must have told him they were back. Not that Tracey knew the significance of this morning's visit to the doctor.

"That depends on you," she said quietly.

He came right into the room. His eyes were very black, lines of tension creasing the corners and his mouth was set in a hard line.

"Stop pissing about, Vanessa, and tell me what happened. What did they say about the test? Have you arranged it?"

"They said there was no point in doing it. They can tell by her blood group whose daughter she is. Or rather whose daughter she isn't."

He didn't speak. It was impossible to tell what he was thinking. She thought he might have gone a shade or so paler, but that could have been a trick of the light. Then, he turned and went back into the kitchen and she could hear him washing his hands in the sink.

He came back and without speaking crossed to where she was sitting, with Isobel on her lap, and knelt on the carpet beside them. She still couldn't tell what he was thinking and nervousness churned her stomach.

He reached out and put his hand against Isobel's cheek and Vanessa saw his fingers were shaking, a fine tremor he didn't try to conceal. Isobel smiled up at him, she'd only just started to smile, and Vanessa felt excluded. It was irrational, but she didn't want to have to share her daughter's smiles. Involuntarily she tightened her arms around Isobel, and Garrin, aware of her movement, withdrew his hand abruptly.

"You're enjoying this, aren't you? For Christ's sake put me out of my misery. Am I her father or aren't I?"

Chapter Twenty-Six

"YOU ARE. BUT THEN I always said you were. You chose not to believe me." She couldn't stop the bitterness from creeping into her voice. "But now it's official. You've got it in black and white. Congratulations." There was a small and agonising silence and Vanessa couldn't stand it any more.

"Well say something then, are you pleased?"

"Yeah – of course I'm pleased." He looked at her and just for a moment his eyes were unguarded and she saw pain and pride and tenderness. Then it was gone.

"We'll have to talk about her future." He got up and moved across to the French windows, so he was silhouetted in the light and she couldn't see his face.

"We're still moving out. I can't stay here."

He shrugged. "We'll talk later. I've got things to do."

"All right," she said, resigned to the fact they were so far down his priority list. "But I won't change my mind."

Impatient for news about the job, Vanessa caught up with Tracey while Isobel was having her afternoon nap. She found her in the feed room, scooping sugar beet into buckets, its sweet earthy smell scenting the air.

"Is now a bad time to ask about your Auntie Laura?"

"It's as good a time as any. I could do with a break, to be honest." Tracey stood up, rubbing her back. "She said she'll see you tomorrow if you're up for it. She's over at Tall Trees herself until she finds someone, which she's keen to do as soon as possible."

"Did you tell her I haven't got a lot of experience as a housekeeper?"

"What are you on about? You've looked after the working pupils all this time, not to mention Grumpy Guts

Garrin. A few old people will be a piece of cake after that."

"Keep your voice down, he'll hear you."

"No, he won't, he's flapping about with Amanda. It's her first show tomorrow and for all the fuss they're making about it, you'd think it was the bloody event of the year." Tracey snorted in disgust and Vanessa smiled.

That was something else they had in common, they both disliked Amanda, although not, she suspected, for the same reasons. Tracey automatically disliked anyone who had what she called an easy ride through life. In Amanda's case this translated literally. Her rich parents paid for her to have horses while she played around at college doing something she'd never actually have to use to make a living. She was studying reflexology, Tracey had told her once, but Vanessa didn't think it would have mattered what she'd been doing.

"It's all right for some," Tracey grumbled. "Amanda doesn't know she's born, whereas I have to slog away from dawn 'til dusk for an absolute pittance. Life is bloody unfair, don't you think? I'd give anything to have half her opportunities – and does she appreciate it? Does she hell!"

"Hmmm," Vanessa said, spotting Amanda walking across the yard and deciding it would be wise to change the subject. "Did your Auntie Laura say what time I could go and see her?"

"After breakfast is good for her. Around ten, if you can make it – Garrin will be out all day so I could sneak out and come with you, if you like."

"No, you couldn't. He'd only find out and then we'd both be in trouble. Just tell me where it is. We'll be fine."

Tracey gave her the address with a smile. "Good luck. Not that you'll need it. I've given you such a glowing reference that it's only a formality. I should think the job's pretty much yours, if you want it."

*   *   *

220

Vanessa toyed with telling Garrin about her interview over dinner, but he didn't come in until late, which wound her up because she knew his mind was on Amanda. Swallowing her irritation, she took a deep breath.

"You said you wanted to discuss Isobel's future. Is now a good time?"

"What?" He glanced at her and she could see it wasn't. He might be here physically, but mentally he was miles away.

"We need to talk about practicalities," she said patiently. "You were the one who brought it up."

"Yeah, I know, but there's no rush, is there? You're not going to find a job overnight."

Resisting the urge to tell him that she might, Vanessa shook her head. After all, it didn't matter what Tracey had said about her. If Laura didn't think she could do the job – and she had doubts herself – then she'd be stirring things up for nothing.

"No, I don't suppose I am," she said wearily. But if Garrin picked up on her anxiousness he didn't comment. He was still bent over paperwork when she went to bed. She doubted he'd even noticed she'd gone. And in the morning he was the same, his mind obviously on the forthcoming show.

Garrin watched Amanda warm up her horse with a feeling of trepidation. Not because of Amanda, but because of her father. He'd been expecting Lloyd might be otherwise engaged, and that's why he'd been asked to come, but Lloyd was here too, and so far he'd been a complete pain in the arse. He was making Amanda ten times more nervous than she would have been and he kept contradicting Garrin's advice.

"Stop mucking about and get that horse over the practice jump," he'd yelled when Garrin had asked Amanda to warm up Shadowman in a corner of the field away from the rest of the competitors. The dark bay horse was sweating and side-stepping and shying at everything and Amanda was getting more and more flustered.

"I think it's best if she calms him down first," Garrin said, giving him a sharp look. "If he gets any more overheated he's going to be difficult to handle in the ring."

"That's exactly what I mean – he's warm enough already," Lloyd argued. "He doesn't need all this poncing about, he needs a good slapping, and a few goes over that jump. He'll be right as rain then."

"With respect," Garrin said, keeping the anger out of his voice with difficulty, "you asked me here for my help. You're paying me for my advice. So perhaps you'd let me give it."

Lloyd looked taken aback and Garrin sensed he was about to argue. Amanda was looking more nervous than ever. There was nothing of the confident girl he'd seen lately. Perhaps, with hindsight, it was Amanda who wanted him here for moral support and not her father.

"I don't suppose you could do me a favour and go and check the jumping times, could you? I thought I heard an announcement just now about a delay to the schedule."

Lloyd looked at him suspiciously, as well he might, because there'd been no announcement, but he went anyway, strutting off across the grass, slapping the crop he was carrying against his boot in irritation.

Breathing a sigh of relief, Garrin went across to Amanda. "How are you feeling?"

"Awful. I've been sick three times already. And Shadow's all over the place, he's not listening to me."

"You're transmitting to him," Garrin said quietly. "Relax. There's nothing in that course that's going to be a problem for him, as long as you keep him steady. Now take nice deep breaths for me."

222

She did as he asked, but she still looked sick with nerves.

"Not too heavy-handed. He doesn't like it. And go easy on the stick, he doesn't need it." He adjusted the position of her hands. "Nice and light. Just how we do it at home."

She nodded and he let go of her hands, but before he could step back, she caught hold of his wrist. "Garrin, if we do well today, will you take me for a celebration drink? We could meet somewhere so as not to upset your batty cousin."

"Just concentrate on the job in hand."

"But, can we? I'd feel so much better about all this if I had an evening out with you to look forward to."

He looked up into her blue eyes. "We'll see. If you jump well today and I mean *well*, give him a good round, we're not here to win ribbons, then I'll take you for a celebration drink."

She smiled and he wondered ruefully if that had been such a good idea. He hadn't yet broached the subject of custody to Vanessa, but he'd thought about it constantly. And if he did get custody of his daughter then he was going to have to change his lifestyle completely. No more womanising, he'd be a one-parent family with all the responsibilities that entailed.

"Penny for them, Garrin," Amanda said, and he jumped.

"Sorry, I was miles away."

"Fantasising about our date," she said, grinning. And he grinned back because at least she was relaxed now and she was likely to listen to him and not Lloyd. He had a feeling that Lloyd hadn't finished with his advice giving yet.

He was right. A few minutes later he saw Lloyd stalking back towards them.

"No delay – you must have misheard. She's on in a few minutes. Right, Princess, remember what I said this morning. We're here to win, not mess about, so ride him as if you mean it. Any sign of hesitation, belt him."

223

Amanda nodded, but as soon as her father had finished speaking, she glanced at Garrin and smiled.

He winked. "Good luck."

He watched her canter round the ring waiting for the bell and wondered what she would do. It couldn't be easy having a father like Lloyd Battersby-Smythe, but Amanda had guts. That was one of the things he'd learned about her, guts and determination, qualities he'd always admired. They would get her a long way.

To his relief, she took the first fence at a steady pace and by the time she was halfway round he could tell she was enjoying herself. Shadowman was enjoying it too. Garrin was beginning to relax when Lloyd, at his side, shouted, "Crank it up a bit, if you go any slower, he'll stop."

This comment drew several disapproving glances from around them and Garrin turned on him furiously.

"Shut up. They're doing fine. You'll put her off."

Lloyd, obviously taken aback by the venom in Garrin's voice, shut up, but the damage was already done. Amanda was slightly too fast at the double and they touched a pole. For a moment it looked as if they'd got away with it, but then the pole fell. Garrin willed Amanda not to look back and she didn't, getting it together again after that and jumping the rest of the round clear.

"Four faults for Amanda Battersby-Smythe on Shadowman," the commentator called, and Amanda rode out of the ring, smiling.

Garrin got to her before her father. "You did great," he said. "Bad luck that pole coming down, but he went beautifully."

"It was my fault. The sun was in my eyes," Amanda said, as Lloyd reached them.

"Sun, my arse – you were too slow." He caught hold of Shadowman's reins and yanked down so that the horse's head jerked up in surprise, the whites of his eyes showing.

"Little sod had better get his act together if he doesn't want to end up as dog meat."

"Daddy, for God's sake." Amanda shot Garrin an apologetic glance, but he'd had enough.

"If I ever see you doing that again, I will personally flatten you."

Lloyd looked so gob-smacked that it would have been funny in any other circumstances.

"I beg your pardon. I'm paying you. You can't threaten me."

"Try me. And you can forget the money. I'll make my own way back." Turning his back on them and shaking with anger, he stormed across the field. Well that was the end of that then. He guessed he wasn't going to be selling the Battersby-Smythes any more horses. Not that he wanted to, if they were going to get treated like that. Perhaps he could buy Shadowman back, he'd turn out well in the right hands. He was still fuming as he stood on the station platform waiting for his train. It was all very well saying he'd make his own way back, but there was no direct train. At this rate he wouldn't be home until far later than he'd planned.

As he sat in the carriage two hours later, watching the countryside reel past, he decided he would talk to Vanessa about Isobel when he got in. It wasn't like him to be so hesitant, but so much depended on it, he had to make sure he picked the right time. In his more optimistic moments he'd hoped that Vanessa might make it easy for him and say she was going back to Richard.

He was sure Richard didn't want Isobel, despite what he'd said the day after Vanessa had given birth. If he had then he wouldn't have let Vanessa hand her over to him in Chandlers Ford. Garrin still wasn't sure what had gone on between Vanessa and her ex that day. She'd refused to discuss it when he'd raised the subject, saying it was none of his business. And she was right, it wasn't.

He sighed. They were going to have to discuss things sooner or later because he couldn't stand living in this limbo. Tonight, he decided, would probably be as good as any other time. Pleased that he'd at least made a decision about this, he settled back in his seat, just as the train began to slow and then finally came to a halt in the middle of the open countryside.

Vanessa gave up waiting for Garrin to come in and went to bed. Tracey had been right – Laura had offered her the job on the spot – and all day her emotions had swung between exhilaration that she could at least be independent, and worry about how Garrin was going to take it.

Laura had also asked her if she could start the following day, which had been a surprise, but it was probably for the best. The sooner they were out of Fair Winds the better, as far as she was concerned. She'd been anxious to tell Garrin – time was running out – but she couldn't tell him if he wasn't here.

She lay in bed, listening for the sound of his key in the lock. But as it got later and later and he didn't come, she realised she'd have to tell him over breakfast. At least that way there wouldn't be time for too much of a row. But when she went down the following morning he was already out of the house.

She sorted out Isobel, put her in the baby sling and headed down to the stables to find Tracey.

"How did he take it?" Tracey asked, pausing from the grooming she was doing. "He didn't look too fed up."

"That's because he doesn't know. I was going to tell him last night, but he was late and I was in bed. Must have gone out with his girlfriend after the show or something."

"Er no – actually they had a row. Well, Garrin had a row with Lloyd to be precise. He came back from Bristol on his own, but the train broke down."

"Oh, well it's probably just as well I didn't see him then. Where is he now?"

"He left early. He's jumping Derry at a qualifying show. I'm surprised he didn't mention it." She began to brush out the horse's tail. "What are you going to do?"

"Leave him a note, I guess. Well, I can't let your aunt down, can I? She's expecting me this morning."

"I think I might go out tonight then. In case he decides to torture me for the details."

"Don't worry, I won't mention your name. For all he knows I could have seen Laura's advert in the paper. He knows I've been looking for a job."

"Sure – and this horse might grow wings and fly around the paddock. I think I'll go out anyway – and pray he gets a qualifying ticket. Then I might just get away with a few black looks and some muttering when I see him next."

Vanessa smiled with a lightness she didn't feel and went back to finish her packing.

Chapter Twenty-Seven

IF ANYONE HAD ASKED Vanessa what her views were on rest homes, she'd have said that they were probably depressing places with a selection of ageing people sitting around waiting to die.

Tall Trees blew these preconceptions out of the window. The television in the lounge remained switched off that evening. Four of the residents played cards and Vanessa realised from the furtive glances she got when she went in that they were playing for money.

"Spices things up a bit," George muttered. "You don't mind, do you? We'll make sure we've still got our rent."

"I don't mind at all," Vanessa said. "You're all over eighteen, aren't you?"

Two of the other residents were reading: a Dick Francis and a Jackie Collins, and Masie, the youngest of the crew, was knitting an angora jumper, her needles clacking away at top speed.

"We don't do telly every night," she told Vanessa. "Dulls the mind, although we do like to watch *Midsomer Murders* when that's on. We like a good murder. Pity they can't make the plots a bit more complicated, though, we can always work them out."

Vanessa was reminded of Garrin. He was probably feeling pretty murderous by now. Or perhaps she was overreacting. He could have won a qualifying place on Derry and at this very moment be celebrating with Tracey on the patio, or making it up with Amanda. Perhaps he wouldn't even care that she'd gone.

*   *   *

"She can't do this. She can't just walk out on me." Garrin stalked around his lounge, Vanessa's note in one hand and a large brandy in the other. "What the hell's she playing at?"

"She hasn't just walked out," Izzy said patiently. "You knew she wasn't going to stay. You didn't want her to stay."

"I didn't want her to take my daughter." He scrunched up the note and hurled it at the French windows, spilling some of his brandy over himself in the process. "Tracey's had a hand in this. Tall Trees is her aunt's place, I'll kill her. I'll bloody fire her when I catch up with her."

"No, you won't, darling. This has nothing to do with Tracey. This is between you and Vanessa. Will you sit down a minute, you're making me dizzy."

He sat reluctantly, but he couldn't keep still. He drummed his fingers on the arm of the chair. What a bloody awful end to a bloody awful day.

"This is probably for the best, lovie. Vanessa needs some space, you both do. You couldn't carry on as you were."

"I'd better go and check Derry," he said. "See how that leg is. Will you be all right here for a bit?"

"I'll stay the night if you like," Izzy said unexpectedly. "Save you driving me home."

So she could stop him having a go at Tracey, more like, he thought irritably, as he went down to the stables. Not that there was any sign of her. Her living wagon was empty so there was no one to vent his anger on. He kicked a bucket across the yard and the noise brought several horses to their stable doors, ears flicking curiously. Garrin went across to Derry and the horse whickered.

"How's your leg, mate?" He let himself into the stable and ran his fingers down the horse's tendon. It was a little hotter than it should be, but there wasn't so much swelling now. A few more hose-downs and a rest and he'd be fine. Or maybe he'd get up early, box him and take him down to the sea. There was nothing like the sea for sorting out minor problems. He knelt in the straw and pressed his head against Derry's shoulder.

I'm sorry, I shouldn't have pushed you. I asked too much of you.

Derry dipped his head and blew on Garrin's hair. *I enjoyed it; we'll do it again.*

We will, mate, we will. We're a winning team, we are.

I know.

They stayed like that until Derry got bored of sharing his living space and nudged Garrin out of the way so he could get to his hay.

Garrin got up stiffly. He ached. It had been a tough course. Only three of the field had jumped triple clears, and they'd managed a double and four faults. Not bad, really. He'd have been pleased in normal circumstances. He still was pleased; Derry had jumped like the champion he was going to be, scopey and strong, but still listening to him. It had been Garrin's fault they'd hit the gate. He'd turned him too quickly, hadn't got him quite straight, too intent on their time, too caught up in the excitement of it all to give him a proper chance.

When he'd realised Derry's leg was up, he'd been stricken with guilt, not so much because of the slight injury, but because of what could have happened. What if he'd put him off jumping? Making sure Derry loved his work was more important to Garrin than anything else. Yet, he'd jeopardised it, the lure of being so close to his dream affecting his judgement.

"Don't beat yourself up about it," Izzy had said. "He'll be fine, he's made of strong stuff, this one." And Garrin had known she was right. All he'd wanted to do was to get home and have his long overdue chat with Vanessa. But he hadn't even been able to do that. She'd taken Isobel away without even telling him they were going.

He switched off the yard lights and went back up to the house. There was nothing he could do about it now. Depression settled in him. Tomorrow he was judging, so he couldn't see Vanessa, but he would catch up with her in the evening. Find out what was going on then.

"Someone rang when you were out," Izzy said. "Amanda Battersby-Smythe, she sounded a bit upset. She said something about wanting to apologise for yesterday."

"Did she?" He slumped onto the settee.

Izzy came across and put a fresh tumbler of brandy into his hand. "Drink this and then get yourself some sleep. I'll sleep in Vanessa's room."

"Thanks." He looked up into her eyes, which were filled with concern for him. "I don't deserve you."

"What did you mean when you said that you didn't want Vanessa to take Isobel with her? What else did you expect her to do?" Izzy's face was serene.

"I want custody of her," he said quietly.

"And you told Vanessa this."

"Not yet. I've been waiting for the right moment."

"Oh, Garrin, there never will be a right moment. Vanessa's not going to give up her child. Not after all she's been through."

"She's my child too."

"Yes, I know she is. But it doesn't work like that. The mother always gets custody – unless she's not capable of looking after the baby for some reason. Or she doesn't want her." Her voice was sad and he wondered if she was thinking of Vanessa's own mother, but she was right. He knew she was right. He could feel his fantasy crumbling. His whole future with his daughter broken into weekend segments, swapping overnight bags and Isobel as if she was some kind of package.

"Isobel would be better off with me. I'm financially stable. I can give her far more than Vanessa can."

"She needs her mum. And Vanessa won't stop you seeing her. You know she'd never do that."

"I don't want to be a part-time dad."

"You don't have a lot of choice, unless there's any chance of you and Nessa getting back together. Is there?"

"No." Pain shot through him and he put his head in his hands. He wouldn't have taken this from anyone else, but Izzy. Even so, he didn't need it now.

"Go to bed," she said again. "This can all be sorted out, but not now. It's too late."

He didn't look up. And eventually he heard her leave the room. She was right, it was too late, but not in the way she meant. It was too late for him to ever put things right with Vanessa, but he wasn't going to let her walk away with Isobel.

Chapter Twenty-Eight

GARRIN WAS TEMPTED TO phone and cancel his judging appointment, but professionalism stopped him. The showground was thirty or so miles away and, with luck, he'd be done by three. Plenty of time to get back, sort out any problems at the yard and go and see Vanessa. He hadn't slept well and he wasn't in a very good mood. He supposed he ought to phone Amanda too. It wasn't her fault her father was a complete arsehole.

Tracey looked guilty when she saw him marching across the yard, as well she might, he thought, leaning on the door of the box she was mucking out.

"How did it go yesterday then?"

"He jumped well, but his near fore's up a bit – knocked himself on the gate, my fault."

"Oh, dear."

"Yes, oh dear. Not a brilliant day, all in all."

She didn't answer, and, annoyed, he fiddled with the bolt on the stable door. "What time did they leave? Vanessa and Isobel."

"I've no idea. Would you like me to hose Derry's leg?"

"Yes."

"Anything else I need to know about?"

"No." He'd have liked to ask her the same thing, but pride stopped him. Izzy was right, he couldn't blame Tracey; Vanessa would have gone sooner or later anyway. It was a huge effort to say nothing more about it.

He drove to the show-jumping, which was being held indoors, tracked down the organiser to tell them he was there and then went to take a look at the course. He was just coming out of the ring when he caught a flash of blonde hair and saw Amanda heading towards him.

"I didn't know you were jumping today."

"I'm not. Daddy is. Oh, Garrin, it's good to see you. Did you get my messages?"

"Yeah – I was going to call you later. Sorry, I've been a bit busy." The news that Lloyd was jumping had shaken him. That was all he needed, another run-in with the man. He could have done with not seeing him for a few weeks to let the dust settle.

"He's entered Jumping Jack in the Newcomers," Amanda went on. She looked worried, as well she might, he thought. If Lloyd tried any of his bullying tactics on the horse, which in Garrin's opinion wasn't ready for this sort of class, he'd get more than he bargained for.

"Does he know I'm judging?" he asked, thinking suddenly that maybe that was what the dinner had been about. To soften him up so he'd turn a blind eye to Lloyd's dubious riding practises. Oh dear, that had certainly backfired.

"Yes. He asked me to come and see you to apologise for the little misunderstanding on Thursday. He said he was stressed out."

"I got pretty stressed out sitting on a train for four hours."

"I'm really sorry about that. We'll pay for the train fare and what we agreed for you to come in the first place. It's only right."

"No," Garrin said. "Look, I can't talk about this now. Forget about Thursday. Put it down to experience. I have." He was turning away when she caught his arm.

"Can we still go for that drink some time? My treat."

"I don't know." Her face fell and he felt guilty. "I'll see you next week, that's if you're still coming for your lesson. We'll discuss it then."

She smiled. "Looking forward to it already."

The judging of the first two classes went smoothly. It was good to have something to concentrate on, Garrin thought, as he marked papers. Sarah Canterbury was judging with him and they'd worked together before. She did a lot and was right up to date with the latest changes in rules. The BSJA didn't seem to be happy unless they were changing things every five minutes, which was probably a good thing, but did make it hard work for the judges.

There were no disputes, nothing that they didn't agree on. No argumentative riders, he began to relax. The Newcomers class started and he looked at the jumping order and saw that Lloyd was number nine out of the eleven competitors. Not a bad place to be. It was the kind of class where, if the competitors jumped clear, they went straight on to the second round, which was also a good thing, as they didn't have to hang around or warm their horses up again. By the time that Lloyd came in, they'd had three double clears.

"Lloyd Battersby-Smythe next on Jumping Jack," Sarah said, handing him the paperwork. "I heard on the grapevine that he'd had a bit of trouble last time he was out. Do you know him?"

"Vaguely," Garrin said, feeling himself tensing as Lloyd bounced into the ring. His horse was already overheated, its neck white with foam. "Looks like he's done a few rounds already."

Lloyd jumped clear, although in Garrin's opinion it was more by luck than judgment. Jumping Jack didn't get so much as a pat for his efforts, but at least Lloyd had gone easy on the whip. Maybe he had taken some notice of him after all.

The bell went for the start of the second round and Garrin watched as horse and rider set off at top speed. This tactic seemed to be working quite well until they were on the final stretch. Lloyd had made the same mistake as him, too sharp a turn into the gate. But Jumping Jack didn't have the experience to right himself and at the last moment he stopped. For a split second it looked as though Lloyd would stay on despite the fact that he'd lost both stirrups and was well up the horse's neck. But Jumping Jack, obviously alarmed at his rider's unorthodox position, shot backwards and Lloyd fell heavily into the jump.

"Oh dear, that hurt," Sarah said, shaking her head and reaching for the bell.

The St John ambulance crew were halfway across the ring by the time Lloyd staggered to his feet. Brushing sawdust off his jodhpurs furiously, he stormed past them, picked up his crop and went in pursuit of his horse, which had stopped by the exit door.

"What on earth is he doing?" Sarah said as Lloyd approached his horse, the crop held high in his hand.

"I've got a bloody good idea and he's not going to get away with it." Garrin was out of the judges' box and vaulting over the tiered seats and down into the ring before he had time to think about the wisdom of approaching Lloyd.

He wasn't quick enough to stop him grabbing the horse's reins and yanking Jumping Jack's head round towards him, neither was he quick enough to stop the first blow. But, as Lloyd swung the crop up for another go, Garrin ripped it out of his hands.

Lloyd turned on him, eyes blazing, "Get out of my way, this has got nothing to do with you. Give me back my property." His face was blotched with rage.

"Not bloody likely. I'm going to make sure you never ride under BSJA rules again, you sadistic bastard." Garrin realised he was holding the crop above his head and that he dearly wanted to smash it into Lloyd's overfed face. With another part of his mind, he registered that they were

236

surrounded by St John Ambulance men.

"Okay, guys, cool it. That's enough. Let's all calm down a bit, shall we."

One of them held out his hand for the crop and Garrin gave it to him and turned away. He'd come close to hitting Lloyd then. Probably would have done if they hadn't been surrounded by people. Christ, what was the matter with him? Beating up competitors with their own crops, whatever the provocation, was not smart. He was trembling as he went back towards the judges' box and, even when a spectator called out, "Well done, Garrin," he didn't look round.

"Nasty piece of work," Sarah said, frowning, as he went back in. "I can quite see why you wanted to hit him, but..." She sighed.

"I know. I shouldn't have gone down there, I should have let him beat up the horse and then the whole thing would be cut and dried. We'd just be able to ban him."

"I expect we still can, but there'll have to be an enquiry. Ah, well. Guess we'd better get on with it. They've just about finished rebuilding that jump."

The rest of the judging passed without problems, but the incident had left a sour taste in Garrin's mouth. He didn't see either Amanda or Lloyd again. By the time he went back to his car, their box was gone. He half expected to find his tyres slashed, but all was well. With luck Amanda would have managed to talk some sense into her father by now. The look in Lloyd's eyes had jolted him. He cursed himself again for his misjudgement in selling them Shadowman.

He forced his mind away from the Battersby-Smythes. He'd been furious with Lloyd – he couldn't stand cruelty – but he was well aware the real source of his anger had nothing to do with horses.

* * *

237

Vanessa was chatting to Masie when the doorbell rang. Before she could move, Masie whisked back the nets and said, "Looks like a double-glazing salesman, shall I go? I love winding them up."

"No," Vanessa said, reminded briefly of Nanna Kane, and wondering what Garrin would make of being called a double-glazing salesman. "It's all right, I know him."

"Ooh, do you, dear? On second thoughts, he's rather handsome. Is he your young man?"

Vanessa escaped without answering and the doorbell rang again before she reached it. Having finally decided to come round, he was evidently now in a hurry. Taking a deep breath she swung the door open.

"Hi."

"Is that all you've got to say? I can't believe you walked out without even telling me face to face. What is your problem?"

"It's not me with the problem. It's you. Shagging that little tart right under my nose, what did you expect me to do?"

Where had that come from? She hadn't meant to bring up Amanda. She'd just reacted to the anger in his eyes. Now he was looking taken aback – good.

"Well, unless you want this conversation in front of an audience, you'd better let me in."

"What audience?" she said, glancing behind her and seeing that Masie and Dora were standing, with their heads round the lounge door, looking fascinated. Embarrassed, she opened the door to let him in.

As they walked past, Masie said in a loud stage whisper, "If you need any help with him, lovie, give me a call. I used to be a pub landlady. I can soon put him out for you."

The image of the five-foot-nothing Masie, putting the six-foot-one Garrin out of anywhere brought a smile to Vanessa's lips, but she suppressed it, and led him through to the flat.

He sat, without being invited, and glared at her. "It's none of your business who I sleep with. You're married."

"Yes," she said wearily. "And that isn't why I left. I seem to remember you asked me to go. This job came up and I'd have been mad to say no."

"I'm not sure it's a very good environment for Isobel – being around all these old people. There must be loads of germs."

"Oh, for God's sake, don't be so ridiculous. If anything it'll be her giving them the germs."

"Where is she, anyway?"

"In bed. Through there." She pointed and he got up and went into the bedroom. "Can you hear her crying from in here?"

"Yes, Garrin, I can. I keep the baby monitor in the lounge." She stood in the doorway, watching him by the cot. "She's absolutely fine. There's no reason for you to worry about her at all."

He didn't say anything, just continued to look at his daughter, and Vanessa felt guilty. After all, she wouldn't have liked it if their positions were reversed, and all things considered, he was taking this very well.

"You can see her whenever you like. I take it that's what you've come round for – to make arrangements."

He turned slowly and she couldn't read his eyes. Then he came across to her and put his hands on the doorframe, either side of her shoulders. "At the risk of having you call Masie to put me out – no, that's not why I'm here. I came to tell you I'm going to apply for custody of Isobel."

For several heartbeats she could only stare at him. She could see he was serious. His eyes were slightly narrowed as he waited for her reaction.

"You haven't got a hope in hell," she said, pulling back from the doorframe because he was crowding her, dizzying her thoughts. "I'm perfectly capable of looking after her myself."

"You're not capable of anything. Let's face it, you didn't even know who her father was, at least I'm not an adulterer."

Vanessa gasped, feeling heat come to her face. "That's hardly relevant to me being a good mother."

"The courts might think it is. I can't see them being very impressed when I tell them what sort of a trollop you are."

"You wouldn't dare."

"Try me. Anyway, she'd be much better off with me. You can't bring her up in some poky little back room in an old folks' home. It's disgusting. This is no place for a baby."

"And you think a stable yard is? A place full of horse-muck and flies and God knows what else. What are you going to do when you're working – tuck her under one arm? Grow up, Garrin. It's about time you faced facts. We're managing fine without you."

"It's not me who needs to grow up. It's you. You've never given a toss about anyone, have you? You still can't make up your mind who you want. Running back to Richard when she was a few days old just because I had dinner with another woman. What happened? Did he kick you out of his bed once he'd realised you weren't such a good lay as he thought?"

"You bastard."

"Yeah, and have you ever stopped to think whose fault that is? You pissed off when I needed you most. Pissed off with that complete wanker of a man, but you couldn't stop there. You had to go and marry him. I wouldn't have minded if you'd picked someone decent. But you had to choose some tosser who enjoys destroying other people's lives. Izzy was heartbroken when you left without a word. So was my grandmother. She had a heart attack. She died,

Vanessa, just a month after you abandoned us. If you hadn't gone, it wouldn't have happened."

"Don't," she said, cut to the core, not just by his words, but by the bitterness that was pouring out of him.

"Does the truth hurt? It's about time someone told you a few home truths. Izzy won't do it. Christ knows why, you hurt her enough. If you think you're taking my child away from me, you can think again. I won't let you do it. I'll do whatever it takes to get custody. I'm not letting you fuck up my life again, Vanessa."

"I think you'd better go." With ice in her voice, she met his furious black eyes and added, "We can talk about this when you've calmed down. I've got things to do." She moved pointedly towards the hallway. "Tomorrow, maybe, after a good night's sleep, you're obviously in need of one."

"Don't be so bloody patronising." He stepped past her, his body tensed into lines, and she stayed where she was, taking deep breaths to try and dispel the shakiness.

When the front door had slammed, she checked Isobel was still sleeping, standing with her hands on the bars of her cot until the trembling in her body stilled. Then she went back into the residents' lounge.

As she walked in a cheer went up and she glanced at the smiling faces of the residents in puzzlement. Then they were all talking at once.

"Atta girl, you told him."

"Such terrible language."

"Germs! The arrogant so and so, I'd have given his face a good slap."

Vanessa frowned and then realised they were all sitting around the baby monitor, which she'd left switched on. She didn't know whether to laugh or cry.

The doorbell rang again.

"It's him," Masie called, an edge of satisfaction in her voice. "That didn't take long."

241

"What didn't?" Vanessa said, going to answer it. If anything, Garrin looked even angrier than when he'd left. "Yes," she said icily. "Was there something else?"

"I need to use your phone. I can't get a signal on my mobile and someone's let my fucking tyres down."

Chapter Twenty-Nine

TRACEY TOLD HER WHEN she phoned to see if she was okay that at least part of Garrin's fury could be attributed to the row he'd had with Lloyd. "He'll probably get banned. I bet he's spitting blood. Garrin was pretty shaken up about it when he got in.

"How did his tyres get let down anyway?" she added curiously. "It used to be a nice area round there. It must have gone right downhill."

Vanessa had asked the same question of Masie and Dora, but they'd shaken their heads and given her wide-eyed looks of innocence.

"Goodness knows, love, we didn't see anything, Masie, did we?"

"Not a thing. Do you think he'll come round again? Listening to you two was much better than watching Corrie."

Despite her embarrassment, Vanessa hadn't been able to get too cross with them. After all, she had left the baby monitor on. And if she were still agile enough to let tyres down in her eighties, she'd be pretty pleased with herself, too.

She decided any future chats with Garrin would have to be at Fair Winds, or better still on neutral territory. If word of their row got back to Laura Collins she might decide Vanessa wasn't the sort of person she wanted looking after her establishment.

Vanessa fretted about this for a few days, but Laura came and went and didn't treat her any differently, so Vanessa decided to stop worrying. Garrin didn't contact her again either. Maybe he'd seen a solicitor and discovered he had no case as far as Isobel went. She was too busy to worry about possibilities for long. Isobel was a good baby, but it was still hard work combining looking after the residents with looking after her daughter.

The only thing Vanessa did find time for was to see a solicitor and file for divorce. She did this with some reluctance because she knew it would provoke some sort of reaction from Richard, but she couldn't afford to put it off. She and Isobel needed some security for the future and it was clear they couldn't rely on Garrin.

Richard's reaction came sooner than she'd expected. She was pushing Isobel along the cliffs in her buggy, as she often did in the afternoons if Laura was about, when she saw a black BMW pulling into the cliff-top car park. Suppressing a jolt of anxiety, she told herself there were loads of black BMWs about – it wasn't very likely to be Richard's – and kept walking.

She couldn't see the number plate from her vantage point, it was too far away. No one got out of the car so perhaps it was a tourist taking in the view. Deciding she was being paranoid, she began to descend the cliff path towards the car park. She had to go back that way and if it were Richard he'd have spotted her anyway. She'd be hard to miss, a solitary figure with a buggy, her hair streaming in the sea breeze. Small stones crunched beneath the buggy's wheels and Vanessa was aware of the haunting cries of the gulls and more worryingly of the fact there weren't many people around. It was too cold and too cloudy for a trip to the coast.

Anyway, so what if it was him, he was hardly going to attack her in broad daylight. She shivered, fear fighting with rationality. The last time they'd met his behaviour had been far from normal. There was no telling what he'd do now she'd filed for divorce.

The driver's door of the BMW opened. It was Richard. He had his back to her, but the sun caught glints of gold in his hair. He stretched his arms above his head, then turned and looked in her direction. And she knew he was waiting for her.

Perhaps she should pretend not to see him. But he wasn't going to let her just walk away – not if he'd come especially.

"It's okay, sweetheart," she told Isobel, "everything's fine." Words of reassurance more for herself than Isobel.

Richard began to walk across, his pace leisurely, as if he were out for an afternoon stroll.

"Hi, Vanessa," he called, when he was in hearing range. "Fancy seeing you here."

"Fancy," she said, determined not to let him see she was shaken. "Sightseeing, are you?"

"Hardly, I've come to see my little girl."

"She's not your little girl."

"I figured you'd had the test done when I got a letter from your solicitor this morning. It would have been nice if you'd let me know personally, but then I really don't know why I expected anything else from you."

He stood facing her, his eyes calm, not looking in the least perturbed at the news that Isobel wasn't his.

Christ, he had a nerve; he was actually trying to make her feel guilty. "I didn't feel very inclined to speak to you after what you did last time we met."

"Oh dear. So you haven't patched things up with gypsy boy then, I am sorry." He jangled his car keys, his eyes still on her face, and she was reminded of the way he'd stood on her hand and tried to bully her into submission.

Vanessa turned the buggy, anxious to get Isobel away from him. "I don't want to speak to you. I've got to get back."

"I knew she wasn't mine the day you told me you were

pregnant." He paused to let this sink in and went on conversationally, "I had a vasectomy just after we got married. I had it done in Spain."

She stared at him, taking in the coldness of his eyes, the slightly raised eyebrows, the utter detachment in his voice.

"But we were trying for a baby," she gasped. "All those months – and you let me think that it might happen. Every single month you let me hope and you knew all along that it was impossible."

"Yes."

"Are you going to tell me why?"

"I didn't want a screaming brat in our lives. I thought we were fine as we were."

Sickened, Vanessa turned away from him. So it hadn't just been her past he'd wanted to erase, but her future too – all of her life. He'd wanted to smash everything to pieces. She thought about the bulldozers tearing up the fairground and even though she hadn't seen any of it, it was as clear to her as if she'd stood and watched the machines moving over the rough ground, destroying, flattening, rebuilding things the way he wanted them.

He'd reconstructed her past like he'd reconstructed the girl she'd been then. Made her into something he wanted her to be, the kind of person who would fit into his life – be one more of his creations, neat and functional, where once she'd been all passion and fire and colour. And she could almost have forgiven him for that, well, at least she could have understood he'd been driven by the fear he'd lose her, but not this.

Her mind flicked back across the years that they'd tried to conceive, his gentleness, his gradually increasing sadness when it didn't happen.

Once, he'd come home and found her crying in the bathroom. "Sweetheart, what is it?" And when she'd poured out her sadness that she could never have another child, that

246

she was being punished for Jennifer's death, Richard had knelt beside her. He'd wiped tears from his own face, said he'd get himself tested, that it couldn't possibly be her, and she'd clung to him, wild with gratitude.

He'd seen a specialist the next week. He'd gone privately so they wouldn't have to wait. And he'd come back, his face bleak, and told her it was his fault. He had a very low sperm count that had possibly been caused by an adolescent attack of mumps. He'd said that perhaps they'd try for a bit longer and then consider fertility treatment, but that he'd much rather have his own child, a product of their union, than have her impregnated with some other man's more fertile sperm.

And she'd understood all this, understood he was a proud man, and she'd said they'd leave the fertility treatment. Leave it in the hands of fate because she hadn't wanted him to be hurt. And all that time he'd known it was impossible, because he'd already made it so.

Vanessa stood in the car park, with the sea breeze fanning her face, and felt too numbed to speak.

He touched her arm and she jumped violently. "I wasn't the only one who lied. You never loved me, did you? It's always been him."

Not looking at him, she reached into the buggy, checking Isobel wasn't cold, feeling her tiny fingers, tucking the blanket around her. "I did love you once," she said quietly. "But it wasn't enough for you. I could never have been enough for you because it wasn't me you wanted. You wanted some fantasy woman who didn't exist. You're the one who doesn't know about love, Richard, not me."

Now she did look at him and his expression hadn't changed. His face was blank and empty. "I've always loved you." Even the words sounded robotic. Perhaps he even believed what he was saying, but she didn't think so.

"You've always wanted to control me. It's not the same

247

thing."

"You don't know what you're talking about." He put his hands in his pockets, then with a shrug, he turned and walked back to his car. The BMW went out of the car park, smoothly and without haste and Vanessa watched it, still not quite believing that everything, absolutely everything about her marriage had been a sham.

Standing there in the cool breeze, she was filled with the deep ache of regret. She'd left Garrin and Izzy and she couldn't ever recapture the lost time, couldn't alter the pain she'd caused, or its consequences. And until this moment the only tiny comfort she'd had was that she'd thought it had been for something real – something true and good. But Richard had just smashed these illusions, sledge-hammered them to pieces like he'd sledge-hammered everything else. He'd stage-managed it all and he hadn't been able to resist pulling down the final curtain.

Chapter Thirty

"So, WHAT ARE YOU going to do, Garrin? You're going to have to sort something out. You can't leave it like this."

"I know that." Garrin rubbed a hand across his face and glanced at Izzy. The truth was he was worn out because, since he'd been told by three solicitors he had as much chance of getting custody of Isobel as he had of becoming prime minister, he'd buried himself in work. It was paying off, Derry was going like a dream and although they still hadn't managed to qualify for the Horse Of The Year Show, he knew they were close. They just needed the right course and a little bit of luck on their side.

"Garrin, are you listening to me?"

"Yeah – course I'm listening. To be honest, I'm not sure I can bear to see Isobel at the moment."

"We all have to do things we can't bear sometimes. It's part of life. She's your daughter. She's growing up and you're missing it. You can't get these first months back, you know."

He stood up, itching to pour himself a brandy, but it wasn't yet seven and he didn't want to see any more disapproval in Izzy's eyes. Any more little jibes about him running away again.

"So you're abandoning her because you can't have her." There was steel in Izzy's voice. "You're acting like a spoilt brat."

"Me?" He shook his head in disbelief. "I seem to remember you were very sympathetic when Vanessa ran off to shag her ex. And letting someone's tyres down because you don't like what they're saying is hardly adult."

"You told me yourself it couldn't have been Vanessa,

you were too busy laying into her."

Shit, why had he told her that? "I was only saying what needed to be said. I didn't tell her anything that wasn't true."

"Hmm," Izzy said. "I can imagine exactly what you told her. She was in tears when she spoke to me, and she's been through quite enough lately without you putting the boot in."

Garrin didn't say anything. He did feel quite guilty about that. Vanessa had looked shattered, which was one of the reasons he hadn't contacted her since. He'd been a total bastard and he knew he should apologise, but the longer he left it the harder it got. The other reason he hadn't been in touch was because he hadn't quite given up on getting custody. He'd been trawling the Net and had found several cases where the father had got care, despite the mother being perfectly capable. The previous evening he'd tracked down a hotshot female solicitor and he'd phoned her and explained Vanessa was still married and there was a possibility she might go back to her husband and that he couldn't bear the thought of his daughter being brought up by another man.

She'd been really sympathetic and had promised to phone him in the next couple of weeks so they could have a preliminary meeting. Not that he was planning on telling Izzy any of this because he knew she'd do her best to talk him out of it. Considering all that Vanessa had done, Izzy was being remarkably compassionate towards her. Bloody prodigal daughter – that was the trouble.

"I'll deal with it," he said now, aware of Izzy's gaze.

"You should sort out some maintenance," she went on relentlessly. "I don't suppose you've done that either."

"I'll go round and see her tonight. But I think I might take a taxi this time."

Izzy smiled at him. "Good," she said and got up stiffly

from his armchair. "Now we've got that sorted out you can tell me the latest on Derry. When's his next qualifying event?"

After Izzy had gone Garrin lay in the bath and thought about what he was going to say to Vanessa. It probably wasn't a bad idea to go and see her and at least apologise. He could avoid the subject of custody until he'd spoken more with the solicitor. At least it meant he could see Isobel. He missed her desperately, but Izzy was right. Staying away was no good for either of them. He got out of the bath, hitched a towel around his waist and shaved. He'd been too immersed in horses lately to bother much, but perhaps he ought to make an effort if he was going to see Vanessa. He didn't feel at all confident about his reception.

He was contemplating what to wear when the doorbell rang. Odd, no one usually called in the evenings, unless it was a working pupil alerting him to a problem with one of the horses. Still wearing a towel and with urgency quickening his steps, he hurried down and found Amanda on the doorstep.

"I'm just going out."

"You don't look as though you're dressed for it. Can I come in? I want to talk to you."

"It's a bit inconvenient."

"Please, Garrin, it won't take long and I've just had the most awful row with Daddy about you."

"Why?" he said, noting that she looked a bit tear-stained. There were mascara traces beneath her eyes and her nose was red.

"Let me in and I'll tell you."

He stepped back and she followed him along the hallway. "I'll be with you in two ticks, I'll just get dressed."

He expected her to make some flippant remark about not bothering on her account, but she didn't and when he came down she was sitting on his settee crying.

"Hey, it can't be that bad." Alarmed, he stepped across the room. "What have you been rowing about?"

"The BSJA have banned Daddy for a year. He's so cross. He was ranting and raving and all I did was stick up for you."

"That probably wasn't very sensible considering it's my fault he got banned." He sat next to her. "I expect he'll calm down when he's had time to think about things. There's no need for you to get upset."

"There is, he's kicked me out. He said I could go to hell for all he cared."

"What does your mum have to say about all this?"

"She doesn't know. She's away at my aunt's. I can't tell her, she always agrees with Daddy."

"I doubt if she'd agree with him kicking you out." Garrin said, looking at his watch. Having made up his mind to see Vanessa he wanted to go now and if he didn't get a move on it was going to be too late. He didn't want to risk winding her up further by waking up half the old dears.

Amanda sniffed. "I'm sorry, I'm holding you up. Are you supposed to be meeting someone?"

"I was going to see Vanessa. It doesn't matter."

"Is she okay now? Has she got over that post-natal depression business?"

He nodded distractedly. He was tempted to tell Amanda that Vanessa wasn't his cousin and it hadn't been post-natal depression, but now probably wasn't very good timing.

"I can go tomorrow. She wasn't expecting me anyway."

"Sorry," Amanda said again, her voice softening into a kitten purr. "I don't suppose I could ask you a really big favour, Garrin. I don't suppose I could stay the night, could I?"

"Isn't there anywhere else you can stay?"

She shook her head. "Not at this short notice. Please. I won't get in the way. I can stay on the settee. Unless you'd rather I stayed with you?" She glanced at him, her eyes sapphire bright, but it was hard to tell if she was being serious, or whether flirting was just second nature to her. "We could carry on from where we left off last time."

"Tempting as it is, I don't think that's a very good idea."

"Why not? Didn't you enjoy it?" She rested her head against his shoulder and he could smell her perfume, which brought back vivid memories of that night.

"I can't go out with you, Amanda, your father hates me. And you're too young, it wouldn't work."

"You didn't mind when you stayed before. My age didn't matter at all then."

"I was too drunk to mind about anything."

"Charming." She looked up at him and now there was a definite hint of the tease in her eyes. "You'll be saying you don't even remember what happened next."

"I don't," he said helplessly. "I'm sorry, but apart from collapsing on the bedroom floor, I can't remember a bloody thing."

For a moment, he thought she was going to burst into tears again. He supposed he deserved it. It hadn't been a very complimentary thing to say. But then to his surprise she smiled instead.

"I was wondering when you'd get round to that. You should have seen the look on your face the next morning when I told you what a wonderful night it had been. I couldn't resist it." She shook her head. "Not a lot else did happen, after that. The mind was willing, but the body wasn't. You fell asleep."

"Shit, did I?" He didn't know whether to be relieved or disappointed.

"I tried to wake you up by various means," she went on, ignoring his embarrassment. "There were bits of you that were still awake – very awake, in fact, but I like to make love to men when they're fully aware of what they're doing.

253

I'm old-fashioned like that."

"Christ, I'm sorry." He laughed despite himself. "I was very drunk. It's no reflection on you. You're gorgeous."

"But not gorgeous enough to risk a relationship with. It's a shame, Garrin. I think we'd make a good couple. We'd have beautiful children, don't you think?"

The mention of children brought him back to earth with a crash. Thank God he hadn't asked Vanessa to come round here. Not that it was any of her business who he had in his house, but he couldn't afford to wind her up. He might not get anywhere with this solicitor and if he didn't, then Izzy was right, he couldn't walk away from Isobel however he felt about her mother. He would have to stay on the right side of Vanessa.

"You can stay on my settee for tonight, but you'll have to sort something else out for tomorrow. And it's on condition you give your dad a ring and let him know you're all right."

"I left my mobile at home."

"Use mine." He pushed it towards her and went into the kitchen to pour himself a brandy, hoping she had the sense not to tell her father where she was. The last thing he needed was a furious Lloyd turning up on his doorstep. He was uncomfortably aware that Amanda wasn't the only Battersby-Smythe he had unfinished business with.

Vanessa frowned and crooked the phone into her neck. Izzy wasn't making any sense at all, or maybe it was her. She'd only just finished the breakfast trays and she was still on autopilot, flicking between seeing to Isobel and trying to eat her own breakfast.

"Are you sure he said he was coming round here last night?" she repeated. "I certainly wasn't expecting him."

"Yes, lovie. I saw him early evening and he mentioned it. I know how things have been between you lately. I wanted to make sure you were all right."

"Well, we haven't seen him." Vanessa rocked Isobel in her arms. "He must have changed his mind."

"I'll phone him." Izzy sounded exasperated. "Sorry to have troubled you, Vanessa. Perhaps something cropped up."

Vanessa hung up. The last thing she wanted was Garrin coming round ranting and raving again. Perhaps it would be best if she phoned him herself, and made sure he didn't. If he wanted to discuss Isobel, she'd far rather it was on the telephone, or failing that, somewhere away from here.

If she got his answer machine she'd hang up, she decided, but it was answered within three rings.

"Garrin, it's Vanessa," she said, before she'd registered the fact that it wasn't his voice. "Tracey, is that you?"

"No, it's Amanda. Hi, Vanessa. I'll just get Garrin for you, he's around somewhere."

Vanessa hung up before she could say anything else, her heart pumping madly. So, Amanda was living there, was she? She wished Izzy had warned her. She'd seen Izzy a few times lately, but they didn't talk about Garrin much because Vanessa didn't want to put Izzy in a compromising position. He'd made it perfectly clear last time she'd seen him that there was no way back for them, even to civility. And the fact he hadn't been in touch since convinced her he'd meant it.

She tossed her uneaten toast into the bin and clattered her plate into the sink. It didn't bother her one bit if Amanda was living with him. After all, wasn't that why she'd moved out, so Garrin could carry on where he'd left off before she appeared on the scene? Ignoring the little stomach swirls of jealousy, she bent to scoop Isobel from her Moses basket, not noticing until she stood up again that the plate had cracked cleanly in two in the sink.

Chapter Thirty-One

EVEN THOUGH SHE'D BEEN expecting him to phone her back, it was still unnerving to hear his voice.

Aware of Masie and Dora, who'd got into the habit of coming into the kitchen for a cuppa and a gossip, Vanessa stretched the phone cord around the connecting door that led through to her flat.

"What do you want? I'm up to my ears in it."

"You phoned me," he pointed out. "But I'm glad you did because we need to sort a few things out."

"Remembered you've got a daughter, have you?" Vanessa said before she could stop herself.

There was a small silence and then he coughed, but to her surprise all he said was, "I don't want to fight. Is it easier if I come there?"

"No." She didn't want him in the house. She'd only just managed to exorcise the memories of his last visit, but she didn't want to go to Fair Winds either and see the evidence of Amanda dotted around the place. "I'll meet you. It'll have to be an afternoon."

"Then let's make it today. Will you bring Isobel? I'd really like to see her."

There was a trace of longing in his voice, which Vanessa ignored. He'd been the one who'd kept away all this time.

"I'm hardly going to leave her here, am I?"

They met in the car park where she'd seen Richard. It was full today, the air heavy with summer. Parents, tiring of their offspring's extended break, were out in droves. Garrin had said he'd pick her up, but she'd wanted to walk. He was waiting by the pay machine and she pushed the buggy towards him and wished the sight of him didn't still tie her stomach into conflicting knots.

"Hi," he said, meeting her halfway. There were tiredness lines around his eyes and his face was unusually hesitant and she would have softened if she hadn't known it was Amanda who'd been keeping him from sleeping.

He crouched by the buggy. "She's grown, I can't believe how much she's grown."

"They do."

"Hello, my angel. How you doing?" He took her small hand in his and Isobel screwed up her face and began to cry. "There's no need for that, darling, is there now?"

Vanessa heard the catch in his voice and decided it would be cruel to tell him Isobel probably didn't recognize him. "She's been grizzly all morning. She's teething, I think."

"How many does she have?"

"Four." Pride warmed her voice. It was wonderful watching Isobel grow. Every little achievement was a milestone – she knew she'd never get tired of the miracle of her daughter growing. "Do you want to walk or go to the coffee shop?"

"It'll be packed, let's walk." He headed in the direction she would have chosen and they walked with the buggy between them. Vanessa knew they must look like any other parents out for the afternoon.

"How's the job going? Tracey said the old ladies love you."

"It's fine." She didn't want to make small talk. She wanted to get this over with and also to tell him this was a one-off. From now on their parenting was to be on parallel lines. Garrin was Isobel's father and that was fine, but she didn't want his fatherly stuff overlapping into her life. Four months had put a manageable space between them, given her the distance she needed from Garrin and she was determined to hold on to this for the sake of her own peace of mind.

For a while he was silent and she hoped he'd got the message. They paused for a woman with a buggy coming the other way. The path wasn't wide enough for two and Garrin was standing so close she caught the faint smell of his aftershave on the breeze. Uncomfortable, she moved away and he glanced at her.

"I said some pretty shitty things to you last time we met. I was angry."

"I gathered that."

"I shouldn't have said them."

"Is that the closest you can get to an apology?"

He gave a quick self-deprecating grin that wasn't like him at all. "No, it isn't. I'm sorry, Vanessa. I really am."

He sounded it and she was tempted to say it was okay, that he couldn't possibly have hated her any more than she hated herself for the mess she'd made by marrying Richard. But then she thought about Amanda. He must be aware that she knew they were living together, which was doubtless why he was being so nice. He wanted to see Isobel and he couldn't afford to wind her up.

"I don't want to rake over the past," she said, her voice tightening, "let's talk about what we're here for. Access arrangements for your daughter."

"And maintenance," Garrin said, his face sombre again and she was aware the space was between them once more and she was glad.

After the walk, they sat in his car, filling in dates in their respective diaries. August 10th was next Sunday, Vanessa saw as she flicked through and pencilled in dates. August 10th, the day of Jennifer's birth and her death. Maybe she would go this year. Maybe it would be different now she had Isobel.

Aware of Garrin's gaze she turned the page, but it was too late. He leaned across and said in a voice that betrayed nothing of his feelings. "I'm going to see her. Why don't you come with me?"

Her instinct was to refuse, she never wanted to be vulnerable in front of him again, but perhaps she owed it to Jennifer. Perhaps she'd like her mum and dad standing there together. And if she could be with him because of Isobel, why should Jennifer be any different?

"Just a thought," he added. "I understand if you'd rather not."

"No, it's all right. I'll come."

She caught the flash of surprise on his face, but all he said was, "I'll pick you up on Sunday then. About two."

Vanessa arranged for Izzy to baby-sit. She would take Isobel to see her sister one day, but not yet. Not with Garrin. When she got back after dropping her off, Garrin was sitting in his car outside Tall Trees. He wound down the window when he saw her. "I figured you must still be at Izzy's and I didn't fancy leaving my car unsupervised. Are you all set?"

She nodded and went across. The back seat was full of pink roses, she saw, with a frisson of pain. They'd had them at Jennifer's funeral and she'd never be able to see their delicate petals without seeing again that tiny coffin disappearing behind the curtain in the crematorium. So terrifying, so final.

She'd half risen from the bench, her service sheet fluttering to the floor, not able to bear it that her baby girl was making this journey all alone. She'd wanted to run after the coffin, throw her body across it and scream that they couldn't take Jennifer, that it wasn't fair, it wasn't time. They couldn't take her little girl away from her for ever. She couldn't carry on living without her.

It had been Garrin who'd pulled her back into her seat, his fingers tight around hers, but it had been Izzy who'd picked up her service sheet and pressed it back into her hands. "She's okay, my love, she'll be well looked after in heaven, I promise you." And Izzy's blue eyes had been filled with such love that Vanessa had managed to control herself, even though she knew perfectly well that Izzy didn't believe in any heaven, or in any god.

And now, in the road outside Tall Trees, Vanessa hesitated, her hand on the car door, looking at the roses, and Garrin must have seen the memories on her face because he got out and came round and opened the door for her.

"Let's get going." His voice was gentle. "You'll feel better when we're on our way."

They didn't speak as he drove through the winding coastal roads. The car was full of the scent of roses, and the fields gleamed gold either side of them. Summer was everywhere. Bales of hay dotted the stubble and when the cultivated land gave way to heath they passed miles of pink heather and gorse, its yellow flowers bright as fire, but all Vanessa could think about were roses slowly being consumed by the incinerator flames.

At the cemetery, he parked and glanced across at her. "Are you okay?"

"Yes," she said, even though she could already feel the memories lifting the hairs on her arms and chilling every part of her.

He reached into the back, gathering up armfuls of blooms, his eyes on hers, but by tacit agreement she didn't carry any and he walked ahead of her, pausing at the gate of the remembrance garden so they could enter together.

At their daughter's grave, he laid the roses on the ground while he cleared a scattering of leaves from the headstone and then he knelt. Vanessa knelt beside him, feeling the dampness beneath her knees, unable to look at his face.

260

Silence gathered around them and she closed her eyes and wondered if Garrin thought of Jennifer as a newborn, still, or whether he saw their daughter as she did, saw her as the girl she'd have been if she'd lived. Growing year by year, always smiling and far away from this place of death.

When she opened her eyes, she realised he was watching her.

"I often see her, Vanessa. Sometimes on forest paths when I'm out riding, sometimes on the beach, sometimes when I'm lying in bed at night. Just glimpses, I mean, of the girl she is now. And she never looks sad when I see her, she's always smiling."

"I see her too," Vanessa whispered, torn into pieces because Garrin never said things like this. Garrin was always practical and cynical and she couldn't bear to think they'd got so far apart, but they still had this in common. Couldn't bear to think that if they'd ever discussed this, even once, then so much of their history could have been rewritten.

He gripped her hand and for a moment she let her fingers stay in his. Then she pulled them away and stood up, clutching her light coat around her because it was too late. Six years too late. And she could see in his face that he understood it was too, and they walked back along the path in silence.

Chapter Thirty-Two

GARRIN WAS LUNGING A young horse one afternoon when he saw a figure hurrying across the field towards him. He shielded his eyes against the sun. Lloyd, he saw with a stab of unease. Oh well, he'd known the prat would turn up sooner or later.

Lloyd, puffing heavily, having just made his way across two fields, came to a halt in front of him. His face looked red and angry – but Garrin had already clocked his body language – and was mightily relieved there was a lunging whip between them.

"I want you to stop seeing my daughter," Lloyd gasped, trying to dodge round the whip.

"I haven't seen Amanda for a week," Garrin said, which was true. He'd told her to leave after Vanessa had phoned.

"She spent the night with you. She told me."

"She slept on my settee – not the same thing. And I only let her do that because she said you'd kicked her out."

"I didn't kick her out. I wouldn't put my only daughter out on the street, for goodness' sake. What sort of father do you take me for?"

Garrin frowned. He wouldn't have trusted Lloyd as far as he could throw him, yet there was a ring of truth about what he said. So perhaps Amanda had lied. Why?

"The relationship between Amanda and me is professional. I'm her riding instructor. That's all. Now if you don't mind, I've got things to do."

"We no longer require your services as her riding instructor," Lloyd said pompously. "From now on I shall be engaging someone whose teaching methods are more to my liking."

"That include beating up horses, you mean? Well, it hasn't got you very far, has it? I thought the idea of show-jumping was to be able to actually enter the classes."

"How dare you. You little upstart…you…" Lloyd was so angry he could hardly speak and Garrin didn't help the situation one bit by smiling. It was the word 'little' that had done it. Lloyd was at least a foot shorter than him. It was a mistake, he realised belatedly, as Lloyd roared and literally leapt through the air at him. The horse, still on the lunge line, which Garrin had coiled loosely over one arm, spooked and gave a half rear and Garrin felt the thud of Lloyd's fist connecting with his chin at the same moment as the horse took off. He felt himself falling and was dragged several yards across the field before he could disentangle himself from the line.

When he'd gathered his wits enough to lift his head from the pile of horseshit he'd just been pulled through, he was subjected to the sight of Lloyd slapping both hands on his thighs and roaring with laughter. The blue sky behind him threw his outline into sharp relief and gave him the appearance of some crazy cartoon character. More furious than he could ever remember being, Garrin scrambled to his feet, reached for the lunging whip, which he'd dropped at the last minute and tore across the field towards him.

Lloyd could run a lot quicker than he'd have thought possible, considering that he wasn't exactly slim-line. He was through the barbed-wire fence and halfway across the next field in about five seconds. Garrin, hampered by the whip, which was several feet long and not designed for being waved about in the air, whilst running, couldn't close the gap between them until they were almost back at the stables. Shouting obscenities, he hurled himself over the five-bar-gate and saw that Lloyd had come to an abrupt halt about a hundred yards away. He was talking to someone and pointing back in Garrin's direction and Garrin thought

263

he heard the word, "maniac".

Shit, he hoped it wasn't anyone who wanted to come for lessons. He abandoned the whip, which had snapped on his way over the gate, wiped a smear of horseshit from his face and fixing on a smile went across the yard.

"Bloody maniac," Lloyd said again, taking a step backwards. "First he seduces my daughter and then he tries to kill me."

He was talking to a woman and as she turned, Garrin could feel his stomach nose-diving towards his boots. She was wearing a smart suit and carrying a briefcase and he'd never seen her before in his life. But he recognized her from the photograph on her website. She was the hotshot solicitor he'd contacted about Isobel.

"Good morning, Mr Tate," she said, her voice only a degree or so warmer than her eyes. "I was passing so I thought I'd drop by and see you in your home environment."

"Right," he said. "I'll just get cleaned up and we can have a chat." He glared at Lloyd and the man stuck his nose in the air and smirked.

"It's about your custody application," Miss Hotshot continued, when Lloyd was barely out of earshot. "Actually, I have to tell you now that I'm very concerned. Your chances of getting a sympathetic court hearing depend so much on presenting the right sort of image. We could call character witnesses, that sort of thing, but so much depends on creating the right impression."

"I do understand," Garrin said, steering her across the yard, painfully aware she was keeping a careful distance between them. "I just feel that Isobel would be so much better off in a country home than being brought up surrounded by old people. Not that I've got anything against old people, of course." The carefully prepared words sounded hollow, even to him.

They passed Lloyd, who'd stopped to do up a shoelace, which, Garrin would have laid bets on, had never been undone in the first place.

He straightened and gave Garrin a self-satisfied sneer. "Well, if you're looking for a character witness you're going to have your work cut out. I wouldn't give him custody of my bloody hamster."

"Surely you can see the funny side," Tracey said to Garrin later that evening. "I couldn't believe my eyes when I saw you chasing him across that field with a lunging whip. Neither could the working pupils."

"No, I can't see the bloody funny side. That bastard punched me. I didn't hear him confessing that to Miss High and Mighty."

"What did you want to talk to her about anyway? Anything I should know about? You're not in any financial trouble, are you?"

"It was a personal thing."

Tracey looked relieved. "There are plenty more solicitors, I'm sure you'll soon find another one."

"Yeah," Garrin said, but he knew it was hopeless. Miss Hotshot hadn't been in the slightest impressed when he'd explained it wasn't him who was the maniac. That Lloyd was just trying to get his own back because he'd had him banned from show-jumping for beating up his horses.

"I can't condone any sort of violence, Mr Tate," she'd said primly. "Whether the recipient is four-legged or two-legged. As a responsible parent you surely know that reason and rational discussion is far more effective. In order for me to represent you I'd have to be sure that you were the kind of person who'd always act responsibly, no matter what the provocation. And frankly, after what I've just seen, I'm not."

She'd snapped her briefcase shut with an air of finality

and Garrin had known that further discussion was hopeless. In the space of five minutes he'd blown the best chance he had of keeping Isobel.

"You're lucky Lloyd didn't try and press charges," Tracey said unhelpfully. "Why was he so angry anyway?"

"He thinks I'm trying to seduce Amanda."

"Well, if you're still trying you must have lost your touch. She's been hanging around you for weeks."

"She's not my type," Garrin said, realizing with a small jolt that it was true. Lovely as Amanda was, he didn't have any desire to go out with her. He hadn't had any desire to go out with anyone, he thought, frowning. Not since Vanessa had come crashing back into his life.

"So you've turned into Mr Sensible, have you," Tracey said quietly. "I'm pleased, Garrin. We all have to settle down eventually, and you've got responsibilities now, haven't you?"

"Yeah." He sighed. "I don't want my daughter to grow up thinking her daddy's a total tart."

"For what it's worth, I think little Isobel will grow up adoring you. And that's just how it should be." Her eyes were unusually serious and he smiled at her.

"Cheers for the vote of confidence. I hope you're right."

There was still the small matter of why Amanda had lied to him about needing somewhere to stay, but he guessed he'd find out sooner or later. In the meantime, he thanked his lucky stars that at least he'd got things back on an even footing with Vanessa. There was a part of him that was glad he wasn't going to have to fight her for Isobel. There had been enough fighting between them to last a lifetime.

The next few weeks were going to be busy ones for him anyway. He had one more chance of qualifying Derry for the Horse Of The Year Show. He decided he would focus on that. It had been Izzy who'd told him he'd have to find new dreams when Vanessa had left. And he'd poured all of

266

his energy, all of his love, into their horse. He would do it again. He might have let himself down this afternoon, but he didn't want to let Izzy down, or Derry. And even though his daughter was barely six months old he didn't want to let her down either – he'd already missed so much of her growing up because he and Vanessa were at war. He might not be able to have her in his life full-time, but he still wanted her to grow up being proud of him.

Amanda turned up when he was schooling Derry in the indoor school a couple of evenings later. He saw her come in through the double doors, but he didn't stop what he was doing. He'd only just got Derry warmed up and he didn't want to break the horse's concentration. Amanda sat on a cross-pole and watched them in silence and twenty minutes passed before he reined in, dismounted and led the horse across.

"He's going well, Garrin, you must be pleased."

"Your father won't be happy that you're here. He came and saw me."

"I know."

"Why did you say he'd chucked you out?"

She looked at him, a hint of defiance in her eyes. "Because you wouldn't have let me stay with you otherwise. Not that you did anyway. And I know why, now. I'm not the only person who's been lying, am I, Garrin?"

"Meaning?"

"Vanessa isn't your cousin, is she? She's your lover. Why didn't you tell me?"

"Because she isn't my lover."

"She must have been once for you to have a child together." She dropped her eyes as she spoke, fiddling with the strap on her handbag. "Isobel's yours, isn't she? Daddy told me all about you wanting to get custody."

"Yeah, well that isn't going to happen, either." Why did

he feel so bloody guilty? There was no reason for him to tell Amanda about Vanessa, it wasn't as though they'd had a relationship. He glanced at her. She looked absurdly young and very pretty. She was wearing a pale blue dress dotted with little flowers, and high-heeled shoes, the heels of which were sinking into the peat of the indoor school.

"I'm sure there must be dozens of blokes nearer your age you could go out with."

"I don't want some spotty teenager. I want to go out with you. You must know I'm besotted with you, Garrin. I've been in love with you from the first time we met."

"Since I bullied you to get back on your horse," he said dryly. "I'm not a very nice person. You can do a lot better than me."

"Daddy's not a very nice person sometimes, but I love him, too. Although not in the same way that I love you, obviously."

Being compared with Lloyd was not in the least flattering, Garrin thought wryly, turning away from her.

"Where are you going?"

"To put Derry away before he gets cold."

She caught up with him at the door. "Please don't let's leave it like this. I know you don't feel the same as me, but we could start again, couldn't we? I mean if you really aren't planning on getting back with Vanessa. I could help you look after Isobel – when you have her, I mean – I'm great with babies."

He switched the lights off and led Derry out into the dusky evening. It was still warm, but it was beginning to spit with rain and he glanced at Amanda, who was dressed for going out, not traipsing around muddy stable yards in the dark.

"You'll get soaked."

"Then… can I wait in the house for you? We need to talk, Garrin."

"No, we don't. Look…" He glanced at her, hating himself for what he was about to do, but knowing she'd thank him for it in the end. "I think you should keep away from here until you get this silly crush out of your system. I don't want to see you again. I can't make it any clearer than that. Now, do yourself a favour and go home before your nutty father takes it into his head to come looking for you."

She didn't say anything. Her face was very pale and as he led Derry across the yard, he could hear her sobbing. He felt like an utter shit as he rugged up his horse and settled him for the night. Vanessa had been younger than Amanda when he'd got her pregnant. They'd thought themselves in love then, but when she'd left him for Richard he'd realised how insubstantial it had all been.

Maybe love was for the young, he thought wearily. Like candy-floss, so full of promise, but dissolving swiftly and leaving you with nothing but the memory of its sweetness. A dream that caught you up in its glitz and its glamour, like the fairground caught punters and showed them for 'one night only' a never, never land of thrills and excitement. All pretty lights that hid the shabby paintwork until the cold light of day revealed the fairground's true colours.

Chapter Thirty-Three

HE HAD ONE LAST chance to qualify Derry for this year's show, but Garrin knew it was going to happen. He and Izzy walked the course, the turf springy beneath their feet, the painted poles gleaming in the sunshine. It was a perfect blue day. Around them, the muted buzz of chatter drifted in snatches as other competitors discussed the course, which angle to take this jump and that from, how many strides their mounts would need, how many corners could be cut. Izzy was quiet as she strolled beside him, but her eyes were lit with excitement and he knew she could feel it too.

"What do you reckon then?" he said, glancing at her. "Got any good vibes coming through?" He pressed his fingers to his head and screwed up his eyes, his face a study of mock concentration.

"Stop taking the mickey, it doesn't do to tempt fate," she said, but she was smiling.

"It's our last chance."

"There's always next year."

"Bugger next year. I want it now, today. All or nothing."

"You've never had any patience, Garrin. All good things come to those who wait."

"Those who work for them, you mean. There's no room in this game for people who sit around waiting. I've worked for this and I deserve it, and Derry deserves it." His voice grew more serious. "He loves it, you know. I've never known a horse who loves jumping so much."

"It shows. And for what it's worth, yes I do have a feeling you're going to do well, today." Izzy stared away across the showground, but he knew she wasn't seeing the people and the steward's marquees and the horseboxes, she was looking further back into their shared past. The time she'd first put him on a horse. He could remember it too.

He'd been about six when she'd first taken him to her uncle's yard. They'd got out of the car and walked across a muddy yard and Garrin, stiff and self-conscious in his borrowed riding clothes, took a deep breath of the horse-scented winter air and felt excitement and nervousness churning his stomach.

In the wooden shack of an office, he was fitted with a riding hat while Izzy chatted to her uncle Bert about Nanna Kane and about how things were going at the fair. Then they'd followed him out to the stable yard and Garrin was introduced to the pony he would ride.

"This is Al," Izzy had told him, leading over a dark brown horse with a long black mane and tail and sleepy untroubled eyes.

"Hi, Al." Garrin stretched out a hand and stroked the horse's neck. It felt just as he'd expected, firm and warm. "Does he jump then, Mr Mullings?"

"Well, he does, but I think you'd better learn to ride him first." He'd smiled at Izzy. "Kids, eh?" And Izzy had laughed and said something he didn't catch.

But Garrin didn't care. A few minutes later he was up in the saddle, being shown how to hold the reins and how to sit and what position his legs should be in. It felt fantastic. It felt, he thought, with a deep sigh of contentment, as if he'd come home. There was no doubt about it; this was where he was meant to be.

The other pupil who should have been sharing his lesson had cancelled so there was just him, riding around the muddy field, with Mr Mullings standing in the middle shouting out instructions, and Izzy, leaning her elbows on the fence and watching. It was the best half hour he'd ever had in his life. When it was time to dismount he cried.

"No need for that," Mr Mullings said, his face all red

271

from the cold and the shouting. "You did really well, Garrin. You're a natural. You're going to be a smashing rider."

He nodded and looked past him to the icy blue sky beyond the rickety stables. He knew that already. He'd always known it. They didn't need to tell him.

Odd, he hadn't thought about that day for years – the day that had started his lifelong passion for horses. Perhaps there was some deep part of his mind that knew it had always been leading to this one. He touched Izzy's arm and made her jump.

"You were miles away."

"I was thinking that your grandmother would be so proud of you."

"For selling the family business. For letting everything she loved be ruined and destroyed, I'm not so sure."

"For rebuilding your life. It hasn't been easy, has it, my love, and you've done it all alone. You're very much like her."

"I didn't do it alone. I had you."

"An old woman with a debilitating illness. I don't think I've been much help."

He looked into her face, seeing all the strength and the passion that had sustained him through so much and he felt suddenly humbled.

"We won't let you down," he whispered and Izzy just nodded.

They were jumping eleventh out of a field of fifteen, which meant Garrin could watch the first few competitors and get a good idea of any jumps that were trickier than they looked.

As he waited to go in, Derry fidgeting and refusing to stand still, he wondered if perhaps he shouldn't have had that conversation with Izzy. He no longer felt confident in the slightest. He felt sick and this wasn't helped when the competitor before him demolished the last part of the combination in his second round, sending poles flying in all directions and writing off the planter so that the stewards gave up trying to stuff the wrecked fir tree back into its pot and just dragged it out of the ring.

It also meant there was a delay and Derry tossed his head impatiently and ripped up the turf with his dancing.

What are we waiting for?

Pack it in; you'll get your chance to shine in a minute.

I intend to.

At least one of them was confident, Garrin thought, as they finally rode into the ring and cantered in a circle as they waited for the bell.

Then they were away and heading for the first jump. He knew when they were a third of the way round that it was going to be fine. Despite the delay, Derry had never felt so focussed. Garrin forgot about everything else and concentrated on jumping until all that existed was the powerful bunching of horse beneath him as they met fence after fence perfectly. It was like music, a conductor and orchestra, but he couldn't tell which of them was which, only that they were in perfect synchronicity. They couldn't put a foot wrong and they didn't and when he came out of the ring after their third perfect clear round he saw that Izzy had tears in her eyes.

"There are only two tickets, someone else might get it," he said, leaning forward and running his fingers along the line of Derry's plaits.

"It's possible," Izzy said, but her eyes told him she didn't believe it. And she was right.

They celebrated at his house, Izzy sipping champagne through a straw and Garrin knocking it back like there was no tomorrow.

"Steady on, you'll be on the carpet," she admonished.

273

"I haven't had a reason to celebrate for ages. I don't see why I shouldn't make the most of it."

She sighed. "I'm glad you're on good terms with Vanessa again."

"Hopefully we'll always stay on reasonable terms for Isobel's sake."

"And you're happy with that?"

"I wouldn't say happy was a word I'd use in the same sentence as Vanessa," Garrin said, refilling his glass. "Do you know if she's done any more about divorcing that dick-brains of a husband?"

"I think it's in hand," Izzy said, wondering why Vanessa hadn't told Garrin about her car park meeting with Richard. But then she hadn't told him Richard had kidnapped Isobel either. She hadn't told him so many things that might have softened the way he felt about her and it grieved Izzy deeply. Vanessa was as proud and as pigheaded as Garrin was, and life was too short to let such destructive emotions get in the way of love. But it wasn't her place to tell Garrin any of this if Vanessa didn't want him to know. If they were ever to be reconciled then it had to come from both of them wanting it. Not because of any interference from her.

"Are you going to tell Vanessa about today?" she asked gently. "She might want to come along and watch you in October?"

"I doubt it. She can't bear to be in the same room as me. She made that clear when we discussed the arrangements for Isobel. Vanessa's happy to be a mother and for me to be a father, but she doesn't want us to be parents."

There was hurt in his eyes and Izzy frowned. I'm not quite with you, what's the difference exactly?"

"Vanessa wants us to do things separately with our daughter. I do the father bit, she does the mother bit, but she doesn't want us doing them at the same time."

"I see," Izzy said, wishing she hadn't brought the subject

274

up.

"It suits me," Garrin said, with undisguised hurt. "Now, let's forget about Vanessa, we're supposed to be celebrating."

Izzy looked at him over the top of her glass.

Oh, Garrin, she thought – so much a man and yet still a hurting child and she knew he was never going to grow up completely while he still held on to his bitterness. He was going to need to forgive Vanessa completely and unconditionally before he could really move on.

Vanessa was going to find it harder than she realised too, Izzy decided, putting her empty glass back on the table with fingers that shook, and feeling weary as hell. Parenthood wasn't something you could divide up like days of the week. There would inevitably be times when you had to do it together, and she hoped with all her heart that Vanessa and Garrin would discover this in a way that wasn't too painful.

Chapter Thirty-Four

Izzy was staying with Garrin the night before they travelled to Birmingham. She'd insisted, saying he'd have enough to do on the following morning without picking her up as well. They'd only be gone two days, but the preparations had started a fortnight earlier.

Tracey was looking after the yard and Suzy, one of his working pupils, was going with him, as groom. It would look good on her CV, she'd said, although he'd better remember she wasn't Tracey and wouldn't stand for any nonsense.

"As if," Garrin told her, grinning. His feelings swung between elation and terror and he was treating the people around him accordingly, which Tracey had told him made him even more of a pain in the arse than usual.

"I'm only staying in case you end up famous," she snapped, as he went through the checklist yet again. "I don't get paid nearly enough to put up with you."

"I'll give you a pay rise if I get a clear round."

"You'll give me a pay rise anyway, you tight-fisted git. One that reflects the fact I'm acting yard manager while you're away."

"You get more than the going rate already."

"No, I don't. Alistair gets paid more than me and he works less hours."

Garrin glared at her. Alistair was Tracey's new boyfriend. He cropped up in most of her conversations and it was starting to annoy him. Everywhere he looked there were couples and last week he'd turfed a lanky, pony-tailed teenager out of one of the working pupils' caravans.

"And there's a job going at the yard where Alistair

works," Tracey added, folding her arms stubbornly. "I might apply for it if you're not careful."

"Blackmail will get you nowhere. In fact, it might even get you the sack."

"Oh, might it. We'll soon see about that."

"Garrin, why don't you go for a walk," Izzy suggested. "Give everyone a break. I'm sure everything you can possibly do is done and you're only winding everyone up."

He took her advice. It was a beautiful evening; the sun was just beginning to set, casting long shadows across the grass and turning the edges of the cliffs to pink. He cut across his fields, ducked under the wire boundary fence and went up on to the cliff path and stood for a moment, looking out to sea.

Far below him the waves pounded the rocks and it was humbling to think they'd been doing exactly the same for countless years, while people's dreams came and went and were forgotten. The breeze touched his skin, bringing goose-bumps to his arms.

The next time he stood here it would all be over. He and Derry would have fulfilled the dream that had taken five-and-a-half years to bring to fruition – the dream that had given him the strength to carry on without Vanessa.

He and Vanessa had spent a lot of time on cliff-tops. Sometimes he felt as though he could measure their lives in cliff-top moments. Once, when they'd been kids he'd scared the living daylights out of her by running up to the edge, holding his arms high on either side of him and saying, "Watch, Nessa, I can fly."

Then he'd jumped off.

Vanessa had screamed and screamed until, worried that someone in the fair would hear her and come hurtling across to thump him, Garrin had popped his head back over the top.

"I'm on a ledge, you wally."

He'd thought it was hilarious, but Vanessa hadn't. When he'd climbed back up again, she'd whacked him so hard he'd nearly tumbled back over.

They'd been on a cliff-top when she'd told him she was pregnant with Jennifer, too. It had been a bleak winter Saturday and they were walking, as they often did to clear their heads after a day spent working in the hamburger bar in Knollsey.

Vanessa was oddly quiet, her beautiful face serene and her dark eyes distant as she looked out across the grey sea.

"What's on your mind?" Garrin asked, thinking she'd had some run-in with a customer. The unflattering red-and-white checked waitress uniform she wore did nothing to hide her slender figure, and the stupid peaked cap, perched on her pony tail, didn't detract from the fact that she was stunning. Men twice her age were always making ribald comments, loving the fact that she gave as good as she got and didn't blush and escape like the rest of the young waitresses. Many a time Garrin had been tempted to vault over the counter where he fried burgers, storm across and give them a good thumping.

"I'm late," Vanessa said, turning towards him, a slight frown on her face.

"Late for what?" he asked and her frown had deepened and then slowly it had dawned on him what she was talking about.

"It doesn't mean you're pregnant. Does it?"

"No, but I think I am," she said sighing, and he'd felt all sorts of emotions flooding him. Worry, cold as the February air; protectiveness because she looked so fragile and young; and pride, a bright thread of it that ran through him, warming as a fire in winter. But he hadn't said anything because he wasn't sure how she felt, he'd just stuffed his hands in his pockets and they'd walked a bit further until Vanessa had halted suddenly and pulled him round to face

278

her.

"Well, aren't you going to say anything?"

"I'm pleased. I'm really pleased. I didn't know how you felt."

"You could have tried asking."

"I know. I'm sorry. It's a shock, but a good one," he'd added, seeing her face crumpling. "Nessa, what is it? Don't cry. It'll be fine; I'll look after you. I'll always look after you. I love you more than anything, anything in the world, ever..."

She laid her face against his shoulder. "I love you more than anything, ever, too."

Garrin snapped off his thoughts. Those days were so long behind them, not just in time, but in emotions, so many emotions that had gone full circle and twisted him into the man he was today. He'd never dreamed he'd end up hating the woman for whom he'd once gladly have laid down his life. For weeks after she'd left he'd believed she would come back. Tell him it had all been a terrible mistake, that she didn't love Richard Hamilton, that she could never love anyone but him.

The sun had all but sunk now, nothing but a bright line on the horizon, until soon that was gone too and he watched the moon take over the sky, throwing its silver light-path across the ocean. When it was too cold to stand there any more, he turned and looked back at the house. Light blazed from every downstairs window and then the front door opened and a figure was silhouetted briefly in the square of yellow before it detached itself and ran down the garden path. Vanessa, he thought, with a little jump of recognition. For a few seconds the past and present interwove and he wasn't sure which was which, yesterday blending with today, emotions bitter-sweet swirling within him.

He was back at the boundary fence – the horses that

were still out at night, darker shadows against the night –
when the figure reappeared at the five-bar-gate on the other
side of the field. Still, with the strange mixture of past and
present churning inside him, he walked across the grass and
the figure came to meet him.

"Garrin – everyone said you were up here, and I came to
wish you luck." A breathy, girlish voice – Amanda's voice.
The realisation it wasn't Vanessa was like a thump in the
chest, temporarily winding him. He shook his head, drawn
sharply back to reality.

"Thanks," he said, feeling weary as an old man. How
stupid to think Vanessa might have wanted to share this
dream, when it was the one that had replaced her.

Amanda curled her fingers around his. "You were right:
I was never in love with you. But that doesn't mean I don't
like you. I hope you didn't mind me coming?"

"No," he said gruffly. "Course I don't mind."

"I'm coming to Birmingham, too. I've got a really good
seat. Mummy arranged it. Daddy doesn't know. He thinks
I'm going to stay with a girlfriend."

"Probably just as well," Garrin said, thinking that Lloyd
had unwittingly already paid him back tenfold for the
humiliation of being banned.

His mobile went off in his pocket, but by the time he'd
disentangled his hand from Amanda's it had stopped
ringing. He squinted at the lit screen – one missed call – but
he didn't bother to see who it was from because Amanda
was chattering on about Birmingham again. Everyone he
knew had phoned him this week – last night Bert had
phoned from his villa in Spain – sounding as ecstatic as if
he'd qualified Derry himself.

Garrin put the phone back in his pocket. No doubt
whoever it was would ring again.

Chapter Thirty-Five

THEY'D BE ON THEIR way now. Vanessa felt a pang of regret that she hadn't tried harder to get hold of Garrin. Izzy had been out, too, and she guessed they'd all been together. Oh well, he had plenty of people around him; he didn't need her good wishes. He'd probably have been tearing around in a mad flap, like he usually did the night before a show. She would think about him tomorrow. He was jumping at eleven. She wondered what he would do if he did well. Would it be the culmination of the dream or just the beginning?

Isobel was yelling for her attention and she paused from emptying the dishwasher and went to see to her.

"That's enough of that, young lady, you'll have everyone coming in to see what's wrong."

Her daughter didn't stop crying when she picked her up and Vanessa studied her face, feeling the usual jolt of concern. Isobel was very flushed and looked as though she was teething again.

"Poor darling," she murmured, rocking her, "I know it hurts, but it won't be for ever, I promise."

By lunchtime Vanessa was worn to a frazzle. Isobel had cried on and off all morning and was obviously in pain.

"Have you tried oil of cloves?" Dora asked, coming into the kitchen with a bottle that looked well past its sell-by-date. "Worked wonders with my kiddies. Poor little mite."

Masie had also been offering advice and although Vanessa knew they meant well she wished they would leave her to get on. She picked Isobel up again and touched her fingers gently to her face. She was awfully hot.

"I've had the oven on, that probably isn't helping, but I

281

didn't want to leave her because she's been so grizzly." Sweat was dripping off her own forehead and running down her neck. "I think I'll just check and see if she's got a temperature."

Isobel did have a temperature and Vanessa felt the familiar sense of panic rising. What if it wasn't just teething? "I think I'll phone the doctor just to be on the safe side," she murmured, half to herself.

The surgery number was engaged and she stayed by the phone pressing redial, casting anxious glances back at Dora, who was leaning over the Moses basket, murmuring soothingly.

"Has she been sick?" the receptionist asked when she finally got through.

"No, but she won't stop crying and she's got a temperature and I'm very worried."

"It's probably just a cold," the receptionist reassured her at the same moment as Isobel started to cry again – a painful high-pitched cry that tore Vanessa apart.

"I'm sure it's not a cold," she snapped, cursing herself; because she was such a regular visitor to the surgery they probably had her down as the kind of mother who flew into a panic at the slightest thing. "She's not crying like she usually does. Listen." She held the phone in the direction of her daughter and when she put it back to her ear again, the receptionist didn't sound quite as dismissive.

"Hang on a minute. I'll see if I can find a doctor to have a word with you."

Vanessa waited, tapping her foot, sure now that something was seriously wrong. By the time the doctor came to the phone Isobel had stopped crying.

"It's not teething, I'm sure it isn't," she told him, trying to force calmness into her voice. "She's got a temperature and I'm really worried."

"Perhaps you ought to bring her down. I'm sure we'll

soon put your mind at rest."

Not waiting to hear any more, Vanessa slammed down the phone and began gathering up Isobel's things. Nappies, bottle, her tiny coat. All the while her breath was catching in her throat. If the doctor thought she needed to go in, it must be something serious. She scooped up her daughter and grabbed the car seat. "I've got to go out," she told a worried Dora. "I'll be as quick as I can. I'm sorry. Could you possibly phone Laura and explain."

At the surgery the doctor took Isobel's temperature and examined her in silence. "You're right, it's not teething," he said. "She's running a bit of a fever. It could be a virus, but I think we'll get the hospital to take a little look. I'm going to call an ambulance. Try not to worry."

Try not to worry. Was he mad? Adrenaline was pounding through her, but she knew she had to stay calm. Part of her brain was on autopilot as she carried Isobel out to the ambulance. She was sick on the way, not normal baby sick – but more violent. Vanessa cleaned her up and kissed her forehead. She was burning hot. Fear deeper than she'd ever known heightened every sense and the paramedic's reassurances did nothing to quell the panic that was growing by the second.

At the hospital she was ushered into an examination room within minutes. She laid Isobel on the examining table, unbuttoning her coat for the paediatrician, and all the while her daughter cried – the same high-pitched cry that tore at her heart.

"When did you first notice she was in distress?" he asked, his face very serious.

"A couple of hours ago, I thought she was teething, but she seemed worse than usual and picking her up didn't seem to help." Vanessa wiped damp hands on her coat. "What is it? What's wrong?"

As she spoke, Isobel started to vomit again and then she went limp on the examination bed. Vanessa stared in horror. "You've got to do something. You've got to…" She was so scared she couldn't finish the sentence, but the doctor had already turned back to the baby. He was pressing buttons on a side panel and suddenly the room was full of people.

Time stopped. Someone was crying. She was crying. There was a woman in a white coat, standing in front of her, her face blurred so that Vanessa couldn't see her eyes.

"Don't worry, Mrs Hamilton. We're going to take care of her. She's in the right place, now."

The woman's face came into focus, but still Vanessa couldn't comprehend. "We think your daughter has meningitis. We need to do some further tests to find out which type it is and then we can start treating her."

Meningitis. It was a word full of terror. Newsflashes streamed through her brain. *Killer disease strikes again*. The faces of newsreaders the world over, sombre as they spoke about outbreaks and death tolls in voices that could convey nothing of what it really felt like, nothing of the black paralysing terror that was sweeping through her now.

"If you'd like to come this way, please, Mrs Hamilton."

They were moving down a corridor, punctuated by waiting rooms where people sat, curious faces turning as they passed. Vanessa could hear sobbing and the world was trembling. The floor was shaking so violently it was difficult to walk. They should do something about that. They shouldn't expect people to walk under these conditions. The hospital air was dry and suffocating, closing her throat. A man went by on a bed, his face covered by a mask, a bottle above his head, dripping something into him.

Once she thought she saw Jennifer darting down a side corridor, but when she turned there was no one there.

Then they were in another room and the doctor was

gently laying Isobel on a bed. "Some of the tests look a little alarming. Do you want to stay?"

She nodded, not able to speak, but it was as if someone else stood watching as they moved around her daughter. The dimness of the room gave everything a dreamlike effect, only the pounding of her heart making it real. They moved with swift, quiet urgency. Isobel had stopped crying now and the silence was terrifying.

Every so often the woman in the white coat would tell her what they were doing, but she couldn't take it in. Snatches of technical information that she couldn't connect with her baby.

She had no idea how much time passed, only that at some point, they brought a chair and pressed her gently into it.

"Is there anyone you'd like us to call, Mrs Hamilton? Someone to be with you?"

She buried her face in her hands, trying to assimilate the words, but it was all happening in fragments: tubes in her daughter where there shouldn't be tubes; people coming in and out of focus; the low murmur of voices. She shook her head, trying to clear the fog, assemble all the pieces that made up this terrible nightmare.

"Garrin," she whispered. "You have to call Garrin."

Chapter Thirty-Six

THE QUICKEST WAY BACK from Birmingham was by taxi. Izzy had wanted to come with him, but Garrin knew she was exhausted from the long drive up.

"I'll phone you as soon as there's news," he told her. "I'll be fine. You stay here."

She nodded, every line on her face deepening with worry.

It poured all the way back. Garrin stared out of the window, he'd held it together in front of Izzy, but as the light fled from the day his thoughts were fragmenting. Vanessa must be panic-stricken. He hadn't spoken to her, but it had been worse somehow hearing a calm stranger telling him that his daughter had meningitis and could he get there as soon as possible.

Would he arrive to find it was already over, that he had lost another child? Isobel should have been with him today, had he thrown away the chance to share the last few hours of her life by going to Birmingham to chase some crazy dream? Guilt flooded him in black waves as Izzy's voice came back to him. "You're missing half her life because of this stupid vendetta with Vanessa. For Christ's sake, grow up, Garrin, Isobel's your daughter."

Please let her live. I'll do anything if only you'll let her live. He didn't know who he was bargaining with. He never prayed. For so many years he'd believed only in cause and effect. You acted and you lived with the consequences. You couldn't go back and change the past, however much you wanted to. There were no Gods, no higher beings who would offer forgiveness for past sins.

They came off the motorway and the dual carriageways

of Dorset, until at last they were speeding along the winding coastal roads of home. Trees looming up in the headlights like great, white ghosts. Rain pounded on the windscreen. The same deities who'd taken Jennifer could snatch Isobel, without a thought for what he and Vanessa had already lost. Garrin forced his thoughts away from such dark avenues. That way led madness. She wasn't going to die. She was going to live. She had to live. He would do anything, if only she would live.

Hold on, my darling, you can do it. He sent his thoughts out into the wet night, begging her over and over to hold on because there was nothing else he could do. He had never felt so afraid – or so helpless.

About a mile before the hospital, they got caught up in a slow-moving queue of traffic. At Garrin's request the taxi driver tuned into the local radio station and they discovered a tanker had overturned on the road ahead.

"It could take hours." The taxi driver's voice was irritatingly calm.

"Isn't there a bloody back way?"

"No, mate, we'll have to sit it out."

Garrin lasted about five minutes before he decided he'd had enough. He stuffed some notes into the taxi driver's hand and got out into the rain-swept night.

"You'll get soaked, mate."

But Garrin was beyond caring. He pulled his coat around him and ran, past the stationary cars, past the policeman directing traffic, past an ambulance, motionless at the side of the road. He was wet through in seconds, but nothing mattered apart from getting to Isobel and Vanessa.

It was half past nine when he reached the hospital car park. Splashing through puddles, ignoring the curious glances of people fiddling with umbrellas at the brightly lit entrance, he hurtled into reception.

They took him to where Vanessa sat in a boxy little side

room off the isolation ward where Isobel was. She sat with her hands on her knees, her dark hair falling over her face as if she no longer wanted to see the world. And in that moment the past didn't exist. All he wanted was to take her in his arms and kiss away her pain. Tell her how sorry he was for shutting her out of his life. But – unsure of his reception – he stepped quietly towards her.

She looked up. Her eyes were dull, as if she were no longer even hoping. Protectiveness as old as for ever rose in him and he didn't speak, just held out his arms and she came to him.

"How is she?"

"The same," she whispered. "Why are you so wet?"

"It's raining."

"Oh, Garrin, I can't bear it. I can't bear it if…"

"No ifs. We're not going to lose her." He stroked her hair and held her tight against him, aware that he was dripping water over the polished floor and that Vanessa was getting wet, too.

A nurse came into the room and asked if he wanted a towel, but both of them ignored her. He cupped Vanessa's face in his hands. "Look at me, Vanessa. We're going to get through this. She's going to be okay. We have to be strong for her."

She trembled, but nodded, her lips moving, but no longer forming words and he realised she was praying.

Time passed. Time measured in breaths and in heartbeats, and Garrin forced away the images of Isobel lying next door, her tiny body attached to drips and tubes while the doctors fought to save her life. Since he'd arrived, they'd been told it was bacterial meningitis and that they were lucky to have diagnosed it so quickly; antibiotics were very effective in the majority of cases.

What about the minority? he'd wanted to scream at the

masked faces. You can't let her die – she's our baby. She's all that we have. But he'd forced himself to stay calm because Vanessa was so close to the edge, she'd have fallen apart without him. If it was meningitis, Vanessa would have to be tested too, they'd said. And anyone else who'd come into contact with her. He should really wear a mask as a precaution, but he'd refused because the world was so alien to Vanessa at this moment. She was locked into God knows where and he didn't want to be separated from her. He couldn't even bear to think how Isobel must feel, surrounded by strangers in masks, away from her mummy for the first time in her life. It broke his heart to imagine it, so he closed it out and held Vanessa's hand and prayed.

Outside the double-glazed windows the rain increased in intensity, but in this little room there were just the two of them, as there had been so long ago when they'd prayed for another miracle to happen. Almost seven years ago when they'd prayed their newborn daughter could somehow be dragged back from eternity.

It wasn't the same, Garrin kept telling himself over and over. Isobel was strong and she was alive and there was hope. He held Vanessa and he murmured platitudes and from time to time she cried, but mostly she was silent and numb. They were offered beds, but he knew there was no way they'd sleep. They were too terrified of waking to bad news. And anyway they'd have carried this nightmare into their dreams. There was nothing to do but wait.

At dawn a doctor came into the room, his face shadowed with fatigue.

"Mr and Mrs Hamilton."

Garrin nodded, amazed he didn't even care about being addressed as Richard.

"Isobel is responding to the antibiotics. She's not out of danger, but it's good news and we're optimistic. Would you like to see her?"

They stood in gowns and masks, looking into the cot where their daughter lay. What looked like a white plaster held a tube into her nose and there were machines beside her. Her eyes were closed.

"She's not in any pain," the doctor said quietly, but Vanessa's eyes were haunted and Garrin knew she was feeling more than the terror of now. Years of fear were condensed into this moment.

"She's going to get through this, I know she is." He whispered the words into Vanessa's hair. "She's strong and she's a fighter. She's going to be okay."

Vanessa nodded, but he could see she didn't believe him – couldn't believe him. He would have given all that he had to be able to put some peace back into her face.

Chapter Thirty-Seven

IT WAS THREE DAYS before they knew for certain that Isobel would live. Three nights of hardly any sleep and of living on the edge of time because they knew they could be told at any second it had run out for their daughter.

"You're very lucky," the doctor told them. "There's no permanent damage and we don't think there are going to be any long-term effects. She'll need to stay with us for a little longer and she'll need antibiotics for some days after that, but she's fine." He broke off, his face serious. "I really think the best thing you could do is go home and get some proper rest. You'll be no good to Isobel if you're both shattered."

Vanessa sobbed quietly. "It's true, isn't it, please tell me it's true and I'm not dreaming."

Garrin got stiffly to his feet and knowing there was nothing he could say that could come close to expressing what he was feeling, he just shook the doctor's hand. "Thanks. Thanks so much."

He turned to Vanessa. "I'll take you home. And I don't mean to Tall Trees. They're right, you need to sleep. You're dead on your feet."

"Laura will be expecting me."

"I phoned her. She said you're to take as much time as you need. She said you were owed some holiday anyway."

Vanessa shook her head. "I can't come back with you. Amanda wouldn't like it."

"What the hell has it got to do with Amanda? Come on, we can argue about it in the car. Just humour me, Vanessa. Please."

Something in his voice reached past her exhaustion. A

tenderness that made her want to unravel against him, but she shook her head. She'd done enough of that already, but she didn't want it to become a habit.

"Garrin, you've been so kind. But you don't need to keep pretending for Isobel's sake. I know how you feel about me."

"You have no idea," he said and she looked into his face, gaunt with tiredness, and saw to her dismay he had tears in his eyes.

"When our daughter comes home, looking after her is going to be a full-time job. I can help. I want to help."

And because she could see he meant it, she agreed to go back with him. "Just for a few days. Just until we're sure she's definitely on the mend."

It was odd being back at Fair Winds. The place was a mess and the kitchen didn't look as though it had been used for anything other than serving up takeaways for weeks. There was certainly no sign of a woman's touch. Vanessa screwed up her face in puzzlement.

"What?" Garrin asked, standing beside her in the archway.

"I thought Amanda had moved in with you."

He shook his head. "You're the only woman who's stayed here for more than the odd night."

There was irony in his voice and Vanessa was too tired to decide whether this made her feel better or worse.

"You haven't been eating properly," she accused him, anxious to change the subject. Perhaps nothing made sense because she was so tired.

"I've had my mind on other things." He went through to the lounge and she followed him. There was a *Horse and Hound* on the table, open on a preview of the competitors jumping at the Horse Of The Year Show. Vanessa picked it up, jolted because she hadn't given a thought to where

292

Garrin was supposed to be.

She caught him watching her. "I'm so sorry Garrin, that you had to come back."

"It doesn't matter. There'll be other shows. Contrary to what you seem to think, I do have my priorities right."

She stared at him. His voice was matter of fact. As if the show was of no more consequence than a normal working day. It had meant the world to him and Izzy. It had been his dream and he'd given it up and during all the time he'd been with her at the hospital he hadn't even mentioned it. He'd just been there, sharing every moment of her pain, making sure she never gave up hope. She didn't remember him even sleeping.

Aching with the enormity of the sacrifice he'd made, she touched his face. "I'm so sorry. I know how much it meant to you."

"I wanted to be with you and Isobel," he muttered. "I'm a selfish bastard – you should know that by now. I was doing exactly what I wanted."

"But that's not true. You've worked so hard and it was all for nothing."

"Stop it." His voice was gruff. "Come on, I'm putting you to bed." His arm crept around her shoulders again and she shrugged him off. Not because it didn't feel right, but because it felt too right and she didn't want to get used to it. They both knew he didn't need to do that now Isobel was going to be all right. They could go back to how they'd been before. They'd got it all sorted, she seemed to remember, but her brain wasn't working.

He looked hurt, but he didn't try and touch her again. She went ahead of him across the lounge, up the stairs. She stopped at the door of her room, but he ushered her past it. "It's not made up. Sleep in mine."

Too tired to argue, she did as he said. She flopped onto the bed, which smelt of him – of his skin and his hair and

293

something less definable – the essence of him.

He knelt on the floor beside her. "Stay there as long as you like. I need to catch up with Tracey, see what's been happening here."

Vanessa nodded, her eyes already closing. She was asleep in seconds.

When she woke up, feeling groggy and disorientated, only an hour or so had passed. She'd never been good at sleeping in the day and being in his bed hadn't helped. He'd crept into her dreams. It was inevitable; they'd been together for three days. It wasn't going to be easy to separate their lives again, but she had to try. She showered and, not wanting to put the same clothes back on, she borrowed his towelling bathrobe from the back of the bedroom door. It was far too big.

He smiled when he saw her. "I'll go over to Tall Trees and get you some clothes. How are you feeling?"

"I'm not sure, but I can't sleep. You haven't either. You look shattered."

"I've had a few things to organise. Tracey's going to carry on overseeing things here for a few days, bless her. She said to tell you if you need any help with Isobel, or anything else, you just need to ask."

"That's good of her."

"I told her we had it covered, but yeah, it is. I've also been speaking to Izzy about the arrangements for bringing Derry back. I was going to go myself, but Suzy's agreed to drive the horsebox back, which will be easier. I've been sorting out insurance and stuff. They'll be back later tonight."

"I didn't realise they'd be stuck up there without you. I haven't given them a second thought. They must have been worried sick."

"You've had more important things on your mind. Izzy knows that. They're both over the moon that Isobel's okay.

I phoned the hospital again just now. They said she was absolutely fine."

"Thanks. I'm so sorry, Garrin – about Birmingham, I mean. It's been your dream for years, hasn't it?"

"Isobel's far more important to me than a horse show." He paused and added quietly, "So are you."

Vanessa swallowed, not sure she'd heard him right and didn't answer. She felt strangely light-headed and empty. It wasn't right. She should be happy that Isobel was no longer in danger. Where was this desperate emptiness coming from? She shivered and he led her to the settee and perched on the arm beside her.

"Did I look like I was going to fall over?"

"Yeah, you did. And I haven't the energy to pick you up. Look, if you really don't want to stay here, I can't force you, but I meant what I said just now. I want to take care of you – both of you."

"You don't need to do that."

"Stop fighting me, Vanessa, please. If you're really not going back to bed then I want to talk to you."

"What about?"

"About being parents. About us."

She flinched, thinking of Isobel in hospital a few miles away. The parents bit she could have dealt with, but she was still too raw to discuss anything else.

He read her face, but carried on regardless. "The last few days have put everything in perspective."

"What sort of things?"

"So much." He looked sideways at her. "I still love you, for starters. I don't think I ever stopped, but I've been kidding myself for a long time."

She didn't speak and he went on in the same quiet voice. "When we lost Jennifer, I let you down. I wasn't there for you. I couldn't reach you, so I stopped trying." He paused and his eyes were black with pain. "I'm so sorry."

295

"Don't," she said, hugging his robe around her. "It's me who should be saying sorry. It was my fault she died – I should have been more careful, I took chances. I was so stupid..."

"Stop it. It was not your fault. It was an accident – a terrible tragedy – I won't let you beat yourself up about it any more. The doctors said it wasn't your fault."

They had said that, more than once, but Vanessa hadn't believed them.

"You have to forgive yourself, Nessa. You have to move on."

"But I left you when you needed me. I walked away from you to be with a man who didn't even know what love was."

"I made it impossible for you to stay." He knelt on the floor in front of her, his voice full of sadness. "I've regretted it all these years, but instead of doing anything about it I let the bitterness eat me up. I blamed you for a lot of stuff that was down to me being pigheaded and arrogant."

"No."

"Let me finish. Birmingham was just a dream I was chasing because I couldn't have you. It doesn't matter. It really doesn't. I'd rather be with you and Isobel. I'd rather be with you than anywhere."

He was close now – his voice barely more than a breath against her cheek, and the emptiness inside her was increasing, and as she looked back into his eyes, she recognised it for what it was. It wasn't food or sleep she was lacking, it was him. For the last three days they'd shared it all: the agony of waiting for news; the joy of knowing Isobel was going to live, and now they'd shared the demons of their past, too. They couldn't go through such a gamut of emotions and then just draw apart again. Trying to put the space back between them now was as impossible as trying to separate the ocean from the shore, the sky from the stars.

She gave up trying, and kissed him.

He wasn't surprised. He cupped her face and kissed her back so tenderly she ached. Then he deepened the kiss and it was as new as the first time they'd touched and as old as for ever. So right, that by the time they drew apart, she had tears on her face and so did he.

He pulled her down onto the floor beside him and the room shrank around them and all she wanted was to stay in his arms. Stretch this moment on. Not go back to the reality of how things had to be.

"You really should try and get some sleep," he said. "You look shattered."

"Sleeping is the last thing I feel like doing." She hesitated and then she put her hands on his shoulders and pushed him back onto the carpet. Pain and desire were fusing within her; it was wrong to feel like this yet she couldn't help herself. She needed him, not to talk, but to be close, to be part of her. Nothing else would do. She straddled him and he rested his elbows on the floor and half sitting, half lying, he looked at her through half-closed lids.

With her eyes on his, she ran her hands up beneath his polo shirt, shivering as she felt the warmth of his skin beneath her fingertips and traced the dark line of hair that disappeared below the waistband of his jeans.

"So what do you feel like doing, Nessa?" His eyebrows were raised, only the slight huskiness in his voice giving him away.

She undid his jeans and tugged them down and let her fingers rest fleetingly against him.

"The same thing as you, I'd say."

He groaned.

"I can stop if you want me to?" It wasn't true. If he rejected her now, she would be devastated.

He sat up, kicking off his jeans in one swift movement and reversed their positions so she lay beneath him, his hands on her shoulders.

"Can't bear to be at a disadvantage for long, can you?" she whispered, looking up into his black eyes.

"No," he said, letting go of her for long enough to undo the towelling belt and push the robe back off her shoulders. Neither of them moved. He was taking his weight on his knees, utterly controlled. She sneaked a glance at his groin. Well, parts of him were controlled.

"I'm still at a disadvantage," he murmured. "Because you haven't told me how you feel about me. I need to know."

"I love you," she said, knowing there was no way she could deny it. "Did you ever think I didn't?"

"There were moments." He kissed each breast in turn, his eyes on her face. "Will you marry me, Nessa?"

She smiled, drunk with desire and happiness. "Is this what you call an indecent proposal?"

"Stop it, I'm serious."

"Of course I'll marry you. But maybe you should ask me again in a week or so. Make sure you really want to. Make sure what you're feeling isn't just the after-effects of the last few days."

"We've wasted enough time already. I want us to be a family more than anything else in the world." He traced his fingers over her breasts, his touch so light it was borderline agony and ecstasy. "How about you?"

She needed him so much she could no longer speak. She pulled him down towards her, feeling the hard muscles of his chest crushing her breasts.

They found each other's mouths again, their hunger for each other blotting everything else out. With each kiss he told her again he loved her. Then at last he was inside her and she knew there could never be anyone else, not for either of them. They had loved each other and hated each other, but now they had come full circle.

And this was the forgiving.

Chapter Thirty-Eight

IZZY FELT EXHAUSTED WHEN she and Suzy finally arrived home, but nothing on earth would have stopped her going with Vanessa and Garrin to the hospital. She watched them holding hands as they gazed at their daughter and knew everything had changed. There was much more than mutual support in their touch. They had the love back; it was so tangible you could practically see it. Like light encircling them. Izzy berated herself for such fancifulness and blinked several times as they stood in the isolation ward next to Isobel's bed. It was wonderful seeing the baby kicking and smiling and staring up at her parents with her huge dark eyes. Losing one child had torn them apart, and coming so close to losing another had somehow made them whole again. What a strange and curious world it was.

Izzy was too cynical to believe that all things happened for a reason. There was nothing on earth that would ever make sense of Jennifer's death for her. But some things definitely seemed to have the ring of karma about them.

She wondered if Garrin had told Vanessa about the letter Cissy Brown had sent him – probably not – they'd had too much to worry about. Now wasn't the time to raise it, Izzy thought, but that letter had proved to Izzy that even though there may not be a God, there was definitely some force at work – as if they were all chess pieces in a great celestial game and someone with a sense of humour moved the pieces.

Garrin and Vanessa didn't tell anyone they'd decided to get married until Isobel was home. They'd both agreed it might be tempting fate, but the moment they got back from the hospital with their daughter, Vanessa said she was phoning Izzy.

"I can't wait any longer," she said, hugging Isobel. "She can be the first to know, apart from this young lady, of course. Mummy and Daddy are getting married, darling. How about that?"

"Gah," said Isobel happily, her eyes bright and no sign of her illness on her face.

"When Mummy's divorce comes through," Garrin added with a wry grin.

Izzy was ecstatic. "I'm coming round right now with a bottle of champagne."

"It's not even lunchtime," Vanessa said laughing.

"So what?"

"Well, don't waste money on a taxi. Garrin can come and pick you up."

"He certainly will not. Anyway, I've got a visitor. She can drop me off. Second thoughts, I'll bring her with me."

"Who is it?" Vanessa asked, puzzled, but Izzy had already hung up. She turned back to Garrin. "She's on her way round with some champagne and a visitor. I'd better give Tracey and Suzy a shout."

By the time she'd found Suzy and Tracey and they'd finished what they were doing and come into the house, Izzy had arrived and was pouring glasses of champagne in the kitchen. "I'm glad you're here," she told Vanessa with a smile. "You can take over – my hands are too shaky for this. I'm spilling half of it."

Vanessa took the tray of glasses into the lounge and very nearly dropped them. Amanda, wearing a pink silk blouse and a very short skirt, and looking as gorgeous as ever, was sitting on the settee next to Garrin. She stood up when she saw Vanessa and came across. "I've just heard your news. Fabulous. I'm delighted for you."

"You are?"

"Yes, I really am. I think you're very lucky. Both of you."

Behind her, Garrin stood up, looking flushed and Vanessa saw Tracey's expression flit between concern and amazement.

Amanda glanced at Vanessa. "May I kiss him? It's probably the one and only chance I'm going to get."

"Feel free."

"Don't I get a say in this?" Garrin said.

"No, you don't." Amanda put her arms around his neck and kissed him full on the lips and Vanessa swallowed hard and tried not to mind.

"What were you doing round Izzy's, anyway?" she said, feeling as though she'd walked into a film halfway through.

"I was asking Izzy if she'd help me by being a volunteer patient. I'm studying reflexology and I needed some volunteers to practise on. Reflexology is very good for people with long-term illnesses."

"I see," Vanessa murmured, digesting this information and wondering if it was true. Or was this some tactic of Amanda's to get closer to Garrin?

Izzy, catching her look, interrupted. "We didn't come round here to discuss feet. We came to celebrate your engagement." She raised her glass. "To Garrin and Vanessa."

Amanda smiled, but her eyes were pensive. "To Garrin and Vanessa." She drained her glass. "Right then, I'll toddle off and leave you to your celebrating. I did rather gatecrash, didn't I? Don't forget to invite me to the wedding, will you?"

She blew a kiss towards Isobel and disappeared.

"God, that woman's got some front," Tracey said. "Are you really going to let her come to the wedding?"

"That's up to Vanessa," Garrin muttered.

"It's okay with me," Vanessa said, thinking privately that, had their positions been reversed, she'd have had great difficulty in being as gracious as Amanda. It was high time she gave her the benefit of the doubt.

They decided to make a day of it and went to Tall Trees to tell Laura Collins their news. George was the only person who wasn't pleased.

"I suppose that means you won't be coming back," he muttered, leaning back in his chair and puffing at a pipe, which was neither lit, nor contained any tobacco.

"Don't be so selfish, George," Masie berated him. "And, by the way, you look ridiculous sitting there with an empty pipe in your hand."

"I've given up smoking. This is to help me through the first stages of withdrawal." George's white eyebrows met as he sucked on his pipe harder. "It's very difficult giving up smoking, I'll have you know."

"You only tried it twice, you daft old sod."

"Well, you can smoke at our wedding if you like," Vanessa told him. "I don't mind."

"Are we invited then? We thought you might not want a load of old wrinklies at your wedding." He coughed and added hastily. "Not that Masie and Dora are that wrinkly, I suppose. It's the rest of them I'm worried about."

"Are you really marrying a double-glazing salesman?" Masie interrupted. "I mean, I know he's very good-looking and all that, but you could do better. He was very rude to you that time."

"He's a reformed character," Vanessa said laughing. "But you can only come if you promise not to let the tyres down on the wedding cars."

"Tyres? I don't know what you're on about. Unless you're on about spare tyres." She patted George's midriff affectionately. "Plenty of them round here."

"It's the giving up smoking – always makes you put on weight."

Vanessa glanced at Garrin, who was doing his best not to laugh. "Come on, let's get out of here," he said. "Before we end up as mad as they are."

When they got back, Izzy had just finished washing up.

"You didn't need to do that."

"Well, I don't like to be idle and young Isobel's been as good as gold. You were a good baby, too," she told Vanessa. She paused and looked at Garrin. "Have you showed Vanessa Cissy's letter? Because if you haven't, I think you should."

"No, I'd forgotten about it."

"Well, that's hardly surprising."

Vanessa stared at them both and frowned. "Nothing's wrong is it, she is all right, isn't she?"

"Oh, Cissy's fine," Garrin said, a little smile playing on his lips. "She's still knocking out candy-floss to the Knollsey tourists. Her letter's about your soon to be ex-husband."

"I don't think I want to know."

"Trust me, you do. It brightened up my day no end when it came."

She waited while he fished it out from beneath a pile of paperwork on the table.

It was only a short note, written in Cissy Brown's loopy exaggerated handwriting. You could practically see the laughter spreading across the page.

Dear Garrin,

I hope this letter finds you and Izzy well and that Vanessa caught up with you. I know you won't mind me dropping you this quick note to tell you that your old mate Richard Hamilton must be rueing the day he ever bought

304

Kane's fun fair. The site has been plagued by problems since he's had it, but this latest one is a biggie. The whole place is collapsing – literally. Subsidence apparently. Half the flat owners are suing him (poor chap, I know your heart will bleed for him!). And he owns the other half so guess he'll have to sue himself too. Seems he was so anxious to get those flats up and make a quick profit he didn't build proper foundations or something. At least that's what everyone's saying. The local press are having a field day. Personally, I think it's down to a gypsy curse.

 I'll finish there.
Your friend,
Cissy Brown

Garrin and Izzy waited for her reaction, but Vanessa wasn't sure what she was feeling as she put the note back on the table. Not triumph, not glee, not even a feeling that it served him right. Perhaps she felt none of these things because for the last few days she'd been so happy there wasn't room for any other emotion.

She thought about the fair and their living wagon beneath the stars, about Izzy's lounge, washed with light and the view across the sea. Then she looked around the familiar room: the squashy leather sofa; the prints of Garrin show-jumping; the French windows leading to the patio outside, and beyond the garden the sunset-streaked sky.

It didn't matter where you were, she realised with a flash of insight. She'd thought Richard had destroyed her, by demolishing the place she'd been brought up, but he hadn't. You could bulldozer buildings and reconstruct lives, but you couldn't alter the fact that love wasn't about places, it was about people.

"I should be dancing round the room and shouting, 'revenge is sweet', shouldn't I?" she said with a half smile. "But I don't feel like that at all. I don't even hate him any

305

more; I don't feel anything towards him. He's history."

Izzy smiled at her – an hallelujah smile – and Vanessa realised the old lady had always known what it had taken her and Garrin longer to understand. Bitterness only destroyed the person who felt it. You could learn to let it go and you could move on.

She glanced at Garrin. He was looking at her, his eyes thoughtful. Perhaps he was thinking the same thing. But he shattered these illusions with his next words.

"Fancy a drive down to Knollsey? I've never seen the flats. We could nip by and see if any of them have fallen into the sea yet. I'd really enjoy that."

It was cold on the coast. The wind chivvied the clouds through the sky, skimmed surf off the grey sea and tossed an empty crisp wrapper along the gutter. They sat on the old sea wall, close to where Vanessa had stood when she'd first come back and looked across the bay at the block of flats. White-painted, but with no sun today to give them golden eyes – or maybe the windows had been shuttered up to stop squatters. Beside them in her buggy, Isobel giggled and stretched out her hands towards a fat seagull that was perched on the railings.

"Gah," she shouted.

Garrin looked pleased. "Did you hear that? She said Dad."

"No, she didn't, that's her seagull impression. Not bad, is it?"

"That's because she's the cleverest little girl in the world, aren't you, angel? Do you think she's warm enough?"

"She's snug as a bug in there. A lot warmer than us, I should think." Vanessa pulled her scarf around her neck. "So have you seen enough? Or would you like a closer look?"

"I've never seen them up close. Let's take a walk up there, shall we?"

"He called it Fairground Court, you know."

"Stupid tosser," Garrin said, shaking his head as they walked along the sandy pavement, past boats tugging at their moorings, past people with their heads down. Past shop fronts, their paint fading beneath the constant salt air, past the hamburger bar where they'd once worked.

"We could nip in for coffee, later," Garrin said, with a sideways glance at her.

"I think I'll give that a miss. I'm not feeling that nostalgic."

"Me neither. I'm bloody glad we haven't got to do that any more."

"No, you'd rather be out in a field in all weathers risking life and limb, but then I always knew you had a screw loose."

"Charming."

She smiled at him, loving every look, every nuance of him and seeing her glance, he put his hands over hers on the buggy.

"I'll push her up the hill. It's steep."

"We must be getting old," she said, when they finally stood outside the security gates in front of the flats.

"Speak for yourself," he said, not even out of breath. "At least staying out in a field in all weathers keeps me fit."

She caught her breath and looked back at the gates, which were padlocked with a chain. The entry phone had gone and there was a board slung up. *Danger, Unsafe Site, Keep Out.*

"It doesn't look unsafe, does it?" Garrin said, frowning. "The flats still look okay."

"Appearances can be deceptive," Vanessa said quietly. "Let's walk round a bit further."

From the side of the building they had a different view.

"Look," Vanessa said, pointing out a crack that ran along one of the balcony walls.

"You'd have thought he'd know about foundations, being a builder," Garrin said thoughtfully. "Building anything on sand must always be a bit dodgy."

"I expect he was probably in too much of a hurry to get the block up," Vanessa said dryly. "Too anxious to wipe out the bits of my life he didn't want me remembering. But he made a mistake there. Solid foundations are everything if you're building something to last." For love, as well as buildings, she reflected. Poor Richard.

"It'll cost a heap of cash to put this lot right."

"And that's when he's finished paying off all the court cases," Vanessa said. "I almost feel sorry for him."

"Well, I don't." Garrin frowned and cupped a hand to his ear. "Can you hear that noise?"

Vanessa listened and could hear nothing but the whistling of the wind and the ever-present sound of sea, and closer by the squeak of an abandoned hanging basket swinging on its chain.

"What noise?"

"I thought I heard a cackle of laughter." He grinned. "That'll be Nanna Kane. I bet she's in her element. She always said she'd have the last laugh where Richard Hamilton was concerned. And I never thought I'd say it, but it looks as though she was right, doesn't it, my love?"

He put his arms around her and kissed her and she could taste salt on his lips and smell the sea in his air and it was as though they were completing the circle. A circle that had been made stronger by being broken and then repaired once more. There were tears on her face when he broke the kiss.

"Vanessa, what's up?" He wiped them away with his fingertips.

"I'm happy, not sad, you wombat. Come on, let's get going. The wind's getting up and I don't think it would take

308

much to blow this little lot over the cliffs and into the sea. And much as I know you'd like to see it, I'd rather be at home in front of the fire."

"Me too," he said grinning.

And so they walked back down to the coast road and she could feel his fingers around hers, spreading warmth right through to her very soul. And neither of them looked back.

About The Author

Della Galton lives in a 16th century cottage in Dorset with her husband and four dogs.
Find out more about Della Galton and her work by visiting her website **www.dellagalton.com**

Also by Della Galton

PASSING SHADOWS

How do you choose between friendship and love?
Maggie faces an impossible dilemma when she discovers
that Finn, the man she loves, is also the father of her best
friend's child. Should Maggie betray her best friend,
who never wanted him to know? Or lie to Finn, the first
man she's ever trusted enough to love? The decision is
complicated by the shadows of her past.

Passing Shadows is also published by Accent Press

ISBN 1905170238 / 9781905170234

Price £6.99